INDIE

INDIE

Paul MacLeod

IGUANA

Publisher: Meghan Behse
Editor: Jennifer Trent
Front cover design: Jonathan Relph

ISBN 978-1-77180-582-7 (paperback)
ISBN 978-1-77180-581-0 (epub)

This is an original print edition of *Indie*.

ONE

Midas stepped over bent tin cans in the brown puddle and onto a fractured laptop to keep his shoes dry, a little island in the middle of floating garbage. The warm rain hit his cheek. He couldn't remember the last night of October ever being so warm, not in this town, but he'd returned from the South just over a year ago and memories morph. Maybe it had always been burning and the ten years spent doing big deals in the South confused his perception of things.

A cruiser glided by, three feet above ground, hovering upon its red glow while he choked on the foul fuel they falsely called magma. It reminded Midas that change had to happen. That's why he'd made a new start. Moved back up north and started his own café called Freehouse, where people would gather to exchange ideas. Good ideas, for once. It'd be an honest buck.

A dog barked from a dark alcove. The long legs of a man in dirty, ripped pants without shoes stretched out upon the sidewalk.

Midas jumped back into the puddle. A heavy chain clanked, and the man pulled the dog's maw back, but not before Midas saw something he wished he hadn't. It would disturb him for some time to come. The dog's head was large and thick; its teeth were long and dripped with mucus. The yellow eyes hated him, like the people who partied this night — they and the canine had it out for his skin.

The dog howled and was heaved by the chain back into the shadows. Midas winced, caught his breath and walked swiftly to his café.

He pressed his palm to the red light, the door slid up and the bells tinkled above. The tables and chairs in the long space were mostly empty. Tonight he had left the café open later given the festivities, but it was obviously a bust. No one wanted to hang out here tonight.

Two costumed youth, one in a pink sequined dress, the other in a wizard's robe, sat at the espresso bar that spanned the length of the café. At the picnic table, a young man dressed as a sad clown with a red tear on his cheek was staring down at the device in his hand, sifting through sites on his Probe. Just behind him was a fallen painting, crooked with one corner wedged into a hole in the old wooden floor while a dangling string held up its opposite corner.

"Ira?" Midas said, projecting his voice into the narrow length. "I got better rope. Let's do this."

"No way, boss," Ira said from the back room.

Over the past year since he'd opened the café, Midas had put the artifacts on shelving along the walls — black-and-white photographs, ancient tools, carved wooden toys, decorated knives, the crossbow, a flute. Midas had found these beautiful pieces while working those deals down South, a kind of hobby, he'd said to himself: to salvage history from destruction that became, over those years, more rampant and lawless. So he came home to Toronto and brought them with him because he thought they meant something. The small café often seemed overwhelmed with clutter, so he kept the bigger treasures in the cavernous, oval back room with its domed ceiling.

No customers went there. It was set apart, on a raised wooden floor behind two pillars such that it resembled an amateurish and forgotten stage, shrouded in darkness.

Midas didn't want Ira in that place. "Ira, what are you doing back there?" No answer. "Can you come here to help me put this painting back up?"

Most regulars who spent time in the café noticed the painting at some point: It showed a port town nestled into forested mountains beyond which stretched a distant jungle, all at the shore of an expansive, glistening sea. Bright brush strokes emphasized the town and guided one's gaze toward its market square. There, within the four stone walls of the courtyard, people mingled, perused, negotiated and traded among the merchant kiosks. In one or two open areas, musicians, mimes, clowns, comedians, jugglers, fire breathers and acrobats performed. At the far side of the market, set into a taller wall, a temple of dark stone with gothic spires towered, and beyond that the sea stretched into a curving horizon beneath a powerful sun.

Ira's head appeared from around one of the pillars that framed the back room. "I told you no way. It's an abomination. You said we'd throw it out."

Midas liked the painting. It showed a world free of the toxic air outside his café bay window, and those greasy streets with their stinking vehicles transporting wasteful supplies that fuelled a trudging economy. He could almost smell the air in the painting, when he paid attention to it. He imagined that air cool and crisp, a bounty that filled your lungs with purity.

He exhaled, exasperated. He never said he'd throw it out. The whole point of this exercise — leaving for tools, returning — was to hang the thing back up. "Look, Ira, you know we can't hang it on the curvy walls back there. It needs to be here. Just help me hang it back up."

"Zora agrees with me," Ira said. "She thinks we should throw it out."

Midas perked up. "She came by?"

"Even she agrees," said Ira cryptically.

Ira emerged from the depths of the back room's shadow and stood at the edge of the raised floor. The pillars on either side dwarfed his thin yet wiry body and followed the ceiling until they joined above to make an arch from which hung short protrusions etched with creatures of the underworld with wings and fangs.

"You can't fit anything else back here," Ira said. "Too many things. You should hide them or sell them if they're worth so much."

Midas frowned. Ira had a point, and he'd always known this was a weak spot in this place. He should never have rented such a narrow space as this, with its useless stage-like arena at the back on a raised floor with a high domed ceiling and curved walls, only to stuff it with all his eclectic art and pieces of interest he'd recovered, or discovered, down south during his business travels. These things were valuable for good reason and yet now, incredibly, they deprived him of money. Because those artifacts, as he liked to call them, didn't drink coffee.

"Just come help here. And get away from there." Midas approached the painting and gripped it on either side, stretching his arms, then stopped, feeling the water at his feet, for his shoe remained wet from the puddle. Dress shoes and designer jeans muddied. "Damn dog," he said under his breath.

"You're right," Ira continued. "The walls are too curvy. We can't hang it. So we burn it to smithereens."

Midas held his rising voice. "Zora agreed with you? What do you mean — she came in and said I should get rid of all this?"

"She said you need to increase sales," Ira said. "She didn't come in today. But I remember she was talking about the back room. She said, 'You either set it up to force lots of people in and out faster, or you add tables. People like to sit in these places, do their own thing.' So she agrees with me. There, boss, see?" Ira snapped his fingers as he leapt down to the floor and walked toward the painting. "Clink, clink, boss."

Midas doubted that she'd said this. Zora liked the idea of making a place for people to gather and exchange ideas. Talk and share honestly.

He glanced at his beeping Probe lying on the espresso bar. That salesman calling again. He walked over and tapped it on. He wanted this meeting over with.

"Midas, how wonderful to meet you," said Hippias.

Midas frowned into the video of a large grinning face.

"You haven't yet," said Midas.

"Yes, marvellous," the man replied. "I'm in town and shan't be long." As usual, his words bubbled with exuberance.

The salesman had been calling for weeks. With each call, the buoyant voice would offer crucial information that, if only Midas fully appreciated it, would save and make him more money than he thought possible. Midas resented his own weakness at being lured in, because he knew this dark art all too well after ten years working for Superior.

"Remember, I told you to hold back. Be patient and only buy from the best," Hippias persisted.

"I don't need advice, thanks. I'll see you soon."

Midas clicked the call off. He turned to Ira, who now stood before the fallen painting.

The youth at the picnic table, in his oversized onesie with big polka dots, puffy orange hair and red tear drop, was fixated on his Probe.

Ira pointed at the painting. "You see this?" Ira demanded of the young clown. "Did you see the centaurs and other things lurking in there earlier? It was yesterday. You were here. I saw you."

Midas wished Ira could reign in his imagination. Wished he would stop drawing bad attention to the painting. And leave the poor kid alone. Ira was wrong, and could only see dark magic in the changes.

Ira was always full of suspicion and mysticism. He came from the outskirts of the city where he'd grown up with nomadic gangs who'd fled the noise and corruption and pollution for a more human life and, potentially, for some of the more innocent of them, to rebuild. But for Midas, and many others, the nomads were just more criminals — out there in the hot winds, cracked earth and barren hills, they could roam and raid the last of the small towns in a new wild freedom made possible by a decaying and weakened state.

The problem, Midas realized, was those boundaries — between this town and the lawless outskirts — were beginning to resemble the deterioration he'd seen down south. The chaos of the cities' corruption and the country's destruction merged at a critical point, the point when he had to come back. But now, to what? To the same convergence, beginning to happen here. And now Ira spoke of magic, but the poor lad didn't know this was nonsense. It was very different than that, and when Midas heard this kind of absurd talk he resented it. Bad magic wasn't the problem. It was the imminent, growing convergence of some terrible things, of bad behaviours and failures. The painting was only a technological sleight of hand by a tech company they all knew as Rinth. It was money and tech.

So shut the fuck up, Ira, Midas thought. It's a distraction from the truth.

And now he was scaring the customers away, because all three costumed youth stood and walked to the door.

Ira's brow furrowed. "It creeps the customers out, boss," he said.

"Look what you did," Midas said, pointing to the now-empty barstools.

"Where did you find that painting again?"

"Lazuli. My bean supplier, Ira. It doesn't matter."

"So if he gave it to you, then it is yours and you can throw out whatever you want."

"It's kind of complicated, Ira," said Midas.

"It's cursed," said Ira. "When it fell yesterday, I swear, it leaked water. I had to get the mop even while serving so many customers."

"I don't think so."

The poor kid — what was he to do but believe his deluded brethren out there, and now the delusion was here. Midas remembered that he'd been there too, in fact, where things had been worse, and not just down south but also what he'd been doing while working for Superior with all those big business deals. When you're in that heady mix, consumed with the temptation and growing wealth — where if you don't take from the scarcity of resources then someone else will, and they'll hurt you if you're in the way and weak enough — you get caught up in the chaos. But it was just chaos, not magic, poor kid.

No matter. He banished the memory, just as the thought that the painting had never been his left him too. He'd taken it after a bad deal, given them forgiveness, then simply stuffed it in his trunk for the final flight home.

No matter.

"Can you help me put it back up on the wall?" Midas weaved through the tables and stood close to the painting. Ira went with disgust to his cup at the bar while Midas sized up the edges and held his hands upon the small candelabra welded into the two upper corners of the heavy silver frame.

"Stay clear, boss," Ira called from the espresso bar. "It's changing again. More now than before so I will prepare the blaze."

"We're not burning it." Midas gazed into the colours of the painting. "And so what if it morphs a bit, Ira? Big deal. It's Rinth technology. What are you worried about?"

"Paintings aren't supposed to change. Decide, boss: It's a magic painting or it's Rinth technology. Pick. But to me, it's bad magic."

"You're too suspicious," said Midas, and he returned to its deep colours, textures and the dying sun in the painting's horizon. "I've heard of those chips that can, you know, kind of download new images remotely. Sort of like the holograms."

Rinth made basically everything internet. It even changed the internet's name to Rinth. Midas liked its hologram imagery, making so many remote meetings seem real. What he didn't like about it was what made others laugh, feel entertained, excuse their unreality. Rinth did all kinds of things like that. *Too big, too many products we're addicted to,* he thought. Too encompassing, depriving us of an out. No escape.

"That's not right. It's cloth canvas. Zora said the same once it fell. 'More junk,' she said."

"She said that?" This was irritating. "Ira, did she come in here today or not?"

This confusing to-and-fro with Ira exhausted Midas, and he stared deeper into the canvas.

The changes happened unevenly and at random times. Usually they were minuscule alterations that accumulated over weeks and even months, except the day it changed twice, he remembered. That was the day he noticed Zora because she kept asking questions, and at one point asked to take a photo of the painting. She admitted what for: she was an artist, drew comics on Rinth to make satirical political points (which in Midas's opinion could border on dangerous at times) and wanted to draw the painting.

A month or so later, she asked again to photograph or draw it right there — this time, on a lark, from its reflected image in a mirror.

Midas refused. "Mirrors distort reality," he said.

"That's cool," she had replied with nonchalance. "It's why I first came in here, to see this stuff. People talk about you, you know." She smiled and looked into his eyes. "I'm just teasing, you know, about the trinkets thing. I mean, aren't they just a little too valuable? You may want to put some of them away."

The bells then tinkled as the front door opened. And there she was for real.

Zora walked in and paused at the doorway while tilting her head, seeming to take in the room. He couldn't quite discern her face while she remained in shadow, for the lighting from the bay window area beside the door didn't extend that far. She might have been smiling as he'd come to expect from her.

Emerging from that annoying dimness into the lit area of the espresso machine at the bar's end, Zora smiled at him and leaned against the espresso bar, resting a booted foot upon the base of a stool. She tightened her ponytail with its streak of white that Midas hadn't mustered the courage to ask about, and put her old jean jacket on the stool. She had a quirky sense of style, by Midas's standards, with her faded black leather pants and that vintage jacket with its colourful buttons and a green ribbon bow dangling off the collar like an abandoned bow tie.

Ira pointed at the painting and raised his voice about it, but Midas drowned out Ira's strained words with a loud effort at clearing his throat, embarrassed in front of Zora. Ira simply had to stop.

Zora smiled, and Midas sensed she was tense. It could have been Ira, or him, or their tension might be palpable in the air. Midas wondered if something else was up.

"Hey Midas, just on my way to work," she said. Her smile seemed a little forced. "Thought I'd say hi. You know, the usual moment of calm before the storm, right?"

This visit, Zora thought, now seemed to be bad timing. Midas's assistant was unusually irate. She liked Ira but he could be cantankerous, and he had a hate-on for lots of things, especially the painting that for whatever reason had peaked his fury once again. So Zora held herself and kept smiling.

"Tea for the road?" Midas asked, bristling as he turned his back to Ira, if Zora saw it right.

"A tea may be the wrong drink given the heat," she said to Midas and partly to Ira. Because it was hot for October 31. Much hotter than last year. "I don't know, I'll just fill up my water at one of the rationing stations on the way."

Midas would rather she have a tea. "Don't worry, Zora, I have good water. Look, I pay for it, right?" He felt some relief from the tension around them.

They stared at one another in a moment that felt good, and then awkward, until the painting slipped again and banged on the floor.

Ira clenched his fists and grated with barely contained fury, "This board with an image is cursed."

Midas was about to yell that it was a true painting — albeit an odd one — but Zora interjected to calm things down, "Why not believe in it?"

This was a mistake, she realized, a dumb question to ask. Ira was obviously furious — she knew what he thought of the painting but today was worse than usual — and would think she asked him to believe in its technology; Midas was frustrated and would think she asked him to believe in Ira's superstition. And they were both mad at each other over something she had always thought was just silly.

Oh shit, she thought. *I should probably go.* Zora regularly said things to people too quickly, at least that was how she felt, and it unnerved her to no end, particularly as someone who'd recently delved into the world of writing on Rinth. Political satire and all that, exposing her rash words. A bigger, longer mistake, probably.

"You're such an artist," Midas said, trying to calm down. "I'm a businessman. We don't believe in magic. We believe in money."

He caught himself. He didn't quite mean that.

"But you believe in good things, right? That's what you're trying to do with this whole café. Do good business."

"So what?" he asked.

"It's a matter of faith," she said, feeling somewhat encouraged. She made a renewed effort to sound cheerful.

"You can believe in good things, or you can believe that the terrible state of the world is just the way it has to be. Come on," she said, and her tone gave off a kind of carefree shrug.

"Hallelujah. You gotta have faith." She laughed with a twinkle in her eye.

"Zora," he said, shaking his head, "there's still no such thing as make-believe." He paused and felt a bit more relief as he turned his attention to her. "The artist in you is taking over again. It's good to see. I prefer you as an artist."

Her neck straightened and she looked cross. "Who asked you?"

He felt bad. "Sorry, none of my business. I just worry, that's all. Augustine and that group he's in — they're dangerous."

She smiled a little.

Meeting Augustine online, somewhere in the realm of Rinth, was a risk, but everyone did this. And he seemed handsome in an image, but in real life he was only sort of handsome. At first it was enthralling, learning so much alluring stuff about the decaying state of the world from a research group in the underground movements — those outliers and independent thinkers and doers who wanted to turn it all around for the better — but it turned out to be enlightening. She wanted to learn and write something down for others to know. About the power vacuum, for one. The ever-widening chasm left by the dissipating rule of law and filled by huge companies intent on insatiable growth. They'd do anything to grow, and more and more people were getting hurt in more insidious ways, as though the customers, numb to the wrongness of it all, would never stop coming. So this revolutionary *cell*, as they called themselves, hunted information for the *higher-ups*, as they called them. The higher-ups in the revolutionary hierarchy.

For several months, her fascination had kept her intrigued — but lately, she just felt unnerved. And besides, Augustine had lied.

"I wasn't in that deep. I just spent some time with them. I regret it. I probably shouldn't have been poking around so much. That's what it started to feel like, anyway." She leaned in to the espresso counter where they'd been talking and said, "Besides, they were good people. At least, some of them."

She was not thinking of Augustine.

"I've seen it makes you angry," he said, thinking of her writing. He resisted with all his might and judgment the temptation to say, *Your ex-boyfriend is an asshole.*

"Just be careful," he continued. "Talking about positive change is one thing, and a good thing. That's what people do here all the time, talk ideas. For good. That's why I'm doing this. It's a coffee house. But it's a bit much when people talk of revolution. You're still writing on Rinth. It's not a safe place. Everyone's watching, and it's pretty clear to me now that Toronto ain't so good anymore."

Zora nodded. The writing made less sense after she'd started into it. No one was listening anyway, and the truth was too hard to find through all the lies.

Ira tapped him on the shoulder. "I'm going, boss. We'll have a burn painting party with Zora. In the alley, behind. Happy Hallowe'en."

Midas could finally relax.

"Happy Hallowe'en, Ira."

Ira disappeared after the tinkling bells, and Zora crossed her arms.

"He's an ex now, Midas," Zora reiterated. The room felt calmer. This felt good, and she needed the feeling just for a moment before her shift at Night started. She'd been working at Night since just before meeting Augustine and, like the cell, it wasn't what she wanted to be involved with, but she needed the money. And working lots of shifts made it easier to distance herself from the cell. Midas was right, things would be fine for now. She'd keep to herself and write about something else, in a way that wouldn't attract attention, especially from those who didn't feel beholden to laws.

Midas rubbed his brow and worried again. *This poor girl*, he thought, *is still at risk. People like Augustine don't just go away.*

"Ignore Ira," he said, shifting the topic. "It's just a damned painting. Got it from nowhere, like the rest of this stuff all around here, hanging on the walls."

"Okay, I get it," she said. He was diverting things again, so often avoiding the obvious, too unhappy when he should know it takes strength to be happy. "We can talk about it later."

Zora stood, waved her hand to him and he watched her leave through the door to the dark street.

Midas sighed his stress out again and went to the back room, lay down on a beanbag chair and waited for the salesman to arrive. He closed his eyes and his thoughts meandered into a dream about clowns and acrobats in a market twirling to furious music and giddy laughter, the incessant barks of dogs amid the clamorous bartering beside tall stone walls, and winding passages made from the stalls of a market full of wares and produce…

TWO

Knuckles rapped against glass, again and again. Midas opened his eyes and turned his aching neck. Moulded into the beanbag chair in which he'd fallen asleep, he rubbed his forehead. He surveyed the floor of the back room from behind the right pillar. Shadow gave way to stuff he'd neglected: Sandino's typewriter, a globe suspended in its silver stand, a lute leaning on a chest, a bookshelf full of old hardcover texts, and a small wooden throne, he thought from the Incan empire, on a raised dais at the back wall. His gaze carried into the café along the espresso bar to the front door and, beside it, the reading area with its low coffee table and sagging sofa. Through the bay window he saw a tall pear-shaped man with a red bowler hat and a beige trench coat. The man's round face pressed against the glass, and his eyes blinked in the rain.

Midas stood, tried to smooth out his collared dress shirt, sleeves still rolled up and regretted the scattered mud remaining on his ankles and shoes. He walked to the door and opened it.

The man surged inside, grinned and held his red bowler hat with both hands against his belly. He put out a pudgy hand. "Hippias. So pleased."

Midas forced a smile, still disoriented from his deep nap. "Yes, at last we meet. Have a seat," he said turning from the outstretched hand. "Can I get you an espresso?"

"It's too late for that. It may be Hallowe'en, but I shan't be partaking in this city's festivities. Black tea, please." The man squeezed his large frame into a delicate metal armchair at a tea table near the espresso bar. It was an antique, apparently from the garden of a noble in nineteenth-century France.

"You're nimble."

"Pardon?" asked Hippias.

"Nothing."

Midas made a cup of tea, placed a biscotti on the saucer and sat down opposite Hippias, who folded his arms and kept smiling. The movement shifted things, and the tea shook on the table. Midas rushed to steady it. He couldn't afford another spill. This water was precious, and a café like this serving gourmet water, as he'd call it in his private thoughts, got the attention of the inspectors. For them it was all about the water licence.

Midas steadied the cup until things settled down.

"Indeed, thank you so much for meeting. My, oh my, we're busy, aren't we? So tough to get meetings these days." Hippias laughed as he flung his head back and squeezed his eyes with mirth. "But busy is good. Yes, yes, now: right to it. I'm a man of select words. Believe me, it's true. And I know you're busy — busy bee — being the small, independent businessman that you are. And what a concept you've developed. So fine, and absolutely unique. Now: I have a proposition for you," Hippias said. "We've been speaking for some time, and—"

"I wouldn't go that far," said Midas. He tried to smile. The salesman was annoying.

Hippias's eyes went wide, then he smiled broadly. "Good point, Midas. I have been calling you incessantly for months now. The purpose for my calls was—"

"To get a meeting." Midas had done this kind of thing too in his own way, which was more subtle. This guy was old school.

"Yes, well, true, and the purpose of the meeting is to demonstrate the fit between our companies. You sell coffee in an independent establishment." He swept his thick arm in an arc around the café.

Midas watched the rain drops trickle down the man's brow.

Hippias kept his smile strong and his eyes wide, ever expectant. Midas imagined Hippias would next show off his research and try to share knowledge, not to get business — of course not, he thought sarcastically — but simply from generosity, to help him. The more he helped Midas, the more Midas would eventually believe he needed him. Midas knew how the game worked. And meanwhile, Midas still didn't know what the salesman had to sell.

"My friend," said Hippias, reflecting to the ceiling. "You're surrounded by conglomerates whose business interests are wide-ranging and whose influence reaches everywhere. There is no such thing as a company that does one thing anymore. Certainly, there are themes. Your old firm, for example. What was it called, Superior? They do investments and properties, to be sure, but there was more, wasn't there? And take my group, *Advance*, as we call it. We tend to the entertainment side of things." Midas had heard of Advance. This guy hadn't said he worked for them until now. He knew they dealt in restaurants, movies, live shows, pornography, intoxicants and gourmet foods. "Products and services that please people," Hippias continued. "Coffee pleases immensely — and immediately — we can all agree. Your brand, especially. I have done some research into your sourcing."

Midas had never seen such a terrible salesman. He should be asking more questions rather than launching headlong into a determined pitch.

Hippias lingered with a pause and a grin. "Peru, is it?"

Midas stared at the man, searching for something familiar. Everything about his face was thick and heavy yet light and fast at once. Midas walked to the far end of the espresso bar and picked up his Probe. He sat with the screen facing away from Hippias and typed the salesman's name and *Advance* into Rinth. This Probe was the one he used the most because he hated walking with the smaller one in his pocket, but the *n* on the big one would stick all the time. He kept his hand-held by the left end of the stage beside the door to his roaster-room office.

Hippias smiled and leaned over the round table. His eyes glowed. "Let's be clear. We want your beans."

Hippias stood with emphatic energy, scraped the pointed feet of the metal chair on the floor and struggled out from between its thin arms. He walked, wet overcoat swishing, to the edge of the raised floor.

Midas glanced up from his screen. "That's my back room. You see all that stuff? I got it in the South. I used to travel a lot with work."

Hippias squinted into the dark oval space. He took in the sculpted stone pillars and the arch overhead. "Was this a small theatre once? It seems like a stage. Are those little devils up there?"

"Don't know," said Midas. He held back from saying anything further, preferring to watch and listen.

"I see the shadows of some curious items in there," said Hippias as he turned to Midas. "Most interesting. You're a man who listens to history? With an eclectic and nostalgic taste."

"I don't know about that," said Midas. "But yeah, I like history. Things haven't always been the way they are now. It gives me some peace." He'd share this with the salesman. It was true, and there was no harm in sharing something personal. It didn't mean he had to let Hippias in any further.

Hippias walked a little farther, planted his hands upon the old, ragged planks of the raised floor and hummed, reflecting, "Yes, yes, my friend, so true."

For the worst salesman in the world, Midas thought, he had a way of connecting.

"Nothing too valuable, though," said Midas.

This was not true. He'd purchased some items and others he'd found in abandoned places.

"You have certainly lived an adventurous life, my friend."

"In a way, I guess."

He had and he hadn't. The artifacts he'd found abandoned tended to have been hidden and forgotten given the state of things down there. Over his ten years working for Superior across that territory, pursuing this hobby was easy, with all those curious artifacts (one simple word for so many diverse things and all of them essentially instruments for so many purposes) just sitting there, waiting to be taken. No one owned them anymore, so it dawned on him fairly quickly that they ought to be recovered. Ought: an obligation to salvage from destruction because they didn't deserve to wither away into nothing. People deserved to know about them, so they could look to the past because the future was bleak.

The condition of the South — unstable with wild currencies and coups d'état — is what made it all possible, and the violence and chaos had become so extreme it left you wondering: How can a coup d'état happen when there's not really a state anymore? Just lots of companies to fill the void. It was almost feudalistic.

And this decay was here now too, in its early stages. So he supposed they were all living an adventurous life, not just him, and a dangerous one. But it wasn't adventurous to have taken these things. *Take* was the wrong word. All he did was rescue them.

"I have never visited or done business in Peru," said Hippias as he leaned over the stage's edge, eyes questing. For a moment, his feet left the ground as he almost teetered like a seesaw. "I have heard things are much worse down there than here in Toronto or Europe." He glanced over his shoulder and gave Midas a sad expression. It vanished as he swivelled back to gaze up into the dome that soared in darkness behind the arch.

"Yeah, they're much worse," said Midas. "Ghost towns. Lots of violence, gangs and the countryside is off-the-charts bad. Some big plots of agro-development, then dried up leftovers of jungles. Mountains are really rough. Crumbled up piles of rocks, when you look at them. Riddled with mines, mainly."

Hippias laughed, suddenly and strangely full of mirth. "They most certainly are!"

Midas clenched inside. He'd sold some mines, helped some companies buy some mines. It wasn't funny.

"And the only thing left to mine, really, is that ghastly magma," Hippias said. "It may be a new source of power, and probably the last one, but my goodness, does it not reek?" He let out a long, deep laugh.

Midas looked down at his Probe's screen and found Advance's headquarters posted as London. He knew Europe had been slower to transition to this "ghastly magma" as this strange man described it. Vast deposits coming from the bowels of the earth that kept some industries doing well, but it was messy. Deep mining, lots of labour and more inputs necessary than the old options like solar, wind, water, nuclear, fusion, all of them crowded out by concentrated, monied interests in this one big resource. It wasn't right. In his humble opinion, it was one thing to ignore the sun's solar power, but it was totally messed up to eat your own planet's heart. The earth's molten core getting sucked out of itself by its own children.

Midas kept looking at his Probe about Advance and found nothing related to power. "First time here?" he asked.

Nothing on coffee either. "Oh, goodness, no. I come all the time. I'm the sales rep for this region, and to the south."

Midas looked up at him. "Really? How far south?"

"All the way south," said Hippias.

"But not Peru," said Midas.

Hippias turned from the back room and walked along the opposite wall of the café, slowly perusing photographs, paintings, wall hangings, small shelves covered with instruments, ancient weaponry and toys. "I should be delighted if you showed me around back there someday."

"Right." Midas followed Hippias and his route along the far wall, past the black-and-white photographs. "What are you looking for?"

"We can sell you better beans, if you can believe it." Hippias faced Midas from the picnic table and gleamed.

"You don't sell coffee." Midas met the gaze hard.

"And in addition," said Hippias, "I should prefer to siphon some pellets through your establishment."

He stared at Midas and Midas stared back at him.

"What?"

Hippias smiled broadly beneath the beads of sweat trickling down his cheek. He walked back into the café, navigating his large frame through the tables and chairs. "Siphon," he said. "Move, you know. Drugs." His face went a little pink. "We're Advance, after all." Then he shrugged, "What do you expect?"

Midas looked for signs of nervousness, but Hippias maintained his confident shine.

"I don't need this." He said this firmly and held his hand up as though an absolute stop sign. Yet despite his resistance, Midas imagined what Hippias was capable of, what might hide in his trench coat pockets, who was poised to walk through the door. Offers like this could not be turned down easily.

"Oh, you know you do." Hippias stood beside Midas with his face close and nodded. "During your tenure at Superior, you would move corrupt pills, potions and powders, wouldn't you?" The words sounded smooth and serene in spite of what they meant, and Midas's field of vision clouded as his heart unexpectedly raced. For a suffocating moment all he could see was the man's heavy lips open and close, hypnotizing him, and inside the mouth the thick pink tongue rolled up and down and around, sloshing like a slug.

"Yes," Hippias continued, "what technology can do! Move this and that, so on the sudden, *n'est-ce pas*?" He chuckled and shook his head in wonderment. "And now here, look outside at the hot winds and the raging rains. The unforgiving sun scorches us, takes our forests and leaves us to bake in our last days. This water, all of it, is rationed, even within a massive underground market in its trade. How times have changed in the last few years. As though here on Earth we have suffered under a hidden debt and now the Sun's become the real banker — a debt that existed all along, between us and that massive burning beast. Or something like that. Unexpectedly, we're called on to pay back. And yet we hold on, don't we?" Hippias spoke louder, his tenor voice stronger.

Midas recovered himself somewhat, straightened his back and took stock of Hippias, who talked like he was saying something new. He wasn't. As though he was orating to an audience in awe of his insights. The debt and the banker part was an interesting twist, Midas thought, but the guy couldn't keep the words from flowing out of his mouth. Sure, it was worsening up here, as the rich North had passed its point of no return like the poor South had years ago — this was more than obvious — but Midas wondered why this salesman thought a speech outlining recent history was the right way to get some kind of closed deal.

"The Earth and us, my friend," he shouted cheerfully and clapped his hands. "In essence, given the state of things, there's really nothing else for you to do. Is there?" Midas's initial offence from moments ago now took on nascent tones of alarm. This felt like the onset of extortion. The man was a drug dealer.

"I don't move drugs. Never did."

Hippias rushed on, "Oh, I'm aware. You had partners. One, in particular. Poor Maverick. Such a sudden disappearance but perhaps he got what he was asking for, hey?" He walked to the stage's edge and strolled along its length as he glided his fingers upon its surface.

Midas reached for a small glass of water on the bar, carefully sipped and thought how he had turned a blind eye to Maverick and the others. They distracted themselves with that occasional thrill. That's all they seemed to want, other than some extra money. But he didn't say anything, not even when they sent watered-down pills and sometimes total duds. He'd always felt uncomfortable about it but it was just another, relatively minor, piece to the bigger problem at Superior he'd had to leave. He was here, doing things better, his own boss doing good. He didn't need this, and it bothered him even more that a stranger walked in, knowing things.

"It wasn't me," Midas said. "He did that."

"True. Again! Ah, such a fine man you are." Hippias leaned in with a sweaty face.

Midas frowned. *This man knows too much about me.* He didn't like what Hippias had discovered. Not one bit. And besides, it wasn't a fair judgment. So he stood tall and nodded at the front door. "And so this sales meeting is over."

"No, dear Midas, no! I ask only that you store the drugs, that's it. We'll do the moving. Trust me. Not to worry." He winked in reassurance and grinned. "My friend, don't worry, we will pay you well. A nice supplement to your little business."

"What exactly is this drug you want me to store?" Midas was growling with resentment, beginning to feel trapped. Because they could always find him here.

Hippias looked to the floor. "Dry capsules designed ultimately for beverages. A little love powder."

"I don't want to—"

"They're small and might be mistaken for coffee beans. That's why we're doing this, obviously. Here, with you." Hippias flopped upon a stool at the espresso bar, relaxed. "You'll be perfect for this," he went on, happy and light. "No one will know. You'll make more money than you've ever dreamt. You'll be the shark, roaming the ocean, taking a little bite out of this, a bite out of that. You get fat, yes—"

"Why me?" Midas's stomach churned. "I'm an indie. Why bother with an indie?" He caught himself wondering, as a business strategist, truly why him. A deep, ill-defined feeling germinated too, because his cash flow was low and being an indie café was, basically, a stupid idea, one borne of a desperation to escape.

"I'm not really at liberty to say. I'm sure you understand." Hippias shuffled upon the stool and observed the opposite wall. "We will bring them in bags and sell another brand beside the one lonely version you sell here. In and amongst them will be our little secret. In specially marked baggies, smaller narrower ones hidden amongst the beans at the bottom of the bags. Can't mistake them for anything else, rest assured. Not to worry! Just to move. From elsewhere to here, and from here to elsewhere. No one will notice and you won't be disappointed, nor will your supplier, Lazuli."

"Well, yes, he would, actually." They had made a deal.

"Well, no, he has been meddling with someone else."

"What?" Midas had been through some harrowing big deals, with lots of surprises, many of them morally suspect, but he couldn't recall a business meeting with as many left fielders as this one. It was a non-stop barrage.

"He's cheating on you, Midas. That's what we hear. With a particularly unsavoury group."

"What?" Midas said. This man was a liar. At the same time, Hippias knew enough about him not to be lying about everything.

Hippias shook his head. "My dear Midas, it's a nasty group of companies, a network. Creed, they call themselves." He stood to gaze again into the back room. "Them you need to watch out for, very carefully." Hippias turned grim. "Very carefully, indeed, Midas."

The dark shadows of the back room behind him whirled with a soundless, invisible wind. It tugged at Midas's spine, as though to suck him up into the dome's high peak.

"Why haven't I heard of this company?"

He had to keep testing Hippias, push the nervous angst and questions over to him.

"A network," said Hippias. He shook his head. "Few have heard of them, and this — system, shall we call it that? — developed very quickly. Almost like a virus, as my director puts it."

Hippias leaned over the espresso bar and took three biscotti from the glass jar beneath the counter, placed as such for the servers to manage. "Not into some very good things," he continued. "We can't figure out who governs them. Probably, power within their — whatever it is — is still diffuse. They will consolidate in due time. We hope they will self-destruct in the process, of course. Although it might help to infiltrate just a little. Tippy-toe in and around, here and there, you know?"

The acidic pit in Midas's stomach churned. He needed the money, but they would dig into him. There was no way Lazuli would get messed up in group like that.

So he thought to ask, to dig a bit and see what truth came through. "I'm sure I'm one of many, aren't I?"

Hippias chewed on a biscotti and crumbs fell to the floor.

Zora typically leaned there, somehow always finding her way to that one spot to perch her dark silver-lined boot on the stool's base, and her round hips would tilt. Midas wondered what Zora would say to all of this.

"But no," Hippias said, and shrugged. "Why don't I admit it? You may as well know just how important you can be. Enjoy the money more that way, hey?" His eyes squeezed with a mirth that, Midas noticed, would appear and vanish in flashes.

"You're not going to tell me who gets this drug, at what price, and what you're ultimately going to do, are you?" asked Midas. *What's the point?* he thought. They were only looking for money and market share. That was their point. Beneath his challenge, Midas felt something close inside of him, a surrender to an old power that once held him for years. He fought it back, buried it from Hippias's sight, yet it tugged with a short, insistent yank not unlike the emptiness from the unnaturally cavernous back room whose shadow engulfing the artifact collection on that stage beckoned his spine. He'd lost the last commission. He'd been let go, not given a package. The people at Superior were snakes. And if he didn't take a cut of this strange new opportunity, as dangerous as it was, he would lose out on one of the most lucrative markets of the times. He'd clear up this nutbar claim about Lazuli soon enough with the man himself. That was nothing. The trade here, though, that was something, as bad as it was.

"Now, my dear Midas. Through your very own bean source, you are linked to a larger and much less independent network. You would do well to embrace your newfound place in this salvaged new world that is coming, or could come, if only we could do it right."

Midas imagined what that asshole Maverick would say if he were still alive: Too good to be true, a gift, take it, work it; and what Zora would say: Do it better than them.

"So please help us close it. Feel it? Do a dance." Hippias put his palms into the air and swayed to a humming music hidden in his head. "You'll get the terms soon, along with the bags. They are rather large. Please do let them in. Meanwhile, I'll leave this sampler for you." From his large inner coat pocket his thick hand pulled out a compact, fist-sized bag of crunchy beans within heavy non-descript plastic. Midas would never put it on a display shelf despite the pleasant aroma. Hippias smiled with confidence, so proud his arms weaved in a dance at his sides.

Exhausted with near defeat, Midas put his head on his arms crossed on the espresso bar.

Hippias smiled broadly again. "Not to worry. We could provide security if you need it. Undercover who come in and pretend to be customers. For a price, of course. Advance does this too. We have to, don't we? In entertainment, things get troubled at times." Hippias put on his red bowler hat and pressed the red button so the front door slid up.

"No," said Midas as he raised his head. "No deal. I'm not giving up. I left all this corrupt bullshit a year ago for a reason."

Hippias's gleaming face fell into a sad frown. "Yes, how true. You are indeed a fine man." As quickly as it left, a smile reappeared. "That's what makes you perfect for this. Just what we are looking for!" He clapped his hands. "Every no is one step closer to a yes. It's just a game, isn't it? So call when you need. I can always help. And believe me, my friend, this is an offer you cannot refuse. Think of the money…"

He bowed, tilted his red bowler hat with a surprising grace for his large hands and strode out the door beneath the tinkling bells while Midas shoved his shaking hands into his pockets and clenched them to stop.

THREE

Just after leaving Midas, Zora found the mermaid statuette in the gutter, in a pool of dirty green water surrounded by plastic bottles, crunched cans of pop and splintered beer bottle shards. She picked it up and shook the water off. It was beautiful despite where it'd been lying, of intricately sculpted blue stone she'd never seen before. She hesitated, wanting to go back and give it to Midas — he'd truly appreciate something like this — but she had to get to her shift. In her heart she knew it belonged in Midas's collection. It could use a good wipe off too, so she decided to take it to work with her for the time being. She'd get it to Midas after.

She hurried through the streets at dusk, and as party-goers meandered by in costume — a tiger here, a pink princess there — one small group passed her and someone whined. Zora sought who had made the sound: the animal resembling a monkey, the bony witch with greasy long white hair carrying a crooked broom, or the man in a tattered suit with holes and rips and spiked hair. As they walked past, the suited one pulled the witch's hair too hard as though teasing, except for the clump of strands in his fist. The witch forced a cackle with fallen, confused eyes.

Then she bumped into Zora.

"Sorry," Zora said. Part of her wanted to tell them to fuck off because she knew this passing trio were hallowers. But as they turned a corner, she felt sorry for the witch, her chosen affront to reality, and the bad friends that came with it.

They reminded her of youth subcultures from the past that adopted strange ways of dressing, acting and speaking, many of them well-meaning in their rebellion yet so often tragically prone to bad consequences. Like the kids last month who joined a sparsely attended protest, blocking the intersection at Yonge and Bloor between two office towers while clamouring, chanting, even singing at times, against the frauds of capitalism, all decked out in a variety of colourful creative costumes. Hallowe'en again, in advance, with a social justice bent she thought to herself at the time with satisfaction, yet even then with a sense of impending doom. Indeed, when one teen streaked naked through the crowd, she cringed as she watched it live on Rinth, for these things rarely ended well. An especially hostile sub-group of protestors surrounded him, beat and kicked him, then dragged his half-conscious body by the ankles to a manhole, managed to open it and dumped him in. A senseless violence where any prior purpose had been lost.

It goes both ways, she thought bitterly. The youthful rebellion and its energized idealism and the twisted world of the mundane adult, the one in the working world well-conditioned and ready to perform, achieve, over-achieve. There and back it went like a seesaw, a lifeline. They depended upon one another, these rebellious youths and those conservative working adults in suits. She felt sorry for the youth because it wasn't their fault. They had to rebel because the world was falling apart and the suits, as she'd call them, could not be trusted. Then they'd grow up and join them. Then, in their suits, they'd harvest a new crop of energized rebels.

Zora pulled out her Probe and typed to Midas: *I got you something. It reminds me of that dream you had. Maybe it's one of those coincidences we talked about. I'll drop it off on my way back from work.*

After her shift at Night it would be nine in the morning, and she would drop in on the way home for a tea and calming talk if she wasn't too tired. Whether with Ira or more hopefully Midas, the whole place had a way of uplifting her. Because Night was bad and everyone who went there was bad.

These thoughts lingered as she walked. With every shift she doubted her bona fides: Was she bad too, then, for wanting this money? Did she have a choice, really, because her comics made nothing, and didn't the values she encouraged in her challenging art compensate for serving those drug fiends, the pimps? Didn't it make up for the violence of the ring, the pit surrounded by an amphitheatre reminiscent of ancient Rome? And similar to Rome, at Night, two men — who'd been starved and whipped and forced to watch terrible things being done to a loved one so they would do anything to free them — beat the life out of each other. A human cock fight, betted upon and cheered by intoxicated assholes in expensive suits and shoes. This club was for Toronto's wealthy elite, so many of them that it was impossible to recognize any regulars. So many that she thought there was something clearly wrong with way too many people.

Zora's thirty-eight years of life had been hard, so she could withstand the brutality of this place, at least so far. Its debauchery was extreme, but she'd seen so much in her journey that the most horrendous moments at Night seemed to her to be exaggerated representations of the world they all lived in anyway, and probably its ultimate conclusion. She hated it.

Then there was the cell. Their ideals kept her afloat for a few months, and she'd felt fortified to be involved in something virtuous. No violence, they said, no crime. Just find important information for the others and then eventually they'd fix things. Make the world better again. That was now gone, thankfully, because her ex-boyfriend was an arrogant prick and she didn't think he was in it for the virtue. Only for himself. So now she was left with her writing — writing for the good, to inspire people and participate with them in doing good — and to figure out how to survive and do good without getting herself killed in this godforsaken town.

After twenty minutes, Zora entered the cavernous hall of Night. Balconies lined the oval walls and spanned some six stories high over a vast stone floor. Her eyes adjusted to the dim light as she weaved her way through dining tables, low-lying brick fire pits and tall flaming torches to her station at the bar. There she found a cloth and wrapped the statuette.

Staff in white robes finished mopping the floor, and those in tuxedos set tables for dinner. Zora kept an eye out for Augustine. He had told her he wanted to give her a surprise before his assignment downtown at the Hallowe'en Ball. He also said he wanted to ask a favour, and all of this bothered her. But for his meagre frame she might have been afraid. They'd broken up over a month ago, and he kept calling and coming around the club. Saying he had a surprise struck her as, yet again, arrogant. She didn't give a shit about a surprise from him.

"Hi there, Sweetie," said Augustine from the other side of the bar.

The light from two torches flickered, and a shadow fell over the nearby booths from the mezzanine overhead where the baths sat. A spiral staircase lined with red carpet ascended to them. Zora gave a disgusted look, walked over and drew the heavy orange curtain tightly around the staircase. She hated what they did to themselves in those steamy tubs. One of the more dangerous drugs available in this place, slider was a terrible chemical liquid manufactured to induce a psychotic coma. Then, if they were lucky, they'd wake up. It was drug mixed with gambling in one and they all placed bets.

"You're here," she said, drawing her attention back to him with some effort. It would be a task to talk him out of here, and she had work to do. She stared at him. He looked paler than normal and wore a formal server's uniform: white shirt, black dress pants, bow tie and cummerbund. What she hoped to do — tell him never to come near her again — made her nervous.

"You're late," he said, smiling with his sharp blue eyes.

Zora thought to call security. Sometimes he'd come around here and not say hello, which was better but also creepy. Like he was watching. How would he know when her shift started?

She quit the cell also because it was inherently dangerous. As calm and quiet as Augustine claimed they were, her conversations with another more senior member of the group named Cisco made it plain there was no peaceful way to spy on powerful people who did bad things. Cisco didn't lie and he was a rough old guy who'd been around the block. More times than she. She admired him and was sorry they didn't talk as much anymore other than the odd message. He respected her decision, and they'd talked about her guilt for seeking, subconsciously he'd thought, knowledge for her own writing. He didn't believe she'd done that on purpose, and knew she'd kept confidences. Midas agreed too when she shared this with him, and despite his opinions about the cell he showed some mild admiration for Cisco, at least her description of him.

Not that they shared much with her. It was all impressionistic for her, and she'd felt more like a groupie hanger-on, amongst them on account of Augustine, which felt more wrong for her than anything. Cisco understood and had said, "Good for you. Remember, there's a difference between knowledge and information. So it's okay. Don't be a stranger, kid."

"The group is onto our next research project," said Augustine, drawing her attention back from her thoughts of Cisco. "We listen, the right people talk, et cetera," he said with a knowing laugh like she knew, but she cringed because she didn't know and didn't think he knew much either. He went on: "As usual, I'm taking the back seat. I'm just picking them up."

"That's wise," she said, not believing him at all. "Why wouldn't you get the information too? What's the problem?"

He bowed his head while his folded fingers clenched upon the marble counter. "It's one quick conversation. Nothing more. They don't need me."

Zora bent behind the counter to rearrange the pint glasses haphazardly placed by a colleague, and fidgeted with the cloth around the statuette. "And here you are, wearing a ridiculous disguise as a server. Don't tell me that's a chauffeur getup. Where're you going?"

she asked as she rose and placed the statuette on the table, wiping her sweaty palms with another cloth.

"I'm sorry, Zora, I cannot divulge."

He'd been saying such things since they met over six months ago.

"Since you're the driver, why don't you do me a favour and drop this off at Midas's café on the way."

Zora immediately regretted asking this and questioned why she would ever ask in the first place. But here it might get stolen, and there was something about it. The statuette was no piece of junk, a word she'd used to tease Midas about all his various collected paraphernalia decorating his café and crowding the oddly-designed back room space. If it was in fact valuable, then she should never trust Augustine with it. Yet she knew where the impulsive request came from: to dare him. Challenge that he wasn't just a driver. Still, a stupid thing to say. This was not a conversation she needed to have, she reminded herself, but here she was letting it linger on, tempted to wield spoken words as weapons against him.

She moved the statuette closer toward her, placed it neatly by the beer handles and wiped the counter. She'd bound it so tightly the thin cloth revealed the statuette's supple shape. So finely sculpted, attractive even, for a piece of stone. She'd have to keep it close for the rest of her shift. Hallowe'en promised to be exceptionally busy.

His smile faltered, until he replaced it with a frozen grin that showed his crooked teeth. His breath was off again today, she noticed. Worse than last week when she'd first noticed it. Augustine muttered from deep in his throat. Zora looked closer at him, for he sounded sick, or deeply bothered. He reached his arm over the wide countertop and pulled the statuette across, dragging it on the smooth stone.

"Not so fast there," she said, and hesitated as she reached her hand to the statuette. His nails were longer, unkept, and in the dim light of the club's flickering fire pits and torches, maybe dirty but she couldn't tell for certain. What had happened to him over the past month? Or maybe he'd always been like this and she'd been so enamoured in the thrill of joining the cell — but no. This was something more.

He stopped and looked down at the thing in his hand. "What is it anyway? Do you even know? Where did you find this beautiful creature?"

"It's just something I found. But I'm afraid it'll get stolen here. You should know that. This place is crazy." Zora cursed herself for answering. Engaging with him was a waste of time, and she had work to do. The club was slowly filling up. Yet her impulse to respond to people never seemed to change. Other people would have called security by now, turned their backs on him as the guards dragged him off with a strap over his mouth to silence his protests. Maybe her words weren't weapons when he seemed unnaturally sick, but minor acts of empathy.

The kitchen door behind her swung open and brought the clangs of pots and hollers of the cooks.

Augustine was holding the statuette by the tail. He dragged it again, scraping it over the stone, onto his lap. Zora winced and held herself from grabbing it back. She didn't know what he'd do. People could be unpredictable, she'd always found, and he seemed now ripe for unpredictability. He shrugged as he stood from the stool. "All right. I'll do you this favour." He straightened his back. "But I need you to do one for me. Will you come with me to a boat cruise next weekend? It's the next big Hallowe'en event."

Zora cursed herself again. She'd not yet retracted her request. He'd never walk off with it, of this she was sure. His arrogant assumptions irked her most.

"Is this the surprise you had for me?"

More minor weapons.

He looked above her head, not quite rolling his eyes, and blinked.

"Isn't Hallowe'en over tonight?" she pressed, although aware this was false. Everyone knew about the Ball this evening and the boat cruise the next weekend, each hosted by a competing company and to which the city's elite was invited.

"Hallowe'en seems to last longer every year," he said. He crossed his leg and clasped his bony hands around his knee.

"Yeah, I guess." She kept her eye on the statuette. "And why do you guys need to serve at a ball to get information?"

The hall behind Augustine was filling up. The wait staff moved faster, and she watched the bar for her customers.

Augustine coughed with a long, deep rattle. "Zora, I keep telling you. That's all we do."

"Gather information." Zora crossed her arms and decided to give the statuette to her boss, Shanti, for safekeeping during her shift.

"That's right. And, next week at the cruise, we need to record something." His head remained bowed at a slight angle and covered in shadow, and he looked up with only his eyes and bore into her forehead. "I'd like you to assist. And you'll have a grand time, Zora. All I ask — we ask — is that for a brief moment, when we know it's happening, you go to a designated place on the boat, sit beside two gentlemen who are going to discuss a deal. Record the deal. All you'll do is sit there, listen and look. And talk a little. You then go about your business and continue to drink and have a splendid evening. Okay?"

This was brazen and out of the blue. She squinted a bit to see his eyes better. Just how sick might he be to even ask this of her, did he have a fever or something? "No," she said. "And I think we need to talk about something else."

She felt dizzy. Part of her felt sorry for him, and she tried to bury the feeling. What his group did, in concept, was alluring and aligned with her values, things she'd tried to make a cause. But in reality it wasn't. It was bad company, other than Cisco. Augustine represented the very kind of thing she denounced, with his arrogance, shifty speech, slippery ulterior motives, and the group was innately dangerous.

Zora knew she had it in her to make a strong point. She found a glass, carefully filled it with water and drank, her eyes fixed on him and his long hands holding again the thing that belonged to Midas. It was time to tell him to stay away, forever.

Augustine opened the cloth and stared at the statuette. His teeth were bared and he held it tightly over the counter.

The statuette had no base, made to permanently float in your hand seemingly deep within the depths of the sea. The smooth scales made of a striking blue polished stone whose sharp edges overlaid one another, hundreds of fine scales that fitted tightly over a perfect waist, not too thin, and covered breasts like a gown one might wear out on the night, over round buttocks and sumptuous thighs that merged within the tail and ended in a wide fin. This smooth convergence from human to animal gave her a magical attraction. High cheek bones accentuated her narrow face surrounded by long hair — it may have been as long as Zora's — going to the top of her back, just past the shoulders. And no matter how anyone held her, she was suspended in salt water, ever floating. Her arms dangled as she plunged deep into the sea, yet remained so still it was stunning because she should have been moving, and already she was so far below the surface there was no light, the only brightness from her eyes.

"What are you grinning about?" Zora asked. She looked up and down the bar. People continued to stream in, taking seats at tables and at her bar. Wait staff moved at a clip and a group in suits huddled nearby at the beer handles.

Augustine moved his eyes up and down the statuette. "Zora, where did you get this?"

She didn't want to answer. "I don't know, the gutter."

"You know what, Sweetie, I'll give this to Midas. Yes, fair enough." He put his hand upon the statuette. "But say yes to next weekend."

"Forget it. I can take it to Midas myself."

There. She said it. A small ripple of relief went through her, and she glanced again around the bar and vast floor of fine dining tables and busy waiters setting things up for the long night ahead.

"We'll pay you." For a moment she thought he referred to the stone statuette he held in his hand. Of course, he meant the job he asked her to do on the cruise. His voice was lower, as though it mattered to keep his voice down. "None of us work for free."

The men in suits by the beer handles gestured to her. "I have to get back to work, Augustine."

"You're calling me Augustine now?" His face tensed, and the red light from the flames of the torches on either side of them flickered long pointed shadows across his pale skin.

"What the fuck else would I call you? So just what are you proposing here?" she asked. "Would I have to snuggle up to someone, prostitute myself? Is that where this is going?" The more the words flowed from her, the more she wanted to grab the statuette and have him banished from Night.

He grimaced and sat back. She reached across, courage bolstered now, and pulled the mermaid to her. The statuette's heavy blue stone scratched the bar's marble surface.

He said, "Just record a conversation. You're clever, determined, and you're pretty Zora, we need you to do this. Yes, you're exceptionally pretty. They'll appreciate that. But you can be a server, to maintain a professional capacity."

"Go to hell." She wanted to say, "You're disgusting," more than ever. The man had no understanding of the fact she was saying no. He could only press onward, assuming she would soon say yes out loud.

His hand stretched for hers holding the statuette, but she put it beneath the counter.

The kitchen door swung open behind her again and Zora started, now nervous they'd be overheard.

As much as he revolted her, if not because of his selfish manipulation then his sickly appearance, whatever the cell was interested in sounded intriguing, she had to admit to herself. But, she resolved, not for her. Not anymore.

He coughed. Phlegm bubbled up and he bent over coughing as he caught a piece of it in his palm. Zora stepped back.

"You're the perfect fit for this," he said when he could manage to speak again.

He's definitely sick with something, Zora thought. But there was something else too, from before. She'd broken up with him because his claims didn't match reality. They didn't fit with the virtue of this *revolutionary* group, and it didn't take her long to doubt what they saw in him. It had come down to one crystalized moment that could seem insignificant compared to the bigger contradictions about revolution and virtue. It's hard to make decisions for oneself based on philosophy, so she remained grateful for the meaningful minutiae of this lone event. It had given her a nudging clarity. At that time six weeks ago, while lounging on his couch sipping a hefty scotch, Augustine had let a lazy lie slip. A week earlier they'd agreed to meet up at a restaurant and he didn't show, messaging her that a job had come up that night: a quick necessity where they — he and an associate in the cell she'd never heard of — had to monitor something. But half-way through his glass of scotch he described the evening very differently: that he'd been too tired, something had come over him, he was feeling out of sorts. For a few days Zora hesitated, doubting whether she remembered the facts correctly, or did he feel shame and had made an excuse for an otherwise still-worthy cause. Soon she'd resolved it was enough, broke up and said goodbye to Cisco.

Zora now focused back on his thin frame opposite her, hunched over the bar where the statuette had sat. His bony, crooked fingers perched beneath a heavy palm with their long nails scraping into the stone surface like a tarantula poised to pounce.

"How would I record these ... these men?" she asked. Asking this question produced a self-loathing she quickly recognized. Too curious about what might happen if she did this, knowing she would never do it, or even let herself be directed to do something, especially when it's wrong. But she had to ask because she was in a conversation, and it was the next logical response. What else was she to do, not follow up with his ridiculous demand? It didn't matter what might happen. Simple: She'd reject it. Still, she wished she could just hold her palm to his face, turn around and walk away.

"A wiretap, of course," he said, nodding with confidence. "We hear he's not such a pig and besides, we'll take care of you. You'll look at him — at them both — with your beautiful eyes. Your beautiful, piercing eyes, Zora."

Augustine leaned across the bar as though to kiss her. His nails scraped the marble. She stepped back farther, found the washcloth and wiped the counter.

"I trust you," Augustine continued. "You'll do great." He hunched over the bar toward her. "This is important, Zora. The bureaucrat is a leader, a mandarin, with great power. As much as one could have in this withered state. And he's a member of a deviant group in government who are plotting … something. It might be a coup d'état. Or not and it's something else. Either way, we need to know what they're discussing."

He coughed again, then straightened his back, his voice stronger like it had been when she first met him.

The anxious vertigo almost returned but she fought it back. She wasn't boxed in, Zora knew she had control.

Augustine stood. He gave a little bow and said, "Come to my place in two days. We'll prepare."

Zora wanted to say no again but there was no need. She'd said no in her own head several times, had said it the first time, and set her eyes to the beer handles down the bar. The men in suits there, blurry in the dusky flame-flickering light of Night, waved to her.

Augustine turned and walked onto the vast floor through fire pits and tables and disappeared into the cavernous blackness while music grew in the room, the clamour of dining tables took over and Zora's crowd of clients thickened. Zora put the statuette into her bag in a drawer below the bar and served them.

FOUR

For Zora, the manner in which the massacre had been orchestrated showed a disturbing level of sophisticated planning.

She stood behind the counter at Night, just hours after Augustine's departure, and stared at the screens, at the horrible images being broadcast in real time from the Hallowe'en Ball — the bloody bodies, the crossbows with their poison tips, the white froth at their victims' mouths, veins bulging, their skin turning dark red and purple. Seven children of government officials had been abducted. And streamed across the window overlooking the expansive ballroom floor below were red viscous lines traced into words that seemed senseless and impossible to Zora.

The pictures posted by survivors showed the attackers in flamboyant costumes — not what one might expect of a sleek terrorist operation: oversized fuzzy animals (a skunk, a deer), a lizard in a white overcoat, a mummy with a crown and cape, a square board game, an angel with a trumpet slung across her back between wings whose feathers scattered as the arrows pierced their targets, and several suited men with tattered cloth, burned and stained with dirt, big hair spiked into heavily-braided lengths and covered in thick paste, and faces and hands marked by variously-shaped bruises. Then, as abruptly as the offenders had drawn their weapons, they'd disappeared, fleeing into

Toronto's underground Path, away from the screams and chaos. Zora had heard these things all night amid her clients' clamour for stimulants, sex, a weighted die, or their jockeying for a spot in the baths, or whatever else, even something as mild as cocaine. The news had barely dampened the party at Night, and it doubly offended Zora that so many clients casually disregarded the horror.

"We have to do something," she'd said. Not knowing at all what that could possibly be, still, it had to be said.

Shanti was next to her, gazing into the cavernous hall as the mass of customers, having digested the initial news, returned to their drinks. "Not tonight, honey. And I think you should avoid it. This is trouble."

Of all the shocking things Zora had seen, this atrocity unnerved her to the core.

"My God, Augustine was there. Did you know that?" Zora had flicked through her Probe to check her messages. The need to know overcame her deep-seated dislike of him. No one deserved to be slaughtered like this. She sent one to Augustine: *????? WTF?? You okay?* And she immediately regretted it.

"It's fine to find out if he's okay," said Shanti. "You're human. It doesn't mean you have to answer back, honey." Shanti had an edgy wisdom about her.

"I'm sending Midas something too."

Shanti smiled. "Oh, really? Why, oh why do you need to do that? Was he there too, waiting tables with your ex?"

Zora didn't bother responding to this sarcastic tease. Shanti had a way of seeing through people, and that was enough. She could see what she wanted. Besides, Midas was just a friend, a precious friend. And if one terrorist incident happened, what was to stop another one from happening, and wouldn't you want to know how your friends are when the sky feels like it's falling? Zora wished she hadn't written Augustine at all, especially the second he replied so swiftly, before she could write to Midas: *Left before it happened. Come tomorrow, my unit, so we can go over details. Lots happening. Amazed.*

Zora reread his reply. "My God, what an asshole," she said. "Don't you say, like, thanks for asking? Instead of, come and do my bidding?"

"Come on, honey," said Shanti. "Customers are back at it."

"I know," Zora said, and clicked off her Probe in disgust. "This guy's a true prick." She pointed to the mermaid statuette under the bar wrapped tightly in cloth. "Can you do me a favour and keep this in your office? Just til tomorrow morning. I'll give it to Midas then. I don't want it to go missing."

"Sure, honey." Shanti took the statuette and walked across the floor through the heavy crowd.

Time passed as Zora kept serving the customers whose exuberance at the thrill of Hallowe'en grew as the hours passed, heightened by the unbelievable crime at the Ball. Zora tried to doubt this perception by imagining they had only forgotten it, that their selfishness focused them on the immediacy of their surroundings. But she heard them talk. Some — not everyone, but enough of them — joked about the absurdity of the costumed murderers, others marvelled at the perfection of a real horror occurring on this night of all nights, at the awesome execution of the event. Zora's disgust, a feeling borne of anger and muted outrage, dwindled over the hours into a defeated dismay. She knew she'd have to leave this place and never come back. Poverty was better than this. She'd find a way.

It took some time to muster the courage to make the decision now, right here during the shift. To walk out. She'd never done this before and, having lived without steady income before, the prospect scared her. At some point during her hours-long hesitation she reflected that the fear of this unknown thing — abandoning her duties on moral grounds alone and deliberately depriving herself of the means to live — became a protective veil, a distraction from the outraged dismay brewing at the behaviour of everyone around her.

She looked across the floor to the entrance where Shanti faced a tall man and woman by the beaded curtain. They wore black uniforms, boots and laden belts. They glowered over Shanti, who pointed in Zora's direction and disappeared behind the beads.

Who are they? Zora wondered. Their faces were unsmiling with horizontal lines for mouths as they crossed the room toward her.

It couldn't be.

I've done nothing, she thought. *Nothing wrong.*

They looked like police she thought, with a slowly emerging feeling of dread. Shanti must have pointed at one of those business suits down along the bar. The dickheads she'd just served pints of beer.

Unless her writing on Rinth had drawn someone's attention, but she'd said nothing very bad there, other than opinions, and never inciting crime or talking of crime. Just progress, ideas to help people, she insisted to herself while denying the obvious as they walked closer: that she'd hung out recently with a research group that kept quiet. *Fuck*, she thought, *everybody does this now. No one likes the world and the world's falling apart. There's no law to uphold anymore so who the hell are they but a private force working for someone. Private security guards with a rich licence to walk around and hurt people.*

They were closer.

She watched them until they stood directly in front of her bar. One of them, the woman, grinned with the notorious metal inserts, some of which were chiselled into fanged points. "You're Zora?" one said.

This was Division Q. A private force with some presence in the city but also rare. Elite, exclusive, expensive and very deadly.

She nodded, feeling they would leave any minute and move on to the real criminal, maybe to her left, to the darker corner past the dining booths and into a passage to the brothel.

"How can I help you?" Zora's high pitch gave her a new level of panic. They would smell it. Yet somehow everything felt still, numb.

The woman, dark and strong, her head held up by a muscular neck, glared. Her teeth glistened in the reflecting glass behind the bar. Zora's blood rushed in and out of her head. Paid well, no doubt from one of the company's deep pockets. Pluto and Oxford were among the biggest. Companies like theirs dwarfed state power, filling a void that people everywhere needed to be filled, giving them an answer for their yearning desire that someone bigger than they be in charge.

It was Pluto's Hallowe'en Ball that had been violated by terrorists, his guests whose children had been stolen. He was probably behind this. And Division Q would get away with anything they wanted.

Here, Hallowe'en meant something, just for a couple of months. So Pluto put on his extravagant Ball, and next Oxford would splash his extraordinary cruise through the waters and around the islands of the Toronto harbour for his influential guests. Big business, politicians, powerful bureaucrats and business associates would congregate to network. And it seemed, given the massacre of the evening, they had gathered at the Ball only to be decimated. After such an offence, someone had to pay, with their private police forces to hunt them down for a fierce revenge.

Everything I've done, an epic mistake, she thought. *Should have stuck to music. No words, no opinions, just sounds and feeling. No distant, vague affiliation with a fucking revolutionary cell. No one gets hunted for creating sounds and feeling, do they?*

"Come with us," the woman said.

"I've done nothing," Zora said, wishing her panic could do more for her than give this numbness.

"Manager over there tells us you met with Augustine earlier," said the woman with the sharp teeth.

Zora wrote about Division Q once, after researching a disturbing story of a small group of young professionals who had donned hallower gear just for fun one evening on the bar scene, and ran into trouble that escalated after the officers arrived. Of the two who remained, one lost her hearing and the other his mind.

This was impossible. Shanti wouldn't betray her. The problem was, it was true: she had met with Augustine and there were video cameras everywhere. They would've seen the footage. Shanti would've been helpless to say anything other than yes, she's the one who met with Augustine.

Zora's thoughts raced as she struggled to find an answer for them, some good way to talk herself out of this. To show them she was not the one to look for.

How the hell do they know about Augustine if they were clandestine and quiet, just researching facts as an isolated cell in a silo? But of course people can find out about all kinds of shit, especially when you're up to no fucking good, you stupid little epic idiot. And a greedy idiot, too, always seeking something for yourself, in the name of social justice. You're full of shit, a hypocrite. It's not social justice if you just take material to show others the truth, but really all just to serve yourself. And now you pay the price with your blood and life.

This internal tirade was all she could come up with. Then survival kicked in, and she looked around for an escape. The brothel's winding rabbit warren of rooms, corridors and doorways provided the closest route. She might lose them in that labyrinth.

Zora ran.

She couldn't bear to turn around and look. There was only one way forward. She forced her doubting thoughts away.

Zora sprinted as hard as she could down an empty corridor, turned left, then down a side hall and right. The moans of sensual delight, the dim lanterns and shadows flickering, the heels of her boots on the stone floor, all this blurred along as she ran and disoriented her in the zigzagging left to right, right and back and around through sets of connected rooms, then through a bathroom area where naked bodies twisted within one another in their oblivious lust. She kept going, pushing her heels into the ground, propelling ahead to the last door leading outside, wherever that might be. She slowed with every turn past hanging beads and drapes as the number of people increased. Deeper into the brothel she went, into more corridors and rooms that only went on and on, empty of a last door leading outside where she might lose them.

Behind her, their hard boots clicked the floor in staccato bursts. The moving shadows, groans of pleasure and soft chatter coming from the dark rooms she passed became distant to her despite their engulfing presence.

I'm not hurting anyone, she thought. Corridors spun in too many directions. *I write comic strips.* She tried to convey meaning to people, to make sense of the badness going on around them all.

The boots clicked louder and echoed.

She had always preferred music, and that time when she was eight in the recital with her grandmother who smiled the whole time even though Zora couldn't get the beat until she had to stop and start over, in front of everyone, mirrored the same tempo as the clicking around the corridor. But music wasn't enough, or maybe she wasn't good enough. She needed something more concrete, to control by writing. But what do you write? How to convince people to do better things in our world? Where does it come from? And then that wasn't enough. She had to go and hang out with a revolutionary cell.

She slipped, fell to her knees. Almost instantly, cold metal hands — chain mail gloves — gripped her shoulders and pulled her up from the stone floor, her back forced against the officer's armour.

What matters, she reminded herself over the accusing words coming through their dreaded teeth, *is that it — music, the fool's errand — had to be replaced. I'm real.* Zora squeezed her eyes shut, mustering all her inner strength. She would change things in the world through another art.

FIVE

Sunday morning after Hallowe'en felt as hot and humid as the day before. Midas took his time as he walked along Dundas Street, enjoying the stillness in the nautical twilight. The streetcars weren't out yet, screeching and fuming as they would, billowing their red mist from the magma, a term he thought ridiculous. Sure it was excavated, but it wasn't natural. The companies had done something to it, a bastardization of a rare mineral discovered a decade ago that soured further what would have been a sulphuric odour. At the time, it was lauded as the salvation from the energy crisis, hailed as the ultimate answer to floundering green power. Desperately necessary after the oil had run out. The trouble was the money it brought in. There was too much of it, and the few companies that wrested control over it bought out the others and buried their technologies, promoted this new source of fast growth, got rich and no one paid enough attention to the long term. More than that, the mining wreaked havoc with its huge swaths of open pits, razed forests and ruined ocean floors whose coral reefs had utterly disappeared.

The more Midas reflected on this, the more his tension mounted again. He needed the calm now, so he banished it from his mind and took in the still peace. For the street remained quiet as the city slept in that precious bubble of time between the dead of night and the early morning.

He tried to enjoy this moment but couldn't because the night didn't cool down anymore. The sky was clear, but the stars remained smudged behind a permanent layer of smog. The rains would come again, and they'd be a violent rush driven by fierce winds. They lived in constant expectation of the next sudden slam of wind: a massive burst incoming from the arctic, or a surging blast from the western wall of the Rockies or the southern Atlantic. The torrential downpour would tear the city's pipes, break its bricks apart, drown cars and even people. The heat would sear their heads and skins, evaporating the water within as their organs became slightly swollen. And then an eerie quiet calmness, like the one he tried to enjoy now, that wouldn't last long. So he stopped for one second and waited, watching and listening. Hold the moment and see.

Surrounded by the structures, Midas thought it was a miracle the buildings of the city lasted as they did. Aside from the occasional brick and beam that had crumbled in recent years and hadn't yet been cleaned up, they had maintained the basics of their old integrity for the most part. Then there were the condo jungles along the lake, midtown to the east by the Don River and northwest by the Humber River: ghost towns within the town — rather, areas that had been ghosted of legitimate renters and owners, emptied into lawless hovels and were sometimes teaming with gangs and lonesome risk takers with no money and not much other choice.

His mood darkened again.

Midas walked into the café and took note of the time. Quarter to seven in the morning. Customers would arrive soon, and he didn't feel ready. He hadn't slept well, disturbed by recurring thoughts of Lazuli and of Zora's message about giving him something for his café. He knew she liked the place but to contribute to it was especially nice. The two thoughts — the darkness simmering within and the niceness of Zora — went to war, and their battleground settled on the painting.

Though irritating, deep down he knew Ira had a good point. It was so odd that it could only become a focal point for people. He didn't want that. Didn't want his café to be defined by this thing.

Tired already and anxious of the time, he went to the fallen painting to fix the one thing he could. He had fifteen minutes before opening to move it, once and for all. And there was no point waiting for Ira to help.

Steadying himself before the canvas, Midas grasped the metallic frame and pulled the weight away from the wall. "What the hell," he grunted aloud, almost buckling. He tried to keep the rectangular mass upright as he dragged its corners across the old floorboards. It hit a chair, and another. He pushed it up on the stage and its backside crashed down. "Shit, dammit." He leapt up, dragged it to the left pillar by the espresso bar and leaned the painting there out of sight.

The front door bells tinkled and Ira called out, "Finally, boss. Good for you. You need help? Here, let me make the coffee." He turned to the little sampler bag the salesman had left.

"Not that, Ira."

Midas turned on a lamp to inspect the painting. The canvas remained intact but one of the small candelabra on the frame had suffered some scratches. He swore again.

Ira sucked his teeth. "Who cares, boss," he said. "Just burn it."

Midas held his tongue.

He decided this was the spot: behind the pillar, in the dark and out of sight. "Ira, can you help me with this?"

There was a pause, and then, "No fucking way," Ira yelled from the urns. "I'm not touching it unless we burn it. And cover it now, boss. Smother it with a blanket."

"Then I'll bring it back out. If I can't hang it here, it's coming back out."

Ira dropped his bag on the floor. Beans clattered. Ira leapt up on stage and produced two strong glue pads.

"Where did you get those?" Midas asked.

"I knew you wouldn't burn it, boss."

After some manoeuvring, they affixed the middle of the painting to the pillar.

Ira shrugged. "For now only, boss. We'll still burn it. Or dump it into a grease trap. Or spray the thing with acid."

Midas thought about this smart kid's passion. Ira got the glue pads because he's a good employee. *Nonetheless, Ira,* Midas resolved, *you will never damage this thing. Never. It's mine and I own everything here.*

Ira leaned closer to the oil canvas and gazed for a moment, penetrating its deep reds, blues and greens. His face almost touched it, and the detailed shapes drew him in even as he cursed it. Midas also noticed a bigger difference this time, not a subtle shift in its textured nuances. The once-bright sun over the bustling marketplace now softened to dusk, and the dancing clown from the daytime became a masked jester with red horns and long teeth. The people laughed, boisterous, and danced, and some performed with breathing fire. Two men with swords duelled, others gambled in circles and in the darker alleys, they kissed and possibly fornicated.

"Things are changing in this wretched thing," said Ira. He pointed, accusing it. "The changes take too long, so it fools you. You might not even notice. But I know. And you, you own it, boss. It's bad magic."

Midas laughed. The last day's tension was done. "There's a lot of detail. That's all there is to it. And I think a Rinth chip."

"But you said you discovered it in a shipwreck off the coast of Peru. There was no Rinth when that ship was made."

Midas resisted the renewed argument, despite Ira's rational point. The ship was ancient, as was the trunk in which he found the painting. Zora seemed to be on Ira's side on this, though he dismissed that fleeting thought as paranoid because she was always a no-nonsense type, albeit often playful. He'd taken her comments as another round of teasing. She'd expressed interest once, especially with her artsy idea to photograph its reflection in a mirror, as though that made some kind of point. He didn't like the attention on it — it was incredibly strange, he had to admit, even for such fantastic technology — and noticed how he'd regularly excise it from his mind, much the way he was doing now by moving it out of sight. At a deeper level he suspected, although he refused to articulate the thought, that his

Rinth theory on the painting's nature and origins was, while palatable to present to his modern Toronto customers, unsteady and missing something.

Ira paced in front of it, stumbled against the globe of the earth in its spinning stand in the midst of the back room, and Midas reached to steady the globe.

"Careful," said Midas.

Ira gazed deep into the canvas with a looming dread. "Boss, she's gone."

"Who?"

"The woman who was in the cage. It was in the pool on that side of the market. You see? Just outside the enclosed alley by the wall."

"I don't know who you're talking about."

"Beside one of the alleys where no one ever fucked. Except one couple, once."

"Ira, how could you ever see that?"

"She was always there, boss. A beautiful woman enslaved in a cage. You would only see her head and floating breasts. Sometimes her arms. I think she was a sacrifice. She went through that tunnel."

"You dream shit up, buddy. To where? The tunnel goes nowhere. It's just a thick wall with some rooms inside. Can't you see? The exit gate to the port is over to the right." Midas shut his eyes in frustration. Floating breasts through a tunnel, clowns breathing fire and chickens with their egg piles. It's a goddamn painting. You look at it, like it and you walk away. A tech wonder, he re-asserted to himself. That's about it. If it was something else, that'd be offensively eerie. As though he'd found a poltergeist, and like a fool decided to keep it. Midas had to hold himself in on this. There was no way he'd found, in effect, a haunted painting and brought it home unaware. The fact remained simple and solid: Ira was scaring customers with his own deluded perception of reality.

"No, boss. It went to the sea," said Ira. His voice was low and grave.

"You can't know that," Midas said with finality and walked away. "There's a curtain from a circus next to the Persian carpets over there," he said, pointing to the column at the other end. "You can cover it up."

Ira tsked. Covering it meant delay. For Ira, burning was the right decision, now. Ira returned to the espresso bar to prepare the coffee. They were late. As Midas inspected the order of things behind the bar, squinting in the streams of hot dawn sunlight, the bells tinkled and through the door walked a trio wearing odd hats, capes and jackets. They were hallowers after a long night — their favourite — and Midas braced himself as they approached the espresso machine.

So young, adventurous and free, these kids. Hallowers, they called themselves. It might have been cool but Midas worried about them when they went about like this. Their image an homage to this night and their cause — was it a cause? — a cause he thought not good enough, but he respected their creativity and spirit. At least they tried.

One dressed in blue tights and a long striped toque stared at Ira, who narrowed his eyes as he sought to interpret their costumes. She weaved on her feet like a strand of wheat on the prairie and held the counter to steady herself.

Midas sat at the espresso bar, clicked on his Probe and flicked to a news channel. He'd let Ira serve them.

"What?" she said, defensive at Ira's stare.

Something's really wrong with these kids, Midas thought.

"What do you want?" Ira asked, ready at the machine.

"I was out with my two friends," she said, and her eyes darted from floor to walls and back to Ira again. "And we wanted to fun around so we went out for — then we saw it — the crackle — and it got, right? So decided then get to something more — like snap — not that really knew we, but got to sharpen up."

These kids are beyond messed up on some bad drugs, Midas thought. It confirmed his worry. Creative rebellion was good. They wore their clothes and attitude as though his generation made a mockery of them — him and everyone in the working world. They dressed up in make believe to say, "Go to hell, you're all unbelievable anyway," and thank God it was just a show. That's what this was. The kids were a show, though an inadvertently dangerous one. While most participated in normal life — went to school, kept jobs — this mess confirmed for him what he had witnessed, from his vantage in the café, since returning to Toronto. This approach to life made them vulnerable, ironically to the very forces they confronted with their art.

"It sounds like espresso, so let's get this done quick," Ira said, and set to work.

The smaller thinner man beside her, dressed in a yellow hat, dirty tuxedo and white sneakers, grabbed her forearm and squeezed. His sweating face quivered. She made a quiet, pained noise but didn't protest otherwise. He held on and implored Ira with his swollen eyes. "Look."

He pointed at the screen of Midas's Probe. Midas stood back, trying to put meaning into the shocking, flashing shapes. It couldn't be.

They all stared, sucked in to the screen's bright square, hypnotized by the exclamations, the harshness, the abrupt statements and the screams of the massacre. All together they struggled to digest what they saw: the recorded memory of the horror.

"How dare they," whispered Ira. Midas felt like stone.

Someone in the trio giggled, then stopped.

A newscaster was speaking over the images: *Last night, criminals in costumes stormed the Ball hosted at the first floor of the tallest tower in the financial core. They first appeared as clowns dancing at the front stage and entertainers emerging from the band until they dropped their instruments and drew weapons, and then, with disguised companions dispersed amongst the costumed crowd, opened fire with guns and crossbows, arrows and bullets poisoned or aflame...* The images kept coming: of tablecloths on fire, of the blaze jumping across sizzling oil pans that crashed amidst panicked guests, fire upon their faces and hair while they scrambled, screamed and scratched one another to run. It went on and on, the chaos and brazen attack.

The children were located upstairs on the mezzanine that overlooked the main floor of the Ball behind a broad window, the newscaster went on, voice clear and stoic.

Midas imagined the scene: There they played, surrounded by babysitters and luxurious toys and protected from the noisy milling below where their parents clinked champagne glasses and talked of deals, trading and, sometimes, art.

Seven children have disappeared.

Midas closed his eyes. Their parents wouldn't have even noticed. They were too busy screaming and clawing for their lives amidst flying bullets and flaming arrows as they punched and kicked and resisted beating batons in vain.

More images, some of wild-eyed men in tattered suits with dark bruises smeared across their gaunt faces, stiff hair pointed up like forked lightning and chiselled yellow teeth.

Upon the window of the mezzanine daycare, looking down upon the dying parents, bureaucrats and business elite, words were scrawled in red smears: *Come and get them.*

Some ran, strong, others screamed, some were stunned and mute but moving, dismayed at seeing a friend fall frozen in disbelief. They shoved themselves into cupboards, closed the doors as fast as they could. Some tried to get there but clawed hands grasped them like iron vices and pulled them away from their friends; they were disappearing, being swallowed up as they lost their voices. They ran away, ran, ran, feet like lead, heads with nothing in them, just terror — toxic with fear.

Ira was frozen next to Midas. *No, get me out please mommy come back where are you,* Ira imagined them saying as he dropped his espresso cup to the floor. He turned to glare at the three hallowers, but they were gone.

Midas leaned against the opposite counter by the sink and hung his head.

SIX

Sunday passed and then Monday too, from that remote nautical dawn it rightly ended in a dark orange, and the crowd at the café cleared. Monday had been busier than usual. To Midas's surprise, many converged with a common need to leave their lonely routines and face the horror of the previous night together. And now they were gone, other than three costumed youths by the bay window absorbed in their Probes.

Ira sat by the espresso machine reading a Probe and, somehow, had a beer.

"Where did you get that?" Midas asked.

"Boss, I deserve it," Ira said. The beer sloshed inside the bottle as he leaned it into his mouth. "I still say you need to start selling this stuff. You'd make the most money." Ira tapped the side of the bottle with his finger and nodded.

"But the man there wants an espresso and doesn't want me to make it. He wants you." Ira shrugged and returned to his reading and his beer.

Past the espresso machine stood a short round man in a brilliant white suit and a white fedora. Midas thought of a stiff balloon atop two stubby legs. The man's tailored suit bulged in the middle and a thick arm rested comfortably at his side while the other stretched in front of him holding a leash at the end of which was clipped a large dog whose shaggy blue hair hung from its big-boned frame. The man stood on the balls of his feet, perched forward and ready. Black sunglasses covered his eyes, the arms squeezed against his wide head, forced over heavy folds of white skin. The lenses gave the aspect of a fly: all-seeing eyes that enjoyed a vast circumference of vision, immutable, never moving and anonymous.

Midas took a step forward. "Welcome to Freehouse."

At first, he mistook the man for a youthful hallower. But he was no youth.

"Yes, an espresso if you please. A single short." The man sang his words in an alto voice thick as honey, lilting them smoothly from note to note. "You're too kind."

The huge dog's black marble eyes glanced up, and for a fleeting second Midas thought he saw swirling purple wisps deep in those orbs.

Midas blinked and shook his head to dispel the stress piling in from a bad couple of days. It blurred his vision, especially when so tired. The dog lumbered around beneath the espresso bar, face out of sight, and pulled the bulbous man's arm by the chain toward the back room, but the man stood his ground with his perched feet set in place. Midas prepared the espresso, taking care to pack the fine grinds into the chamber. He tested the steam, checked the pressure and temperature. "Nice dog." Midas cleared his throat. "And that's a terrific suit. I love fedoras."

The man stared up, at and through Midas to the brick wall behind him. "I hear your espresso is the best in the city."

"Oh? I'm glad word is getting out. I'm Midas, by the way."

The man still didn't look at him. "Caesar," he said.

Midas tapped his espresso machine. "This baby I found myself. It's an import from Peru." He tried to focus on the espresso and noticed a weak crema. He kept the first one and prepared another.

"Yes, I realize." The man's lips curled.

"It's got four drips and lots of pressure. We have it hooked up to good water, too." Midas paused but the man said nothing. "Which is rare, right?"

The man continued to stare straight ahead.

Midas forced conversation. "You wouldn't believe what research I had to do to find this thing."

Ira's near-empty bottle echoed one last slosh. The rest of the room was dead quiet but for the soft giggles of the three hallowers by the bay window. One packed a bag and nudged his two friends to leave.

Sitting with legs crossed and settled comfortably in the love seat beside the sofa, a thin man in a suit with a somewhat dishevelled fedora stared out the bay window onto the traffic of Dundas Street. He had taken it upon himself to move the love seat a good ways around the coffee table there, and Midas noticed some board games and a few precious books — incredibly, hardcovers from his small collection he'd placed out for customers — had fallen to the floor.

Caesar moved his head slightly in that direction and turned back to the brick wall behind Midas.

"Don't mind him. He's harmless."

Midas tried to take this in and understand. He decided to assume the books were an accident. But a lingering doubt festered because the suited man — a well-tailored suit, from this angle, and expensive shoes from the crossed leg that put them in view, but for what seemed like a muddy stain, no doubt from the unpredictable rains these days — had moved the love seat quite a bit. No one did that.

"What, he's with you?" Midas asked Caesar, and looked to Ira who was packing his bag by the end of the espresso bar, sitting up on the raised floor with his feet swaying. Midas looked back at the lanky gentleman, noticed a rip at the back of his fedora, a rip surrounded by burn marks and asked, "Your lawyer, I suppose? Accountant?"

It was a poor attempt at humour.

Caesar nodded once and raised his free hand to give a little dismissive wave. "I'm here on business, you'll see. Business development. Brings me to town, you'll see. There's a well-attended cruise this coming Saturday night. Wonderful opportunity, isn't it. To spread the word."

Finally, the drip finished. Midas took a deep breath, deciding he'd have just a few more minutes of this odd duck and his rude assistant, and that would be it. The guy's words sounded like his eyes: vacant and deadpan, yet they carried something. Midas asked, "So where are you from?"

The bug-eyed man stared at the brick wall behind Midas. "Here, and recently somewhere in the South, and a few other places. I'll stay here a time," the man said, and sipped. "Important business going on up here in the North, what with the opportunities. We spread ourselves, you'll agree, far and wide."

There was something about this man. He made cryptic comments and spoke with a slow cadence in a kind of thick minor harmony. His gaze, which was annoying for its apparent arrogance, went past Midas.

The three young hallowers stood, slung their bags over their shoulders and hurried out the door.

Midas nodded to the departing group then turned back to Caesar, who was now staring down at his cup.

"Such coffee," Caesar said. "What's the brand?"

Midas drank water, wishing it were rum, and worried his shaking hand would show. "Thanks. Small producer I sourced myself."

The vacant bug eyes moved slowly from side to side above a grin of disdain and pity. "Oh, I don't think so." The honeyed tone went quite minor.

"No one else sells it here," Midas said, irritated for speaking so quickly, and looked across the room for Ira, still at the end of the espresso bar, who buttoned his bag shut.

Caesar placed the espresso cup upon the saucer with a reckless clatter. The spoon fell to the floor. He said, "I should like to have another. The Lazuli brand, if you please, this time. Meanwhile, I should like to have a look around."

"A look?" said Midas, and caught himself. "Anyway, I don't get what you mean. I sell only Lazuli's beans."

Midas bent beneath the counter, took a handful of beans that had been dumped into a bowl for ready use and studied them for the dark, oily texture and the unique glint of dark red, even as he resented feeling such unwelcome pressure from a simple customer. But the man was right. The beans he'd used to make his coffee were different.

Midas walked by Ira and asked with a low voice, "That salesman, Hippias, left a sampler. Have you been using his stuff?"

Midas strove within to forgive him. Ira was a good guy, and Midas knew his reaction to all of this offence was his own fault, not Ira's.

Ira gave him a languid gaze. "Boss, it was very busy. I think it was the student. She brought it in from the back. You said we could use it."

This couldn't be true. Before he could respond, he saw Caesar and the blue dog weave through the tables and chairs. The leash remained taut, and the dog veered toward the stage while Caesar held back to peruse the paraphernalia along the far wall near the far-right pillar that framed the stage.

"That's not a place..." Midas tried to say but the dog growled. Caesar pulled the leash, yet the dog tensed its muscles, unyielding.

Ira walked past Midas to the espresso machine. "I'm turning it off," he said and flicked the switch. As he left with the last garbage bag flung over his shoulder, he said, "Need help with this guy, boss?"

Midas shook his head and waved Ira off. He nodded toward the dog. "What's its name?"

"Madame Blue," Caesar answered. "She finds your collectibles curious." He reached for the string that still dangled where the painting once hung. "So do I."

This sounded almost intimidating to Midas. He spoke as though Midas's artifacts were his business, that he was entitled to know more about them. This kind of arrogance got Midas's back up. It all reminded him of so many deals while at Superior. Whether his very own clients or the other party to the deal, they'd get too confident with their money. He'd see it cloud their perception of things, whereupon they'd put themselves on a pedestal. And they were always ready to take something from you.

"What makes you decide to put one item out and keep another hidden back there in the darkness?" Caesar walked to the stage and scanned it from one side to the other with his blank dark glasses, it seeming to Midas that he looked without seeing.

Midas wished he would get away from the back room. He should have covered it with that curtain by now. "Listen, I'm closing up. I have to ask you to leave." The dog made a low sound from its throat. "And before you go, I'd like to know how you know where I get my beans."

Caesar waved his hand dismissively again, and this grated at Midas. His back remained set to Midas as he perused the stage, then changed his mind as he gestured with his fingers to come closer.

"I rule Creed," said Caesar. "My business network continues to expand. Quickly, too, these days. You've heard of Creed?" His voice lingered on the name.

Midas's spine tingled then seized like someone yanked at its base. Only a feeling, he insisted to himself and shuddered. Hippias had warned him about this name. But that was just Hippias and Midas had never heard of them. Surely, he would have heard of them.

Midas stepped around a table closer to Caesar but couldn't read the other man's face. The sunglasses, round cheeks and still mouth deprived him of any expression.

Midas kept his cool on the outside. He'd negotiated with some intimidating people in his time, over a lot of their money. This should be nothing. "Afraid not," Midas said. "Are you new?"

In situations like this, Midas was perfectly fine with lying. In fact, for a moment he managed to find a brief solace in his pride on this point even while this odd duck's honey voice shook his nerves.

Caesar's mouth twisted into a crooked line. "Oh yes. As I said, we are growing fast. Making lots of people queasy, if I may say so." Caesar crooked his mouth upward, ever so slightly. "I don't mind the effect and, in fact, quite enjoy it. Don't you enjoy unnerving people, Midas?"

Midas steeled himself. This was no longer odd duck territory. Sometimes, he knew, the wealth of some degenerated into a source of delusion. Just because they sat on a mound of gold like bad dragons should never justify a sick desire to unnerve people. It was common in business that in a negotiation one might put forth a threatening comment — a position, sure, but for a strategic purpose, not to unnerve alone. The nervousness would come naturally, of its own accord. All you did was state your position. Now he heard *queasy*. This was different. He opened his mouth to say something — take an assertive stand, make a claim — but instead the blue dog shook its shoulders and turned to Midas. He turned to it.

Its eyes delved into his. Things slowed then as their blackness expanded. Even from this distance, Midas swore the dog's eyes swirled a hint of purple. He tore his eyes away and looked back at the annoying, arrogant customer to focus on making the man leave.

"No, I don't enjoy that," he said. "And I'm closing. You're going to have to leave now."

The blue dog growled.

"That's fine, for now, that is," said Caesar. "Of course, you'll change too, Midas. Like everyone. Your concept in this little shop really is too simplistic. A much bigger business plan is afoot, and you'd do better to mind it. If you know what's good for you."

Midas's blood pressure rose. Who says such a thing? In a peaceful place such as this?

Forcing a calm, he asked, "What's Creed?" while reminding himself he didn't need to have this conversation. But he did, didn't he, he thought. He had to know more: whether Hippias lied about Lazuli's betrayal of their contract, and whether Lazuli now worked with Creed.

Caesar's face contorted again, and his bulging cheeks squeezed within the tight straps of his sunglasses.

"Your future."

"What are you talking about?"

"Creed has business with you, to be sure. You'll see the merits of our business plan." Caesar's grin curved upwards, in a heartless effort to appear real. "You've been highly recommended by your associate, Lazuli. You'll come on board, just like the rest of them. In fact, not much choice, really. You see, Midas, you're the perfect fit for Creed. We've seen your business practices, your ways over the years. Perfect."

Perfect? Not much choice? His future? This was outrageous. He knew this kind of arrogance. This man was already staking claims over him.

The blue dog jumped onto the stage by the left pillar. The leash stretched almost to the breaking point and Caesar stumbled. He resisted and tried to pull back, but the dog maintained its close gaze behind the pillar where he'd hung the painting. Caesar's arm remained in the air as the two struggled in their tug-of-war.

Midas imagined how pleased Ira would be at the prospect of the dog's sharp jaws ripping through the painting's canvas.

And it seemed that Hippias was, indeed, on to something about Lazuli. Apparently, he may have met Caesar. Still, he doubted a man like Lazuli would affiliate with a guy like this. "So what exactly is this idea, this business plan?"

Caesar laughed but made no effort to smile, only one horizontal line.

"Creed," he said. "It stands for so much. First and foremost, Creed is a way. A set of methods and a mindset. You just need to free yourself and embrace it. Maintain contact with your network, and the assigned ones."

"Sounds like a cult."

Midas meant it. Cults grew and disappeared, thrived or died, all over the place. They were more common these days given the unsteady circumstances not only south but here too. He thought of Ira's past, of Zora's former cell and its ideological bent, of business elites and how they framed their missions. This, however, was next-level.

Caesar turned away from him. "So many fascinating collectibles," he said.

Midas began to feel panic as Caesar clambered onto the stage toward the dog and the pillar. Why not just let it go, he pressed himself, for the dog might take a swipe at him too. The low noise from the back of the dog's throat grew louder and its shoulders bunched into rippling muscle.

"Easy there, doggie," said Midas.

The blue dog bared its long teeth at the painting. Midas stepped back and turned to Caesar who maintained his stoic stance, arm raised with the leash while he stared at Midas like a frozen, stuffed insect.

"Look, bud," said Midas, mustering himself. "I'm not interested. It's time you left."

Caesar emitted a long slow chuckle. His strange laugh offended Midas like nothing he'd heard before. "Let me be clear," Caesar said at his slow pace. "This is business. I now own Lazuli. As he's your business partner, like so many others, we visit them. All of them, in the spirit of business development, you'll agree. You're simply one of many but you, Midas, deserve a special one on one with me. So everyone, in an ever-expanding network, joins Creed because it simply makes the most sense, you'll agree."

Midas's nerves prickled and he sensed the whole room become seized with an alert stillness. Eyes widening, they flicked over to the lanky suited man on the love seat and back to Caesar.

"You'll join us too, just as Lazuli recommended. And don't hesitate. We promise great riches, boundless opportunity freed of the moral constraints that have held people back for so long."

His voice grew stronger as he spoke. Despite the bland face, made anonymous and bereft of empathy by the wide dark sunglasses, he now showed passion. The paleness of the fat folds of his face took on a pink hue that reddened. His free fist clenched and seemed to pound an imaginary podium before him.

This guy really thinks he's convincing me, thought Midas. He tried to say this to himself with dry humour and instead his spine only tingled more.

"In fact," Caesar continued with a rising voice consumed by a distant promised glory where his blank eyes shone. "They're all just beginning to come on board. The drones of Bay Street, as you people here might say. It's spreading, and we at Creed need to accelerate the spread. Because there's a path forward. In fact, a pathway. All we need to do is master it. So join us now, Midas. Get in early. You'll be at the top of the heap. Consider it to be a kind of enhanced networking. You know the drill as a successful businessman, don't you? We meet Lazuli, we meet his associates, partners, suppliers, they join our network and they grow forward in the same manner as all of their associates, and then theirs and then theirs in turn, and so on and on. And finally, in fulfillment of this great pathway — once the legend we've uncovered is at last found — we expand through it, to the endpoint, and we then bring those riches and ways back here."

At this point in Caesar's monologue he softened his tone, convinced he offered a balanced reason for his argument. He opened both palms upward before him toward Midas, as though in mock supplication. Then his voice swiftly rose again into a fevered pitch. "So you see the plan: We grow here, we link to them, we grow with them. And then—" He paused and the reddening pink hue consumed his entire bulbous head as his exclamation echoed through the empty café, across its narrow length and invasively into the back room's dome. "We rule. All of it, Midas."

His fist slammed the air before his rotund belly, and his mouth broadened into a wide slit that might have been a victorious smile on any other human being. Here, it reminded Midas of the awful slit of a mouth on a great white shark that, when opened, revealed a rushing range of jagged fangs.

"So join our network, dear friend. Truly, you see, you really have no other option."

Midas looked away from Caesar, to the lanky man in the suit. He sat still as a stone, staring out the bay window at the cruisers gliding by on Dundas, oblivious to this exchange. Midas looked more closely and noticed tears in the man's suit, burn marks here and there, and a long, thick spike of dark hair that fell out from beneath the fedora. Midas backed farther into the darkened stage area, and his heel bumped an ancient radio. As he fell to the floor on his buttocks, it began to play jazz through static, a distant big band from way back in the last century. Midas turned on his pained haunches to the blue dog, who growled and showed its long canines as a thick line of drool dripped to the floor, and back to Caesar.

"All right, bud, that's enough. Get out of my café." But as small and absurd as this stranger and his words were, Midas felt unsteady as it dawned on him that he didn't know what either of these men or the dog were capable of. The strange man was presumptuous and demanding, the dog growled fiercely and a tall man in a tattered suit who looked like he'd just walked out of an explosive traffic accident sat calmly nearby, watching with his back turned to them.

Caesar faced him. "You owe Lazuli. Because he gave you so much. So you'll do this. For him, and for me, and for yourself."

"I don't owe him anything. And I don't know what you're talking about. The only thing I got from Lazuli was beans." The blue dog faced Midas with its intense fixed gaze, other than the slight movement of an arched eyebrow. He held himself as steadily as he could, but he knew he was anything but confident. The dog growled and drooled, Caesar made claims and a quiet man in a suit sat still as a tiger, poised for something.

Caesar shook his head. "Some of these precious artifacts came from around his ranch. I know, Midas. In fact, you roamed the South, taking things, didn't you? Even as a wicked hobby? He told me."

Midas cringed at the accusation. It was offensive and overstated. In fact, it was twisted. He reached for the broken radio and fumbled with a dial to turn it off. But it was stuck. He turned back to Caesar, this odd man who made such demands of him.

"No wonder Lazuli recommended you," Caesar said. "The perfect fit for our network. And here you are, up here in the North where new opportunities abound. And I haven't even made it to the cruise yet." Caesar let out a delighted cackle. "Whether you like it or not, want it or not, you're joining us. So make it peaceful, Midas, you see?"

The air went from Midas's lungs and he suppressed a gasp. "Get out."

Caesar stood unmoving. His mouth gave up its vain attempt at a grin and settled back into a still, flat line. "You haven't been transparent, Midas. Not to me, or to Lazuli. First, the beans. And you refused, back then, to admit your responsibility for a certain swindle."

"Yeah, what was it then? What are you talking about?" Midas felt his voice rising. He knew he was guilty of dishonest business dealings. Happened all the time. That's why he got out. And the first deal with Lazuli had been messy, but he smoothed it out. He reminded himself he had no interest in finding out what, specifically, this creepy predator meant by his claims.

Midas got to his knees. The dog growled.

Caesar ignored him and continued, "So yes, the perfect fit with us, Midas, you see? The ability to say what you need to say to get through a deal. Very good. We at Creed celebrate such talents. Well, Lazuli didn't get too far into the details, or couldn't by the end of the conversion…"

Midas felt nauseous. This strange man showed genuine curiosity for how Midas had lied. As though he admired it. The technique, the skilled application. He looked across the narrow expanse of the café from his stance on the staged area of the back room, saw the lanky man in the tattered, ripped suit and was struck in that moment by its similarity to some of the murderers' in the Hallowe'en Ball massacre.

The blue dog's muscles bulged and it turned to Midas.

Midas thought to hurl something at the dog — anything from his precious collection back there — to disable it, even for a moment while he took on Caesar. But the dog was large and perhaps somewhat trained. "Well I don't know what you're talking about," Midas said.

"At first, Lazuli was defiant too," Caesar continued. His head kept turning from right to left, surveying the back room from pillar to pillar. Midas took the opportunity to pull his Probe out of his pocket. "Denying his true nature. Pretending to be a good man. A powerfully good man." He shook his head with pity. "And then after a time — and it did take a good long while, regrettably for all the horrific pain we had to subject him to — he saw the light. Our light." Caesar's head stopped shifting.

If the creepiness of this odd man's business proposition wasn't enough, then the lanky suit who sat by the bay window, his image harkening back to the massacre, was enough to convince Midas to do something. He knew enough to sense danger, as amorphous as it was with Caesar's mere talk and the lanky man's mere sitting while he stared at Midas's blurred, distant reflection in the bay window. Midas saw that gaze and stared back at the man's shadowed cheeks and chin beneath the fedora.

Midas glanced down at the Probe in his hand and typed fast: *Urgent. Need your guys now. Being harassed. Unfriendly intruders here. I'll do the deal. Need you RIGHT NOW.*

"You'll agree," Caesar said, "deep down, your boss had it in him. Maybe more than most. The stuff of Creed, that is. He just hadn't had the opportunity to come up with the idea himself. Unlike me."

"He wasn't my boss," said Midas. "Get out."

The blue dog growled and glared at him. Throwing something would only goad the dog on, and he imagined Caesar might have a concealed weapon too, which reminded Midas of the ancient pistol stored somewhere amongst the artifacts. He stumbled, half on knees, half on fumbling feet. Midas glanced at the small Probe in his hand, desperate for a response, then up at the immovable man standing all too comfortably before the stage, his arm still outstretched, and back to the dog.

"You must be wondering what exactly happened to your boss?" said Caesar.

Midas quickly recovered his footing and stepped back, deeper into the back room, watching all three of them — the stubby man, the blue dog who sat staring at the painting like a golden retriever at the ready, and the lanky man in the suit at the far end by the window — as he stepped slowly around a chest, a bass drum and came to the bookshelf where lay a nineteenth-century Remington revolver.

"Not interested one bit," he said as he stood and pointed the pistol at Caesar. Midas cocked the gun. It surprised him, with a mix of dismay and added confidence, that it was in fact loaded. With some relief, he saw the scene more clearly and now with some measure of contempt. Caesar stood staring at him, and Midas was oblivious to the dog's whereabouts other than Caesar's outstretched hand at the end of the dog's leash. What had turned disturbing and borderline predatory, at least in words, now seemed with this loaded gun in hand a little more absurd.

But for the lanky man in the tattered suit at the far end of the café who stood and turned to face them with his fists at his waist. So, now a clear offence. How dare they. Midas felt his field of vision cloud into shrouds of red rage.

"Come join us at our next sales meeting," Caesar said, sounding calm and inattentive to Midas's outrage behind the gun. "The Torontonians are coming in clumps. They see the value. The unique proposition will appeal even to you, or perhaps especially someone of your experience. For we may have a special guest call in, your very own Lazuli, if he's ready and up for it after his recovery…"

He looked at the blue dog and tugged at the rope, but the dog dug its old claws into the wooden floor and bunched its heavy frame in resistance. Caesar sighed and said, now looking at Midas again, "What we promise has the capacity to lead Creed to the most awesome resource, perhaps to the largest and most dense source of wealth and power. So come to our meeting. And these meagre chattels will mean nothing to you. Come find your new self and wealth. You know what to do Midas. You've done it before. It's called taking. And it's okay to take. You can have it all, Midas. See Creed's goals, live with them, see what's on the other side, that beautiful land of milk and honey, and still do what you're doing. All at once."

"Fuck you, get out," Midas said.

The blue dog surged but instead of tearing his flesh to shreds, it veered away and leapt off the stage at the same time that the front door of the café tinkled, opened and through it walked two large men in black leather coats each carrying two bags of coffee beans in either arm. They marched past the lanky man who stood — moving slowly and calmly as though to convey nothing was going on here at all, that they were just about to leave — and they continued along the length of the espresso bar toward Midas's incredulous eyes while Hippias burst through the door behind them.

"So pleased to provide the first formal delivery!" he exclaimed with a swoosh of his hand in a wide arc.

"Ah, what have we here?" Hippias asked as he strode behind his men along the espresso bar. The lanky man in the suit bristled and moved forward. Before anything happened, the blue dog bolted to the front door, pulling Caesar whose face twisted again as he resisted, white-knuckled, then relented and followed the dog with the suited man quietly trailing. At the door beneath the tinkling bells, Caesar turned his vacant glasses toward the café and said, "You can't run, Midas." An alto cackle bubbled out of the slit that was his grin. "The trouble with indies is: It is retail. I know where to find you."

They disappeared into the street and the door slid down.

Midas lowered the pistol, went to the roaster room and found an old bottle of rum. Midas didn't drink much but the stress called for some kind of immediate relief. Hippias and his delivery men could wait a moment. He poured a tumbler half full of it, sat on a stool at the end of the espresso bar and drank. Shaken and numb, he drank and drank again.

"Oh my, my friend," said the cheerful Hippias as he patted Midas's shoulder. "Whatever happened? Good thing we were nearby. Well, to tell you the truth, I was on the way to pay you another sales call. And drop off the first delivery."

He held out his hand, then shrugged with smiling abandon as he laughed and gave Midas a strong bear hug. Midas couldn't help but grin.

"Oh, you poor man," Hippias said loudly into his ear. "All is well. Not to worry. Got it? I told you we have security. You could be safe now."

"Yeah, sure. You saw them, eh? A weird short guy and a blue dog and a creepy assistant from Bay Street." Relief washed over him. "Seriously. Looked like he'd been to hell and back."

Hippias held him by both shoulders and nodded. "Were you at gunpoint?"

Midas grinned again and pointed to the pistol on the espresso bar. "Nah. The reverse. I scared them off."

Hippias's eyes widened and he exclaimed, "Ah, good for you, my good man! So, you need security. We're quite good at it in fact. You may or may not want my folks around, though. They can get quite ugly what with their fake, chiselled teeth, the chain mail and all that nasty stuff. Nonetheless, you're interested in our little arrangement after all then?"

"Well, I don't know."

Sending the note felt like a mistake in this moment of elation at having defeated Caesar and his dog. But then, Midas knew they would return. The mistake was turning himself into an indie café.

Hippias frowned. "You know we can help you." He nodded slowly, as though he imparted something rare and wise. "And I know this town. Why, there are madmen running about, massacring random people and stealing their innocent children. You, moreover, are a sitting duck. If I may, I think you've just learned that you need us now more than ever."

Hippias smiled broadly. "Midas, come now. This can be simple, and we can start with a pilot period if you prefer. This is the exchange: you get free security — they're more expensive than you think — from us, and we get to store some pellets in your room back there. To boot, you get a supply of real beans, same as the sample I gave you. Recall, Lazuli is, well, not as reliable as he once was. And when this is all said and done, we can re-evaluate our relationship. Fair? Useful? Right? Say yes."

Midas knew he could only have one answer.

"Yes," he said.

SEVEN

"What do you know?"

Zora saw blurred humanoid shapes and a bright light. Smoke wafted through the air. She smelled nicotine and choked as a bulbous clot caught in her lungs.

"There is no revolution. Only terrorists," said a woman into her ear.

"Speak."

This came from a man in front and to the left. He wore a tall hat. It was striped with indiscernible colours.

A fist pounded the table.

"Tell us how you know him," said a harsh voice directly across the table. Zora raised her hanging head to the square, chiselled face that leaned toward her.

Augustine had warned her not to talk to the police. She had told him this was a useless comment. She knew that already from some years on the road in her teens, dodging the state's feeble attempts to rescue her after the death of her parents. There was only one thing she truly feared: not death, not war, not disease — the police. Mostly because the police forces were in such disarray, splintered into private security companies, some large and bureaucratic, some small and fraudulent, protecting no one but their clients.

"Why did he come to see you?" asked the woman, again into her ear. Zora shivered. The blurring that surrounded the man with the tall hat sharpened into stripes of red, yellow and black. A long top hat. It seemed far too long to be real. She blinked through the blur, and it still looked three or more feet tall.

They make you think you're crazy, she thought, fighting back the fear with the last sliver of strength she could find in her innermost core. Must not let them get to her. *So later when you tell people what they did to you, no one will believe it. Close your eyes and find your true self.* "No," she said. A throbbing in her head, along the right side near the front and in the middle, muffled her perception of her own voice. Zora wondered if they heard her or even if she'd moved her mouth. Exhausted, the fear surged again, unpredictable as lightning, and seized the back of her throat so much that she gagged. Zora resented this overwhelming domination where her own body defeated her.

Resist. Hold on.

The man with the top hat bore a warm expression. It muted the fear in that instant, and she fought it again because she couldn't trust it. He couldn't be friendly. She struggled to remember what had been happening. She'd been unconscious. They'd held her in a vice. Couldn't move. Needle prick in arm. And before that — questions about a vehicle, or something like that. At first calm questions, then more demanding, pressing, almost frantic and insistent that she had answers. But she had no idea what they were talking about. So much so that the words they used in their asking felt inaccessible to her: their questions about Augustine, and repeatedly about this vehicle. It moved, fast, moved you fast, flew you without even a plane. What did it look like? What did he say about it? Who else was he talking to about it? Come on, Zora, we know. We've been watching. Everyone knows, everyone's watching. Come on, Zora, just tell us. They were crazy with their questions, coaching then screaming. Hostile, then nice. Mean, hunting as though starving, then friendly. Then nothing, and now this.

Something almost clogged her air pipe. She coughed it out and swallowed.

"Give her water," said the woman whom Zora could only hear, for she wavered in a blur as a thin, wispy humanoid. Zora tried to lift her heavy hand and realized steel clasped her wrists behind her chair. *Handcuffs?* she thought, or maybe she said the word, but her face felt too heavy to have moved. She tasted blood.

She felt cool water splash against her mouth, and it soothed the dry cracks of her lips. Zora blinked and winced. The right side of her face was sore and swollen, though she had no memory of being hit.

"Tell us how you know him," the harsh voice repeated. A strong fist pounded the table and rattled the legs. She was too numb to jump.

"What did you do to him?" Zora heard her own words in an inside-out order. She meant to respond by asking about Augustine, put the questions back on them, but she felt jumbled and incoherent: *did you what to him, what did he say to you, I just work there know nobody who are you saying I don't know what this is just found a stupid toy friend has stuff like this what revolution it's just a café.* They would never understand her. And she couldn't tell what she said and whether they were simply thoughts. She hoped she didn't say anything about Midas, about going there to drop that thing off. Then they'd know where he was. He had nothing to do with this but all police like this want is to find a crime out of nothing. Shouldn't have been on her mind at all but everything was so hard with them slamming the table — the big guy with the chiselled face did that — the others whispering and someone yelling, accusing her of things she knew nothing about. Augustine talking to her right before they came, at some point before they came. Fight off the numbness for a real hope of a crystallized rational thought to make sense of this. These bastards had no right to do this to her. She'd done nothing wrong.

"More water."

A metallic bottle arrived again, more conservative this time. She swallowed gratefully.

"We don't have him. But we're glad you're feeling better now," said the calm voice with the tall hat. He sat, legs crossed, at a distance from the table, to the left. "Let's be reasonable and discuss this comfortably now, shall we? That's best, isn't it?"

In this moment Zora didn't trust, his tone settled the room.

"What did you know about the kidnapping?" he asked.

"I was just working. I told you. Didn't I?" She wished she could remember. Now they were coming back at her, probably with the same questions. Helpless to previous statements she may have made. Either lying then or lying now, they'd claim. She knew how they'd do this, and as her heart sank, she kept on: "I had nothing to do with it. I only know what I heard on the news." Zora felt a sudden self-loathing. She had just answered another question. With a glimmer of strength, she sought to turn it around. "Did they take the suits too?" she asked. "Or just the children?" If she asked real questions, the ones everyone else was asking, they might leave her alone.

"Why *those* children? For ransom? For leverage? What are you planning?" said the harsh voice from across the table. He almost whined, not begging, but pressing at a high pitch. He dragged on a cigarette and blew toward her over the table.

She spat at him. "Don't smoke in my face."

He sat backward, perhaps shocked, then his fist hit the table hard again.

She remembered the fear. They would kill her. Earlier they almost did. Unless it was a nightmare. That hatred in his face — pure, direct and unrelenting — assured her they didn't care. She remembered now, the slaps, pulling her hair, shoving her cheek on the table, the thick book over her head. Holding her there, and then the needle in her arm. She didn't want to remember. It didn't happen.

"We know where you come from. We know who you associate with," said the steady voice from beneath the hat. "We know about Augustine's revolutionaries. This is no mystery to us. But why on Hallowe'en? Was there a symbolism to this? To underline the horror?"

The heavy breath of the woman from her left side rasped into her ear, "Take them instead of giving them candy? Were they your candy last night?" She thought she heard a quick giggle. A lightness behind the idea.

Zora jolted back from the lank, crooked lady who remained blurry in her tired eye's narrow field of view. "That's sick. You people are sick." She choked again. "So did they take the parents too? Any of the bastards?" Zora asked, spitting again to her right on the floor. She couldn't stop seeing those scared children as the door crashed open in their room. Their play invaded by an unknown force, a trust violated, strong arms grabbing, hitting them with clubs, brandished knives, tying them with rope, subduing them as they screamed. She could see them running, struggling to escape, to put objects between them and the invading monsters, to find closets and shelves — any receptacle — in which to hide.

"Ah, there we are," said the man in the hat. The thin woman giggled with greater wind in her lungs, a rolling wave of delighted sounds from the back of her throat. "You mean any of those bastard parents?" he went on, still calm. "You have violent tendencies, don't you? We can tell by your writing on Rinth. Angry enough to aid this horrific crime?"

For the nature of his accusations, the man remained steady, almost thoughtful. She remembered a reflective professor she'd had, and how his inflection could soothe.

"I didn't do it. I told you." Zora's cheeks and lips shook like a child caught, when she was in trouble. She fought it, to keep her jaw still and sure, hoping she wouldn't bend to their will.

"You've been hanging around with Augustine and his little troupe as they've poked around very important things, haven't you? Haven't you, Sweetness?" said the woman, still a thin, wavering blur as she put a Probe on the table. Her hooked nose hung in front of Zora as she bent forward with the rest of her pointed, quick face.

"In your writings," said the man under the hat, "you said the children were made of the same evil moral stock as the corporate thieves, as you called them, and had been hopelessly corrupted just as their parents. The rapists of the planet must be stopped at all costs, you once said. True or false, Zora?"

This didn't sound right. She might have written of terrible children and some of it she wrote in fictional form, sometimes portraying hyperbolic scenarios and caricatured characters. People took crazy liberties in their art, she thought. Whether political or not. She didn't mean it. Only in a metaphorical way, to make a bigger point. Zora implored this to herself, and she was so exhausted.

"Prove it," she heard herself say with a nearly spent burst of defiance. Her lungs gave out and heaved a muted sob. "I can't see the screen."

The thin lady moved, her long body weaving in the blurry air as though she revelled in a misplaced sensuality. Her long fingers pressed the Probe's screen. An account opened showing emails to and from Augustine.

"See? Your idea," said the lady. "True or false, Zora? True or false?" she repeated with a colourful intonation.

Zora tried to read through her tearing. She could discern her words from her thoughts a little better now, but she kept having to blink amid the throbbing pain in the right side of her head. Somewhere in behind there pulsed an ache she'd never known before.

She forced herself to understand what these wrong-headed assholes accused her of. Only able to see from her left eye, everything around her felt two-dimensional, lacking depth.

"That isn't true." She bent her head and sobbed. "You made them up. I never wrote those things. I wouldn't hurt anybody."

"You've written a lot more than this, my dear," said the smooth voice. He continued, and she could almost see him lean back to regard the ceiling. "A talented artist with a comedic bent, you seem. And a political drive, critical of the state of things. Is this fair? Might I venture that you assess the world through not only private and public frameworks, but also through a judgment on good and evil? Compare things as absolute or relative, with a dash of instrumentalism? A quest for the ultimate conclusion to post-modernity? We looked you up while you took your nap. Lots of comics cast with a dark, sarcastic humour. What are you really up to in this work?"

I don't know him like that I didn't do these things, she may have said but for the numbness and echoing. Her head felt like a spike of ice had rammed into it.

"I don't think so, Sweetness, I don't think so," said the spindly lady to her left. "That's what you tried in the beginning of our little chat today." Her intonation bounced up and down like a mad flutist leaping from high note to low. "Then things became more true, my sweet, and now you're back to this? I don't think so. I don't think so."

"I watched, just an observer." The edges inside her skin curled.

"The comics were a means to influence people," said the man with the tall hat. "To incite them to do things, to defeat legitimate government projects, important efforts to salvage what desperately needs improvement. Isn't this so?"

"No, I have ideas of my own." She hated herself for responding. She knew she should just sit here and say nothing no matter how they lured her to answer. They'd twist any word she uttered to their own ends. Exhausted, her instinct to fight back and resist weakened. She doubted herself and resented this abiding insecurity she'd fought all her life, especially now when she had to admit she'd written angry things critical of the state of the world, of people who hoarded concentrated wealth and power.

"Ideas of your own? Ideas of your own? Ah, so you work for this terrorist organization and you feed on them too? So creative, Sweetness, so creative." The spindly lady continued to weave in a murky blur at the edge of Zora's view.

A taunting parrot, a bird-like humanoid, Zora thought, and she tried to ignore this confused image, but the lady's strangeness, made stranger by the blurring, clung on.

"No, he was just a friend. Not even, I just knew him. Please, stop." He thought, or said, he was going to save the world and she knew he was wrong. His arrogance and contempt would never allow it.

"Why should we?" asked the man with the hat. "The blood smeared across the window: 'Come and get them.' Do you know what that means?"

"I can read what you wrote if you like," breathed the lady into her ear. Zora's skin prickled with the giggle. "They have sucked the ecosystems of life for centuries. Only to get coin to trade, calling it profit to gain the confidence of other thieves, and for power on top, only in turn for more coin to hold, all in a complex descent to desolation. What other species self-destructs like this? What terrible force compels them? To tear human beings from their innate rights and to twist others by exploiting greed, gluttony, pride and sloth. You, my friends, have one path ahead." The bird-like lady stroked Zora's hair. "You wrote that to Augustine with hatred in your heart." Her rancid breath went into Zora's ear and Zora winced. "A good little idealist, aren't you, Sweetness? Aren't you? And then you wrote this: 'It's not just for rights we do this.'"

Oh my God, what did I say? Zora thought.

The inside of her skin was like water freezing at a sudden winter's air. She wanted to respond that she wrote it in another context, but the ice pick feeling in her head intervened. The woman's breath was like putrid garbage, and they were convinced she was bad, so they would only use her words and hurt her with them. She couldn't do anything but be their friend.

Zora choked and as the power she'd always had ebbed away, still she pushed back. "But that's my writing. About other things. Nothing to do with him. Before, even." She felt so tired. "Why are you doing this to me?"

Everything appeared as cardboard cut-outs then, and she a distant observer, detached, her unsteady thoughts waxing and waning.

"After, Sweetness, you wrote about how they should pay back. About that ancient Robin Hood. To take from them and give to those who have suffered their thievery and exploitation. You wrote this. Pay back. Pay back. You wrote this."

Zora clenched her eyes shut — winced at the pain on the right side of her face — and resisted the growing, awful sensation of detachment. She coughed into the air above everyone, almost daring them with the loud noise.

"What did Augustine write?" she said. "I can't see it."

The calm man continued, relentless. "He said you were hateful. You wanted to hurt them. It's clear from your words. That's why there was blood smeared on the window, the blood of children, the luckiest of whom have been taken away to fulfill this corrupted revolution's next operation. Which child was torn open to share its blood as ink to smear a threat to their parent upon that window looking down upon them all? What did you do with the rest of that child, and their blood?"

"I don't know about the blood!" Zora screamed. The little ones would have run and scurried. It couldn't have happened.

"You tell me about the blood!" burst the square, chiselled man. From his perspiring pores across the table came a burning, pungent odour.

She choked again and sobbed, quieter and spent, "Those poor innocent little children." She moaned, and from somewhere deep within found the will to spit toward him again. The bloodied mucous bridged a long line of red drool, suspended from her lip to the edge of the table.

A few moments passed. She blinked tears and looked up at the top hat man.

"Get to the point, Peacock," he said.

The blurry humanoid shape at her side straightened herself, as though shaking her feathers, and for a fleeting moment, through the aching pain of the deep ice-pick throb in the right side of her head, Zora perceived a narrow multi-coloured parrot of red, yellow and black, with a curved, pointed beak. This thing asked, "You encouraged Augustine to take this abduction on, didn't you? You'd get good material writing about it, right?"

"No, I won't." Zora felt numb as she sat bent forward, heedless to the stained saliva hanging from her lips to the table. That's what they thought because that's all they understood, she thought, so tired and spent she was now panting, and the thought didn't become words in her head. Just a concept that flashed and she tried to grab it, hold on to it as the invasive bird-like lady ruthlessly pushed her words into Zora's ear.

"I won't? I won't?" the spindly lady said. "So you did it but it's not going to give you anything? Only now you say this? But isn't that why you paid Augustine? We saw you both at the bar, Sweetness. What was wrapped up so tightly in that cloth but a big wad of cash, yes? For the opportunity, yes?"

Zora didn't say anything for a while. They had her all wrong. "I didn't pay a thing. I hate that fucker," she said. The hanging spittle dropped.

"One more time, now, Sweetness." The blurry lady's breathing seethed into Zora's ear like the long, furious hiss of a mad, hunting cat. "What did they say, what did Augustine say, about it? No wheels, faster than anything, ever? What did it look like?"

Zora's tired memory remained a complete blank. It was a stunning feeling: to be accused of something from out of nowhere. To have no idea what someone was saying, or why. *So this is what it feels like to turn around and see a predator glaring at you, about to pounce and rob you,* Zora thought. The surprise emptied her. She couldn't move. She just stared back.

The man with the tall striped hat put up his hand. "We want to trust you, Zora," he said.

Zora willed herself to force words over her parched tongue. "I don't know what the fuck you're talking about, motherfucking pricks," she said. "Who are you, some dumb-ass hallowers lost in your fantasies?"

"Now, now, dear Zora," he replied, comforting and disapproving at once.

She squinted at him and his tall hat, trying to imagine what he might be caricaturing. But they couldn't be hallowers. They were too old. He just wore a tall hat with three horizontal stripes.

The spindly thing weaving next to her kept on: "If you're willing to pay him — them, this bullshit revolutionary cell — then who are you? Working on both sides, are you? With a government department that wants to keep quiet from the big guys who run business, and some other gang? Who, Sweet? Who do you really work for?"

Now they're going to kill me if I don't give them what they think they need. Inside this hazy, invasive envelope, she hid inside her mind like the children would have hidden inside those cupboards. "What the living hell are you talking about?" she said. Her whole body shook in the chair with the clinking metal around her wrists. Shaking with fear and suddenly so cold, she knew more than ever at this point that her anger had dwindled, was possibly overcome. The metal clasps around her wrists clamped behind the chair's back dug into her skin.

The calm man appeared at Zora's right. "Hush. That's enough Peacock," he said, waving a dismissive hand toward the spindly lady. "It's clear she doesn't know. I'll finish this." His hand laid softly on her shoulder. "Zora, you have a recording device, now."

Warm breath melted over her left ear. "Remember?" the bird-like lady giggled. Zora wanted to beat her.

"Fuck you," said Zora, but it came out as a tired whisper.

The man pulled a chair to sit beside her. He gave her knee a pat. "Do you understand the consequences that must flow from your refusal to do as we ask? We would love not to have to do this, but we have no choice. You agree? My dear, it might be helpful for you to comprehend the social significance of what we ask. This isn't mere law enforcement."

The icy pain stabbed through her head as she listened to his version of the truth. Hers, she knew, as the hazy envelope converged, was in jeopardy.

"You'll speak with Augustine, attend the cruise with him too," he said.

Her mind clearer now, with the fuel of the anger, she realized they must have seen video footage at Night. She'd seen various recordings in Shanti's office a couple of times, and the audio would always be chaotic with hundreds of voices clamouring in the background. This time, that conversation with Augustine had been early in the evening before the noise.

"We know he has a plan, as crazy as it is and doomed to fail, no matter. We've been following the cell, and your ex, for some time. Many have. Well," here he paused and granted himself a chuckle to share with her, "many have been watching many these days. The hunt is heating up, as you'll soon see."

This she took as a gratuitous ploy to lure her into trusting them by their sharing confidential information with her. She tensed.

"We just want evidence," he continued, "from the wiretap now on you. We want clear proof he and his gang are the terrorists responsible for the massacre at the Hallowe'en Ball and the abductions of those children." The man's voice became rushed and heated. "Get the information we need. We need to stay ahead of this game, don't we? Then, you'll not be charged, convicted and faced with the ultimate punishment. Do this and you'll be spared, Zora."

Hot breath in her ear again. And the giggle. "Remember, there is no revolution."

The man leaned in. "Remember the real revolution, Zora. Yours. You have things to write about. Don't let them corrupt the good cause. People deserve better. We all need this information, dear Zora, please, we implore you. Many people are interested in this, looking as we are. We need to know, as I'm sure you understand, what is really going on. And the best way to get information is to ask nicely in the normal course and listen, because when one does it by force, well, those conversations tend to be briefer. Vital information is lost."

His face settled into a wise, contented smile. She might have slugged him in another circumstance, but she was tied up and exhausted.

"Water?" she asked, spent and empty.

One of them produced a bottle of lukewarm water, pushed its nozzle into her mouth and pushed out two short, measured spurts. "Not too much, Sweetness. It's precious."

Zora's breathing slowed, and the room went still as they watched her. She'd denied Augustine his request and now faced the wrath of his enemies who apparently had watched unbeknownst to him. She had no choice but to comply, if only to get out of this room, these handcuffs and save her own life. She'd figure out a way. She'd always found her way out of a threatening mess. The children had scurried in their innocent terror as though trapped in their worst nightmare, but it had been for real this time — into cupboards, behind a couch, beneath it. And the one who would have been caught against the wide-open wall, exposed with nowhere to hide, who could only hide his face in his hands, quaking as the long bony strong hands came down. There were children still alive out there, somewhere.

"Okay, I'll do it," said Zora, wondering, and almost resolving if only she could muster the true strength despite her terror and desperation, whether she could turn this whole awful thing around, at least find the kids. For if Augustine were guilty, he'd know where they were.

The man in the tall hat stroked the nape of her neck and said, "Good for you. That's better, isn't it?" He laughed. "The wiretap is this clip under your hair affixed behind your right ear. You cannot turn it off. Take care of it. If you toss it, we'll know and will come for you. You're strong, my dear Zora. Go forth and do your duty."

EIGHT

By late Tuesday afternoon virtually every table in the café was occupied. Ira stood behind the espresso machine, and his hands whirled around cups and little spoons as he crafted shapes with foamed milk. Two students navigated the tables serving coffee. Midas squeezed through the line at the front door.

"Shit," he said to Ira.

"You should be happy to make so much money," said Ira, frowning. He returned his focus to two espressos, eyes intent.

Midas was exhausted. He'd lain awake most of the night, worried and regretful with the growing confusion around him, his mind wandering back to his last days at Lazuli's ranch … the day after his deceit was exposed. He'd tried to get away with it — the images in his mind were dizzying — the secluded bay surrounded by twisted rock formations … the hidden shipwreck lodged on a sandbar … Lazuli cutting him out of the deal … his anger … exploring the bay and taking what he found on board that ship as recompense.

No one knew about the shipwreck, and it was just a piece of garbage, the same as so many other abandoned wreckages across the coast. The taking was possibly wrong, he knew. But at the end of the day, he was paid properly and he and Lazuli made good. He'd even offered to hand over the various artifacts he'd found, however worthless. Lazuli laughed it off and told him to keep "that garbage." So they made a new, fresh start. Indie.

And now he had to call the guy and get his take on Caesar's bizarre claims.

He hadn't thought of this for a long time. Preoccupied with doing something good with this café, he thought he'd buried it fine and well where it belonged: to be forgotten. Instead it invaded his dreams now and, in typical dream fashion, mixed images, people and things in a mess. In last night's dream, it was the Incan throne and then the entire domed stage area of his café that he'd discovered, impossibly contained within that wreck like a yawning, infinitely dark attic.

Ira yelled over the counter through the din of the café. "Boss, you have a business to run. No spacing out allowed today. I'll make you an extra espresso to refuel your focus."

Midas smiled as he passed Ira toward the back office. "Did anyone come while I was gone?" he asked, thinking of Zora.

Ira's hands kept moving as he finished a cappuccino, delivered it to one of the men at the bar's end and said, "What do you think, boss? They have a curious name. We call them customers. At least, those of us who work here bestow them this title."

Despite the real defence that he'd left only an hour ago to buy a new hologram device because his old one's constant blank face of doom was made more frustrating by the persistent sticking of his Probe's keyboard, Midas felt shame. They didn't expect this volume, not on a weekday.

"Listen, real sorry, Ira. I have to call Lazuli and that old hologram wasn't working. It's important. A Rinth message isn't enough for this."

Over the hissing steam, Ira muttered bitterly, "Why don't you just use that telephone in the back? Go antique. You seem to like them. Now you want to videoconference. Oh, has to be perfect, always, right boss?"

This stung because it wasn't true. There would be nothing perfect about the call.

Midas said, "Look, I'll just be five minutes."

Midas walked along the crowded espresso bar, unable to feel pleased at the unexpected success.

In the roaster room, he aligned the new device to his Probe and buzzed Lazuli.

He picked at his nails as it connected. The lines of yellow and blue drew themselves in the air above the countertop before him, at first broken, meaningless crackles until the image coalesced into a chair's broad arm, a forearm and a long bony hand. The responder — Midas thought it must be Lazuli — did nothing to fix the angle.

"Lazuli? You there? It's me, Midas."

The electric image achieved three dimensions yet remained only yellow and blue. Midas cursed. He'd just wasted his money on another shitty hologram device.

"Lazuli? I can only see your hand. This is important. We have to talk."

The hand lay still on the wide arm of the chair he recognized. Lazuli would sit in it like a king, usually behind the oversized desk in his office, sometimes in the dining hall for meeting guests with certain business.

"Lazuli, I can't hear you."

But the hand just sat there, still.

Someone turned the camera on, Midas thought. He can't be asleep.

"Boss." Ira's strained voice pierced the distance from his place in the café's clamour.

Midas didn't know what to do.

"Boss," came the word again. "Please. I'm swamped out here."

Frustrated and desperate to speak with Lazuli, Midas ignored Ira and pushed the door almost shut.

Lazuli's hand then moved, and Midas felt a new tension. "Lazuli?"

The camera shifted up, shaking as it went, and showed Lazuli's face, chest and arms through a distorted, crackling image of hologram lines, yellow and blue. The image focused and then splintered again.

"My boy," said the old man. Beyond the artificial lines of electric energy, Lazuli gazed at him with his characteristic intensity. It may have been the effect of the unsteady, thin electric lines of the hologram, yet Lazuli seemed bony, even gaunt. Midas imagined what Caesar and his associates may have done. Caesar had sounded cryptic, but Midas had taken it at the time as the disturbed claims of a psycho. Yet now here, Lazuli had changed. It wasn't the hologram.

"It's a new beginning," Lazuli continued with a grate in his voice, as though he had a bad cough. "They came and showed me the path forward."

"What do you mean? You're your own man, Lazuli, you're strong. You always were." Midas strained to see Lazuli's real face past the hologram's falsity. "Listen, a man who calls himself Caesar walked into my café and claims he bought you out or something like that, and expects me to get involved with whatever he's doing. I don't even know what his business is." Midas tried to stay steady, keep this cool, simple and rational, like all he needed to do was clear this up quickly. "Do you know him? What the hell is this?"

"They came a month ago. The Hallowers." Lazuli reared his bald head up to face Midas, accusing with his eyes. "Caesar came too. They're Creed. We're all Creed, Midas." He paused, and maybe sighed behind all the zigzagging rays of the disturbed hologram. Lazuli leaned forward perhaps energetically and said through the sparking noise, "Accept it. We always were. This is a phenomenon, an inevitability, a logical fulfillment of our nature."

Midas thought he discerned a slight grin flicker across Lazuli's face, but the unsteady hologram lines made this only a fleeting possibility.

Lazuli coughed, bent over as he clutched his gut. He heaved air in, and phlegm rattled his lungs. "Midas, I had to give up your name. I gave them several and I'm sure they have paid most or all of them a visit. That's how we do business, don't we?"

He was silenced by a fit of coughing. On recovery, he continued in a low hoarse voice, uncharacteristic of the business leader Midas knew him to be, "You'll like this plan. It's absolutely fascinating and holds so much promise. What did Caesar say?"

Midas stared at the hologram, shocked.

He was hoping to hear Lazuli deny everything and set it all straight. Instead, his colleague — he might have called him a friend by now — spoke admirably of this. Lazuli bent over again and coughed. Spittle spewed forth, he leaned to the side and spat, then gripped the wide arm of his chair. "You might find what they did to me, in the early stages as they go through it with you, to be somewhat unpleasant." He hacked again. "The things they say. But their plan is solid, Midas. Ride out the rough patches. I know that sounds opaque," and here Lazuli laughed but Midas noticed it was too sharp and quick, and as the man shook his head. Through the ragged snaps of the hologram's dysfunction Midas thought he shook in dismay, but the closer he looked he could see the grin on his shimmering face. Midas was fairly sure of Lazuli's satisfaction. So he listened more carefully than ever.

"I see now what I didn't before," Lazuli continued. "And yet it's still all so wrong." He slumped in his chair, as though tired. "You should join them." This last comment was disturbing.

Lazuli shook his head again slightly, and the grin turned into a grimace. Midas tried to read the man's face, like he normally could with anyone in a conversation. The broken hologram made this difficult but not impossible. Lazuli's pained face betrayed eyes glowing, intent and determined. He was sure of himself even as he was sick and appeared on the verge of disease. The skin on his face bore blemishes, a darker mark ran along from his cheek bone down past the jaw. A bruise? Midas wondered. "Just give in, let them have it. The café. All of it. Take what you can, with them. Save yourself and join Creed now." He stared at the camera.

Midas saw red again. The same fog that surrounded his field of view when Caesar invaded his space. "Why am I getting dragged into this?" He almost yelled. "Why did you send these creeps to me? Just tell them I have nothing to offer. They're looking for business in the wrong place. What exactly did you tell them about me?"

The hologram sent sparks and zigzagged around Lazuli's image, distorting it into inhuman shapes in brief seconds only to return to his real form. Lazuli sat back and laughed with a calm confidence, despite the phlegm bubbling out of his lungs. As though this was funny. Like he was doing the right thing, so confident. "Just gave them names. And underlined yours in particular. Midas, you're so good at this. Very few others are quite as perfect for it. And gave them the dog, only to get them to stop. Some of these initial conversations with Creed can be uncomfortable. Because they're inexorable. You get used to it, though, once you're in. It feels normal. Midas, a larger force is consuming everything around us. They'll stop at nothing. Understand that Creed is a sound business proposition, with an incredible almost mystical bent. Evangelical, without the angels of course. No need for them." He laughed harder this time and slapped his knee with a sudden delight. "Useless little fuckers."

Midas was never a religious person, but this offended him about as much as Caesar did. Everything Lazuli said was so out of place. *Gave them a dog?* What dog? Midas shook his head.

Lazuli seemed to be lost in his own deluded world. Problem was, as Midas thought it through, this was not only Lazuli's world, it was Creed's. And a new reality began to dawn on him that it was concrete and growing.

"I could barely speak, much less think by that point," Lazuli went on, his eyes gleaming and gleeful. His excitement grew as he spoke and told the story of this encounter. A negotiation, a business meeting, conversation or whatever it might have been called in a normal world. Or a hypnosis, a spell even. Something different had happened between Lazuli and Creed, its Hallowers and Caesar, that had changed the man fundamentally. In a very bad way. Lazuli kept on his rant as Midas's angst deepened. "So they took the dog, left a Hallower here to watch over me..."

The quivering waves of yellows and blues made Lazuli solid — a sudden image of his real strong self — only to splinter into a disjointed homage to what he was. The large man with eyes still piercing in the chaos leaned back, stroked his chin. Lazuli held up his hand as though to stop everything and take note. "Wait. What did Caesar tell you?"

Midas would answer, get as much information as he needed for now, and leave this conversation. It was all so painful.

"He talked about a promised place of wealth, opportunity and riches, free of moral constraints." Midas's voice shook as he spoke. Caesar's message felt worse when he repeated it.

Lazuli laughed again, coughed and doubled over. "I'm surprised he said that much. Certainly, he's there to do deals, develop his network, and you're one of many who deserve an early introduction. Did he talk of the legendary place then? What it looked like? Everyone's selling something, aren't they. But this, Midas, is real. This pitch is the final one, and a very good one. They don't stop. My boy, these Hallowers don't stop. They do one thing: take. And the plan is to open the pathway to that legendary place. We know it's out there. We know there's a pathway there. We know because they're already here. They're the Hallowers. We're changing into them, can't you see that? It will happen with or without our active participation so I decided what you will inevitably come to decide: to join now, to get in early, get the good stuff."

Midas almost kicked the hologram to the wall, and regretted doing all of this, the ridiculous café he'd built. "Well, whatever they think they're looking for, they're not going to find it," he said. "There's no legendary place full of riches. That's stupid. There's only Earth. What's left of it." Midas sighed, almost done with this but had to ask, "What did they do to you?"

How dangerous are they? These psychopaths posing as a business.

"We used to call it growth," Lazuli continued, oblivious to the question. "We go there, through that passage to that awesome place, we take, and they come here. Just take, Midas. That's the plan." He bent over and hacked again, then calmed. "They were right, I see some of it now." He coughed. "They were so convincing."

Lazuli looked at Midas, up to meet his eyes, and behind the psychotic zeal Midas sensed, he also saw something worn in this tired man, dusted and beaten.

Midas couldn't trust him with anything anymore. There was no point in speaking further. The man had gone mad. The trouble was, so had everything else. He might have disbelieved this all as an unfortunate coincidence: Hippias showing up, talking of Creed, then Creed actually showing up, then Lazuli confirming their claims. The trouble was, he'd left his last job at Superior because he'd seen, in essence anyway, part of the germinations of this so-called Creed or what it seemed to represent and once back home here he kept seeing it. People killed at Night. People dredged this mineral-constructed magma artifice out of the bowels of the earth and abused it, abandoned the rule of law and drowned themselves in intoxicants and debauchery to forget, embraced privatized policing, cared nothing for their ruined water supply and made profits from destroying the atmosphere. So Midas recognized with some growing horror that what Lazuli described was not completely deluded, at least not in essence.

"But what am I supposed to do now?" asked Midas, in one last attempt to extract as much as he could before Lazuli descended into total incomprehensible madness.

Lazuli didn't seem to be listening. "I just gave them everyone's name," he rambled. "They took the dog. A funny blue dog with strange eyes. I called her Madame Blue. Don't ask me how I came up with the name other than it seemed the most obvious and it just sort of settled in my head, so naturally. As though the dog itself thought of it! Rare species that it was." Lazuli paused and leaned back again. "That specimen is a wonder, Midas. Its sense of smell is remarkable, even for a dog." Through the uncertain flickering of hologram lines, his image disrupted constantly by sparks and crackles, he continued. "Yes, that dog's sense of smell was almost magical. It could smell lightning before it struck. Once we were in a boat at sea, and it smelled a giant mutated beast of a shark far below the surface — and barked in victory once the thing arrived near the side of the boat. It could smell rare radio waves even, emitted from a distant satellite owned by a space agency whose illegal experiment later made the news. If anything can smell out whatever might lead Creed through the mysterious passage they seek, it's that fascinating blue dog that came to me not long ago. Out of the blue, I guess." He laughed again. "Just after you left, actually. Nonetheless, that's for them to take care of in due time. All you need to do is follow the Creed plan, my boy."

"What the hell does that mean? Smell out what?" Midas gave up. All Lazuli could do was repeat his plea to do something Midas would never do. Creed may be real and Lazuli its latest imploring victim, but Midas would suffer no more of this.

He watched as Lazuli's image fizzled with the disconnection.

Midas looked back to his busy café, at poor Ira through the crack in the door, and then into the image, this shadow of the man he'd admired so, and felt his gut twist into a terrible knot.

The yellows and blues flickered spastically in every direction, cutting Lazuli into pieces, reformulating him, and destroying him yet again before Midas's widened eyes. Something was changing all around them, on that Lazuli was correct, and something was very wrong.

"Lazuli!" Midas yelled.

The camera shifted back to its former position to show only a limp hand upon the broad arm of his chair.

"Boss!" cried Ira's distant voice from the clamour Midas only now once again could hear. "I need you out here." The milk frother screeched somewhere in the distance.

Midas felt numb. Yet the image of Lazuli was gone. And Ira and the café needed him. Heart heavy and with a lump in his throat, he walked back into the boisterous café. Ira and the students moved swiftly, determined and sure. Midas picked up a plastic bin to gather dishes, and as he meandered amongst the tables, the conversations persisted about the massacre and abductions. Everyone ignored him as they debated, drank coffee and imagined the motives, the perpetrators and what might happen next. Midas kept moving, feeling empty and anxious. They — Creed, Lazuli and Hippias — were acting consistently with one another. Not together, but he sensed they represented a pattern. Something was happening and it gnawed at him even as he kept trying to say to himself they were just in their corner. He was here, separate and apart, doing good and independent business.

He weaved and stumbled through the tables and chairs. He'd lean over around someone, ask if it was okay, and aim for a saucer, careful of the crumbs because on the floor they would just add to the growing chaos. All a numb blur, and time passed. The music hummed behind so much noisy chatter, and he wondered how they could possibly be so interested in such a horror as the Hallowe'en massacre as gradually the crowd thinned.

Midas stood behind the espresso machine and said to the students seated at the bar eating unsold sandwiches, "You two can go. Thanks for your help. Here, take the rest of the sandwiches."

They hurried out past the machine where, at the espresso bar, a red bowler hat moved upward from Hippias's bent head as it lifted from his bowl of soup. Midas felt an exhausted pang and turned to Ira who leaned, relaxed at last, against the back counter with a bottle of beer in his hand.

"When did you give him soup?" Midas asked.

Hippias said, "I also asked to speak to the owner of this fine establishment. Where might he be, and would you please introduce us?" He smiled broadly and winked at Midas as he leaned down to the base of his stool and produced upon the counter a heavy plastic bag sealed at the top with an orange fastening.

Ira took a long sip from his bottle, eyes half closed, and pointed his finger at Midas.

Hippias shifted his hat back, chuckled and said, "Ah, my good friend. So good to see you again. I thought I would do you the courtesy of arriving in person for the next delivery. The real one this time." He winked again. "Not mere samplers."

Midas forced a smile at Hippias's little joke. Still feeling uneasy, he reminded himself this was not Caesar. It was the affable Hippias. The real one? The sampler was supposed to be real. That's why we call them samplers. And the first batch yesterday was supposed to be a real delivery, not a sampler.

He must mean this one has the drugs in it.

"Let's move this quickly, please," Midas said.

"Try them," said Hippias. "Well, maybe not now. Do it after you've completed your day's work. Maybe this chap can imbibe." He nodded at Ira, who gulped long and kept his gaze steady. Hippias chuckled again. "They're quite simply magical."

"I thought there were going to be drugs?" Midas said, leaning close to him with his back to Ira. "Included, you know, sealed and hidden in there."

"Ah, yes, a normal assumption, but don't worry, dear friend." Upbeat and jovial, Hippias said, "It's coffee, after all. And you're a café."

He snapped his fingers in the direction of two large men, the same two in long leather coats as before, who lingered by the door and the espresso machine, blocking the way as Midas noticed with even more frustration. "We've got about a good, what, twenty bags?" He seemed to ask them but kept looking at Midas. "Of what — of coffee, my good man! That's right! Coffee. They'll bring them in to your back room there. No, don't worry!" He winked and whispered, "Not the stage. The little one to the side. Your office. What is it? The roaster room? How charming. You really should offer an historic tour for the clients, too. You know, a sort of show and tell of all the wonders you've collected here." Hippias couldn't contain his delight as he grinned with pride.

Midas was still frowning. "It was supposed to be coffee with some drugs hidden in there. In baggies or something like that. I agreed to hold it for you, sealed separately among the coffee beans. That's different than giving some kind of new drug-laced coffee to my customers. Is that what this is? That's a different deal." Midas heard his voice growl. This salesman was infuriating. Who lies like this? A deal is supposed to be a deal, and Midas was sick of incorrigibly bad people running around in the marketplace making preposterously shitty deals. "You can't do that," he said.

Hippias grinned and shook his head dismissively. "You worry too much. The people will love it, absolutely adore it and come back for more and more." Hippias threw his head back and laughed. "In fact, we could call it something like *Come Back*. What a brand!" He slapped the table with glee.

"So, what," said Midas, "you haven't sold this before? It doesn't already have a brand name?"

The two men re-entered under the tinkling bells, each dragging a trolley with boxes of coffee beans. Hippias pointed to the roaster room.

"It's a new product and we need to sort of market test it, as it were."

"You want to market test it on my customers?" This was wrong.

Hippias took off his hat, possibly aware it accentuated his reddening face. Midas looked around the café, and as the customers dwindled, the room became quiet.

"I sell coffee. Real coffee." His voice was hoarse. Midas thought back to that little round man, Caesar, and how he might have resisted instead of agreeing to this.

"It is coffee. It's coffee with a twist," pressed Hippias. "In fact, truth be told, I only said *drug* rather recklessly. I mean, coffee is a drug, isn't it? We don't drink it for nutrition, I'm sure we agree. Therefore, it's a drug. Done." Hippias settled upon his stool. "Now, let me clarify please: this coffee has been genetically modified. It does something somewhat special to one's inner feeling and sense of self. I call it — admittedly, at the risk of sounding hyperbolic — the God drug." Hippias bent over his soup as he giggled. "You feel like you're God," he went on, a little loud and rushing his words, "or at least I do. But others more likely just sense it, you know, up there just above the crown of your head. Don't know for sure, maybe it depends on who you are and some DNA aspects lurking around here and there. It's truly marvellous and wonderful, Midas." Hippias smiled broadly. "Believe me."

"This wasn't the deal," said Midas. He tried to maintain a steady voice and kept his shaking hands in his pockets. "This changes everything."

The two men left with the empty trolleys, returned with others, and slid them along to the roaster room.

Midas nodded toward them. "People don't want that when they think they're buying regular coffee." They'll never come back, he thought with dread. And they'll sue my ass.

"No." Hippias shook his head with vigour and insisted. "They'll just like it more, that's all. By God, well," he maintained in earnest, "I suppose that sounds rather extreme, doesn't it? Truth be told, it's really more like euphoria. Coffee plus a kick. Or, well, I suppose a hell of a kick. Plus, it's tasty. And, this."

Midas waited and watched.

Hippias raised his finger. "One hundred per bag or a percentage of our total profits, which will be at the numeral one."

"I can't sell drugs like this."

"Oh come now, Midas," he said, exasperated and now strained. "It's not that bad," and he slapped his hands upon his knees. "You don't have to give it to everyone. My goodness no! Just those who want it. You have to be upfront." His eyes rolled. "And it doesn't make you high. It's not like slider. I said the word *God*, I know. Did I use that word? It was the wrong word."

The man talked far too quickly. Midas also thought, as his mind raced, how rare coffee was, that Lazuli's supply was not only excellent but difficult to source, that he'd given up a long sales funnel for a narrow, risky and far too specialized retail play. But now, Lazuli was too far gone. He couldn't do business with him, not unless he did business with Creed.

The two large men in black leather returned from the roaster room and stood behind Hippias.

"Midas," he said, pointing at the two men. "You need them and we need you. And you need the beans. Take the percentage. That way, you don't buy them, you're just one of us, we own them, you keep your cash, and you get a cut. Deal?"

There were inherent risks, including the question of ownership, but he was low on cash and stuck with a café without any coffee. His racing mind couldn't keep up. He could accept them, as he implicitly already had now that they'd been stored in the roaster room, for now. He'd never serve them. They'd have to talk further, and the ill-gotten assets would either move elsewhere or be returned if they couldn't come to another arrangement. Today, he was too tired. And feeling surrounded.

"Deal."

Hippias let out a loud quick laugh, squeezed his eyes shut with unconstrained mirth and slapped Midas on his chest. "Oh yes, my friend. Exciting times ahead."

He put on his red bowler hat, went to the door with the two men and turned. "By the way, there's one bag that's extra special. I've labelled it *Tea Party*. It's all red. Little joke of mine. Can't miss it." Flushed, he turned to the door that slid up and open. "Keep it secure. It's for a private event in a few weeks for a select group of special guests. I'm sure you'll be proud to host. They're powerful people in this town."

Midas watched them leave and shook his head at how any of this could have happened, and how he could get himself out of it. He had some Lazuli bean supply left. It would do for just a little while yet.

NINE

Zora knocked on Augustine's door.

"This is bad," she said to herself. Her vision had cleared but an ache remained in the right side of her head. After the interrogation, Zora sat on the streetcar for a while and returned home where she slept still as stone until the nightmares came: hazy yellow light in an empty white room and a cold table, fists pounding it, hot whispers in her ear and children scrambling, crying, "Mommy, no, no, no," and she fought back: *Focus*.

She was no longer in that room. She was awake and away from the nightmares. She'd had coffee, then a second, while sitting in her small, cramped kitchen. She'd walked along the path beside the tracks past Dundas West and back at least twice. A day might have gone by but she lost track, focusing on her innermost reserves of strength built over a young life of uncertainty. She'd never been so close to raw danger like this before and found herself staring out her window for long periods. Out there, from her eighth-floor vantage, spanned what felt like a jagged plain of shingled rooftops splintered into crooked grids of grey, greasy streets. The brightest colour moved in flashing lines and stank the most: red burning magmatic fuel from cruisers, some flying recklessly in the high lane just above the houses, and one that came too close to a treetop's barren branches that might have caught fire. This desolate scene almost caught her and brought her down again, but she refused to let it take hold. She looked up into the darkening sky and the setting orange sun moved down below the horizon, but she found solace in knowing it would always come back. Then they'd all start over again, try one more time. For a moment, she felt better. She even messaged Midas.

I'll get there in a couple of days. Sorry, something came up, she wrote. She felt guilty for lying a little.

He replied immediately which surprised her because it'd been 10:00 p.m. Tuesday night.

He messaged back: *Just checking after what happened at the Ball. Just making sure you're ok.*

This was sweet of him and she liked him a lot. But he could not possibly handle what she was into. He was a simple business guy, here to re-create himself. Or, rather, recover himself. She, on the other hand, had been sucked into some kind of revolutionary vortex.

The awesome fear resurged, and she'd again pushed it down until it crystallized into a determined state of steadiness. The terror and shock reduced merely to fear. Intimidated by the task to ask that bastard Augustine enough questions to satisfy her oppressors, yet preoccupied by the fate of those abducted children.

Then Division Q invaded her Probe. *Stop staring out the window, Sweetness, start the job...* Zora pressed her Probe to get out of the message, but she was locked there. They'd frozen her account in some way, to stay in front of her and dominate. Even more offensive was the totality of it because the woman whom her colleague called Peacock couldn't see her, or rather, what she saw. They'd called it a wiretap, after all.

Focus, she said to herself with a renewed intensity. The kind she was always used to. Zora turned away from Augustine's door and stared out at the street. "I have to be strong," she said into the growing wind that spanned a vast dark park, and she barely heard, through sheets of rain, a raging saxophone in a distant bar. She tightened her ponytail. "This is fucked."

"What are you saying, Zora?" asked Augustine. She spun around. The door was open.

Augustine stood in the cramped hallway lined with paintings and two mirrors, the widest of which hung above a walnut pedestal table crowded with flowers. Beyond the hallway was a living room, its puffy white sofa, a dead bear's back for a rug and a new kitchen. To the right of the entrance to the living room was a small bar, stuffed with bottles.

Keep calm, she said to herself in defiance of a rising panic. Her mind flew from thought to thought. *What am I going to say? What happened to those children. Are they all right? They might be.* She had to ask him enough to get an incriminating response, if in fact he was truly involved in the crime. Except she had no idea how to do that.

Zora hesitated, even as the rain crashed behind her and she pushed through the dull ache lasting in her head, dispelling the images of Division Q's interrogation, searching for what dialogue might lure him to a confession.

"I've been reading," he said, and pointed to the thick text on the table in the hall. He held a half-full tumbler of scotch. "I know you must be wondering, 'Oh Augustine, where do you find the time?' But I find it soothing. Things have been rather stressful, as I'm sure you can imagine."

She suspected disgust darkened her face at his luxuriant arrogance, his indulgence in scotch, the riches of his wealthy home. As though he hadn't recently escaped a massacre while so many others didn't.

He turned to walk back into the hall. She kept standing at the doorway.

"Are you coming in?" He stopped at the doorway to the living room. "The winds are fierce, all of a sudden. They say it's another bout, then we'll get some heat again."

She knew Division Q wanted her to enter. *No, I can't do this*, she thought, and felt trapped. They had frozen her Rinth account; they were everywhere; they would see her balk.

She took two steps in and looked at herself in the mirror. It couldn't be real but it was: Her wet, bedraggled hair, baggy eyes and high-strung exhaustion, surely exasperated by the vodka, made her look like hell. And behind her reflection in the mirror, several small paintings, cheap fakes of the Canadian wilderness and others of impossible images — of people contorted and melded with images of something else, walking here and there, reaching for something. She had to tear herself away.

Focus, she said to herself again. Zora struggled to think of something to say, to ask. But the hell in the mirror drained her of any smart words.

"Have a drink," he said, and coughed. "Take off your raincoat."

She'd prefer not to but that wouldn't work. She had to encourage conversation and standing awkwardly by the door, dripping from rain, wouldn't do that, so she unbuttoned the long dark-red raincoat and dropped it on the shoe mat. Still, she couldn't bring herself to walk fully inside.

"What are you reading?" she asked. "That's a hefty book there." She nodded at the text on the pedestal table.

He sighed and rolled his eyes. "Nothing, Zora. Too complicated to explain, really." He sounded languid, like he'd had several glasses of scotch already.

Zora felt like slugging him upside the head with such a disparaging comment. She glanced at the small, dense letters that packed the open pages. There was no clue here, nothing to speak about. Just a textbook on esoteric law at a chapter titled "*Mens Rea*" and on the next page a section on "Excuses."

He'd been a lawyer, she recalled. What area, she never understood clearly from him. "Why are you reading this?"

He laughed like they shared a joke, but it came out as another frustrated cough.

"There's no criminal liability without fault, Zora. And even if there is some fault, if you don't know right from wrong then you're innocent."

He smiled at her and his mouth glistened with liquor.

"That doesn't sound quite right to me," she said. "You never practised, did you? Not like in one of those fancy offices above where the Ball was held?"

"I told you. I'm better than that." He coughed suddenly and bent over with a brief fit.

"You're still sick?" she asked.

Recovering, he stood straight and looked to her image in the mirror, "That tragedy has taken a toll on all of us, Zora." He shook his head and his eyes went vacant as though remembering. "I discovered something significant at that event, just prior to the crime, and it got me thinking. In fact, I'd been looking into this phenomenon brewing for some time now on my own — without the cell involved of course for they'd never understand it — some things I'd come upon that simply coalesced into a rock-solid realization at the Ball."

"What did you see? Did you know in advance what was planned? Is that what you were looking for? This so-called information?" She paused and suppressed an anger growing in her.

Shit, I'm an idiot. That was too fast.

"No, we left almost immediately after we arrived."

"Why?" she said, trying to contain her pitching voice. "What am I missing?"

He leaned against the doorway. Zora's nervous eyes darted from him to the mirror, to the open text beneath it, the chaotic paintings reflected in it and past him into the apartment.

He was a tall man, thin and well dressed in a collared short-sleeve shirt, designer jeans and expensive slippers, all draped with a light bathrobe. Her view of him changed. Maybe he'd always been sickly without her noticing it. Now it was clear: His face was more gaunt than their last encounter at Night, the skin even paler, with shadows — long ones — stretching downward from his baggy eyes. His hair was a mess, like a hallower.

Her nervousness swelled and she fought it back down. Yet she remained at the rainy, open doorway, vowing to get through this, unable to step forward.

"You know, Cisco. He's good at seeing things. Some costumes looked a little too odd. He took a closer look at them and ordered the rest of us to abandon the plan."

Zora scrambled to think of what must be asked. What would sound like a legitimate question.

"So what brought you there in the first place, Augustine?" Zora tried to control her tone. With her thumping heart, this wasn't easy. "I mean, how'd you guys find out about it? Not the Ball, but whatever you were looking for. And what were you looking to find out, anyway?"

Shitty spy, she thought. *How's this going to help.*

"So curious, aren't you, Sweetheart? Truth be told, it wasn't me. It was your good buddy Cisco. He had a former contact who got involved with a business network" — he cleared his throat with some show of disgust — "called Creed. Fascinating concept, and I'd taken an interest for some time now. The cell," he scoffed. "They know barely anything about what this is, what this phenomenal new power means. Only I know."

Zora tried to keep her face neutral against the fear at his wavering back and forth between what seemed like a contradiction for him: disgust at what he'd discovered and pride at having discovered it.

"We found a poor lad about a week before," he went on, "at the bar on College. Simply asked some questions in the back alley behind — looked like one of those damn hallowers. Well he was in conflict with Creed, and honestly I don't blame him. Needless to say, we don't know what ultimately happened to him. After the others left, I returned an hour later and we had a quick word. We connected, for lack of a better word, then and there, he and I, and the rest is history."

"And? What were you thinking you'd find out?" She felt her sweat gather as though it was pouring down her neck. Surely he noticed her frantic eyes popping out of her head. "What was the tip?"

Zora moved into the hallway toward him and looked at his face with determined eyes as though to push him with her will deeper into his suite, out of the rain into comfort where he could speak more. Despite feeling like a complete idiot, it worked. He moved further into the living room and flopped himself upon the couch.

He chuckled. "Oh, he said lots of things. I had to impose some sensible order on his frantic babbling, but I could do it. And then so much became confirmed just a week later with the massacre," he said. "So I thought to look it up, this phrase here: *mens rea* in the Criminal Code of Canada. What is a crime, after all? Was it that, or something else? In any event, I discovered something absolutely pivotal just moments before the tragedy happened. Met a few of those suits, as you like to call them if I recall, past the base of the stairs in the Path and around a bend in one of those labyrinthine hallways. I could put it all together by then, having digested what the poor lad had revealed in that back alley behind the bar on College Street. A revelation almost too perfect, to tell you the truth."

His tone, so calm and nonchalant, was sickening, but she held there and forced herself to ask through a spastic choke in her throat, "What did you learn? This game changer, what was it? From the poor lad, as you call him, or at the Ball?"

Oh my God I can't interrogate anyone to save my life.

Augustine couldn't help the smile that spread across his face like a thin slit with pointed teeth lining its edges, discoloured yellow. "I can divulge this only: I mentioned a company earlier when I asked you to do this project. Creed, the very one the poor lad had become so embroiled in. Like I said, I've been doing my own research on them, on the side, and when I say we discovered something significant, you know, really, it's just me. They think they know. But they — oh, Cisco and the rest of the group — don't know half of what Creed really is. What it can do. What it has waiting for us."

Augustine rose from his white sofa, reconsidered the walk to the bar and gave Zora his glass for a refill, then fell back amongst the cushions with a satisfied smile. Zora, now standing within the living room just beside the bar, poured them both a hefty glass of liquor — more scotch for him and the most expensive cognac for herself.

Something was about to be said, she thought, and sought to keep calm. She gulped the cognac to keep her hard-pounding heart from leaping out of her chest and leaned against the bar while Augustine spoke about Creed and his research. His eyes shone bright, intense and fervent.

Zora turned to the bar's bottles behind her and topped up her tumbler once more, dropping a small cube in.

There. Now she might be able to listen without continuing to freak out. As it settled into her blood, the cognac let her give a mental "fuck you" to Division Q, wherever they were.

Augustine kept on with his story, so engrossed he appeared in love with it.

"I'd been questing these things for some time," he said from the other side of her cognac as it settled into her veins. So soothing, a wall beyond a moat protecting her from the offence of his words. "You see," he was saying as she became just numb enough at the growing, ominous prospect of his fervent belief, "the kid in the back alley told me about it. I'd learned before, anyway, as so many of us had been learning in our respective investigations. We all know something is afoot. All of us — companies, investigators, guys like me, the cell — know it, something awful and terrible. Some want it for what they can understand: like a territory, or a piece of wealth, a business opportunity. Others hunt for a madness. And this is what I thought I'd discovered, a madness, a delusion — until I met the kid. Well, he confirmed all that was too true to be coincidental. Or rather, too coincidentally and wonderfully true to be false."

So they're hunting for something, she thought. Him and others. A vague thing, a goal. This success they sought: What were the clues for them to find what they sought? Unless Augustine had gone completely mad.

"This company is striving to do a deal with a group of errant bureaucrats. For a vehicle of extraordinary potency."

A vehicle? Didn't Division Q say something about that? Zora strained to focus on his words.

"The lad — told me — about it — a vehicle with extraordinary technological capabilities such as to put airplanes and cruisers to shame. Makes the magma irrelevant. Hah!" he laughed for himself at his thought.

"It has the capacity to salvage this wretched world. Turn the ecological decay around, and let enough survivors reverse this god-awful mess. And that rebel group inside government — they're nothing to snuff at. You know as well as I that the state — the bigger apparatus that employs them — is weak. They show power but despite that, I know, deep down, they're thieves just like the rest of us. At the same time, they have something. And it's worth something. So somebody stole the kids. This became enlightening too."

"Children are dead and kidnapped." She glared at him, shaking so hard everything was almost blurry again, just like she felt earlier at her apartment when she tortured herself over this offensive assignment with vodka and coffee. Her stomach clenched. She had no choice. Division Q would kill her if she didn't do this. And there were kids somewhere and now it was real. He — Augustine — had something to do with this. He knew something about it. *And there are kids at stake.*

She gulped cognac again even though it obviously wasn't calming her down.

He lifted his scotch and regarded her from deep within the sofa's cushions with dull eyes and laughed softly to himself.

"Dead?" he asked, glancing with surprise from his glass as he sipped again. "Oh, the children aren't dead. They kidnapped them, to be sure, but they've had to keep them alive, if they are to extort what they want from their parents. Because that somebody," he said, staring past her into the intermittent sheets of rain, "is a very bad man. A cunning man."

"How can that thing you're talking about — vehicle or machine or whatever the fuck it is — salvage our world?" she asked.

"Creed has a plan. And we need to know what that plan is."

He stood, hands pressing into knees to push himself up off the sofa, and walked toward her. He twirled the ice cubes in his waning glass and beckoned her again to fill it.

"What's the machine?" she said as she dumped the bottle of scotch vertically downward, filling his glass.

Oblivious to her question he nodded at his glass and said, "It's completely wild."

His laugh transformed into a phlegm-filled rattle, and his whole frame doubled over. With this burst of air from his lungs she stepped back. His breath was rancid, like he'd been infected. The dark patches under his eyes didn't come from lack of sleep, or makeup. They were longer than exhausted bags, stretching down, with more blotches on his neck. Etched in and organically part of his skin. Injured or sick.

"What's the technology?" she asked again, for he sounded like he knew but he maintained he didn't, and she believed truly he did not. She heard him, the bastard: Others were seeking something, a broad-based quest he'd found out about only weeks ago. It was a hunt. A big, bad hunt.

"We don't know yet." He wiped his mouth with the back of his free hand.

"But you must have some idea. This is really important to you, right? You guys must be intent on doing whatever it takes, right?"

She felt stupid for speaking so quickly. A spastic series of attacking questions. He would catch her in her ridiculous ploy at any moment and the thought alone sent her eyes bulging wide.

"Zora," he stopped her and held up his hand. "We need you to broadcast the deal." He walked back to the sofa.

"Broadcast? You mean not just record?" Zora felt the vertigo come back.

Augustine rubbed his pale forehead and scratched his dishevelled hair. She'd never seen him in such a tired state although she was sure the liquor didn't help. And yet, he was not drunk.

"Yes and yes. Zora, we need to incite a revolution," he said. "I'm sure you appreciate this. And we now know something more about the company poised to negotiate with that errant bureaucrat group. This should appeal to you, Zora, so just do it, won't you? Get the surveillance device implanted, won't you? Children were stolen from seven—"

"Abducted," she said. "People steal things. They abduct people. That's the right word."

Zora filled her glass with yet more cognac. Surely he would say something more about the Hallowe'en Ball. Get him drunk and keep calm. She could do this, she vowed to herself.

She drank half of the glass and thought of the hallway behind her. It gaped and beckoned her with its mirror and noisy paintings reflecting upon themselves.

Then he began to ramble. The scotch at first had everything to do with it, although his whole rant confused her even when it might have made some sense. He spoke of a key, that the kid he'd interrogated let some words loose, maybe under enough pain although Augustine didn't admit to anything. The kid, or this asshole Augustine, she'd lost track at this point who was talking to whom, but somebody had a knife and it wasn't friendly.

She took another gulp of her cognac. Preoccupied by her horror at what he was saying, she felt herself missing details, struggling to concentrate to make sense of something that ultimately must be senseless.

She stared at him and listened but it didn't matter much for Division Q, she thought bitterly, because this had nothing to do with the damned confession they wanted about who was responsible for the crime at the Ball. So she gulped some more, because Division Q was obviously way off in their investigation. Augustine was still babbling nonsense.

They got the wrong guy, she thought.

He was slurring now: "'Some call it a passage,' the kid said. 'Some call it a portal.' He'd been hanging around with them too much, trying on their slim suits and working their circuit, making calls, you know, picking up things about them as he worked."

Zora shifted, impatient — *What is he on about?* He was drunk on a mad delusion, and she was beginning to feel more than a little tipsy herself.

"I said, you tell me about this portal," Augustine continued. "I had him on the ground by then" — he grinned — "he was pretty scared. He knew about Creed … He told me, 'The key is a guardian.' And he laughed, even in the face of my knife. I think he was cursing me or something… 'A mythical beast protecting any passage. A beautiful blue woman,' he said, and he began to giggle like a child burying his fear beneath something else twisted in his head, seeing something incredible without understanding it."

This is totally messed up, Zora thought. *Come on, dumb-dumb, get more out of him. More? Yes more,* she thought. It wasn't enough, apparently, for this godforsaken assignment that he might have murdered a kid. She had to extract yet a *different* confession out of him. She said aloud into the air at the ceiling, to the bloody Division Q on their line, "Are you fucking kidding me?"

No one answered, of course, and she burst into a short bout of a sob, then stopped herself.

Augustine's grin wavered, then he sat up straight in some effort to recover his composure. He waved his hand in the air. "Calm please, Zora. I digress. Back to the business at hand. Violence is now everywhere, Zora. Look around you. Society needs a major recalibration. Surely, if we've thought of it then others have too. Someone is going to do something, soon."

Zora needed to leave. She turned around to look down the front hall and watched the rain and wind building outside, cruisers gliding by on the red magmatic power that stank and ruined the last of their air. She turned back to him to say one last thing. She couldn't help but express herself on this.

"But you need to do good things," she said to him. "That's the only way for better change. Are you sure you weren't inciting something with what happened at the Ball?"

I can't believe I just said that.

Augustine snorted, and then began to hack. "I didn't incite anything." His rattling calmed and he became reflective. "We fled the scene."

"Right. You fled the scene of the crime. Funny way to put it."

"We left before the crime," he reminded her.

The rain outside beyond the end of the hall pounded upon the pavement behind those distant Coltrane sheets of sound. She buried the comforting thought of her music, forcing herself back to this sick man's grating words that wouldn't stop.

He drank an amount of scotch that carved serenity into his face.

Zora yelled at him: "And you want me to go to a fucking boat and broadcast this meeting?" Zora felt she had to leave the room or she'd slug him. *But just hold out a little more*, she said to herself. *One more minute.*

"Well honestly, Zora, it simply must be live," he said, oblivious to her growing outrage. "We have this tech, it gets placed there by your eye and we experience everything you see. Not a stupid audio recording with its distractions and fuzziness. And this means you must be there and not waver from the task. Everyone will be watching."

His long finger, and its dirty nail, reached for her brow and she shirked from it.

"What if I don't do this? Are you saying I'm somehow now committed? Are you crazy?"

Augustine was still thinking of the tech they were planning to use. Or he just didn't care enough about her to answer. "I mean really, Zora, anyone who uses a simplistic recording device alone remains in the stone ages." He laughed and slapped his knee, as though beside himself with glee. "Sounds like a radio. Or a turntable. At least those you can find. How about a typewriter. Ha! Do you write with a typewriter, Zora? Maybe got it from your silly friend?"

I already have a wiretap in my hair, she thought. *Now Augustine wants to shove something into my eye. Or by my eye. This is fucked.* Zora's panic swelled up and she breathed to regain control. She said,

"If you know so much about this, why do you need me? And what's their plan? And whose plan is it?"

"Good questions, Zora," he said with a wooden smile. "We need you to get close to them. As for who they are and what they want — well we have some ideas, but your broadcast will finally determine who they really are and as for their plan, well just imagine: Each child belonged to a key dealmaker in government and business. Seven of them. It's extortion. The message in the blood made that clear: do the deal with us or they'll die. What parent would not comply?"

She turned again to face the rain, long drops crashing from the relentless night sky.

"Zora, go to Cisco at the docks. He's in the Cherry Street strip. Just watch your back there. You know that neighbourhood. He'll keep you safe and set you up and we'll be ready for the meeting. At the cruise, meet me at the main bar on the large deck. We'll go from there."

His smile slit again across his face with his yellowed teeth.

She stepped away, turned to the park's dark expanse and the dense city lights beyond it, and leapt down the stairs. She ran into the sheets of rain to the muddied grass across the street until she fell against the tall black iron fence bordering the park. The rain came upon her, and the soaring notes battered like a ram from a bar down the night's lamp-lit street. Zora put her face into her hands and she wept over the music.

TEN

Midas woke in a panicked sweat. He turned to his right side and looked at the open window, felt a warm breeze with brief relief, and raised himself from the bed. Glad he was awake, but he knew he would never fully escape because this wasn't just a dream. It was a memory. About his café, Lazuli and something that should have been irrelevant. The painting.

That damned thing that came from the damn ship, so long ago. The afternoon he went there, the ocean was somewhat troubled, dipping and rising in troughs and peaks as they rushed against the high crags. Midas had been furious at how he'd been betrayed in the deal, and not sober at all on whatever stimulant he'd taken... He rowed the boat through rocks and foamy sea, climbed the ship's sides, rummaged inside and found chests inside the short narrow room.

Despite his inebriated state in that moment, part of the adventure had been terrifying. At any moment, a shark could emerge from the murky depths and consume him. Or some other beast, for much had changed in these waters, and in the forests and mountains too. No one kept track anymore of how so many species had morphed under the corruption of climate change, destruction and pollution. Especially in stateless places.

Strong, mindless and angry, he'd jumped into the sea, thankful for the bright sun and blue sky, and tied rope to the handles on either end of the chest that floated as he cursed in the water, choked on the salt and floundered. He'd struggled over the hull of his rowboat, knocked his head on the oars as he scrambled, and heaved the heavy chest up and inside. And felt like a demi-god, despite his dizzied state. For a moment, he'd told himself divine forces had sent him there.

The chest's lid flew open to reveal not only coins and necklaces but also fascinating sculptures and two paintings.

He shouldn't have done this. The ownership over the shipwreck was dubious — it was an abandoned piece of garbage, just like so many other abandoned things in the country. If you could call it that. Across the South, states had deteriorated into nothing but grand swaths of land occupied by chaos. The cities were a terror in their own right. In the countryside, however, the chaos spread out across jungles, mountains, savannahs and pampas gradually and steadily, leaving farms in ruin, small towns ghostlike. Some occupied by gangs or used by companies. Both roved around and took what they could. So this ship, though it technically sat within the lands Lazuli had purchased, represented only another abandoned wreck.

"I'm sorry," he said later to Lazuli.

"You can have it," said Lazuli from his wide-armed chair at the end of the long oak table, referring to the chest full of artifacts. Lazuli lifted a hand and waved it dismissively. They were of no value, and he paid no further attention.

Midas breathed deeply to calm himself and let the memory slip away. He needed to focus. He needed to save his business.

He took his hand-held Probe to call Zora. His heart jumped at the sight of Zora's message staring back at him: *I'll get there in a couple of days. Sorry, something came up.*

She must be calling from Night. It was close to midnight. She'd never done that — call during her shift. He replied immediately, unable to help himself. *Where are you? Haven't heard from you in a few days. That dickhead do something? Just worried cause of the Ball. Feels like you're too connected.*

He reflected on how she might take that and rewrote: *Just checking after what happened at the Ball. Just making sure you're ok.*

This would do.

The blank screen in his hand filled him with dread. The Probe remained quiet.

Do you need help? He wrote. *Where are you?*

After a long tortured minute, the colour red overwhelmed his screen. A return message appeared, blinking at the bottom, from Rinth. He was blocked.

This couldn't be right.

He went to the kitchen, made an espresso and after several minutes of fretting, decided to go for a walk, maybe wander near Night, and probably try her one more time.

The heat might have been pleasant had it not been so wrong. Queen Street West was dark and still in the November night with its big moon, grey trailing clouds and heavy humidity. Midas walked to Night first, almost worried he would find her, for she would frown at his deal with Hippias. He imagined walking into Night with relief that she was fine, explaining everything and her turning away in disgust.

He hurried between the street lamps' cones of light.

Cans clinked along the road in the strong winds. Two cruisers glided quietly above, and the fuel's stench descended as they passed. It sickened him every time because that fuel would run out too. Then they'd have nothing. He heard Zora's claims again: *Those days are closer than most people realize… No power, no good water, and the lights will blink out one by one. Then the real violence starts.*

A scuffle interrupted this train of thought, and something else: a deep-throated chuckle.

Midas slowed and turned to a filling station to his right. It had a smart, vintage look with its tall magma cylinders by a car wash. Past them, deeper into the property, surrounded by trees and beneath a leafy canopy sat a pair of derelict gas pumps.

Another chuckle echoed. A chuckle with no happiness. Then it barked hard into the air.

He paused and peered, sorting out whether the sound was from an animal. As though embarrassed at its outburst, it silenced itself into the night's quiet.

Dirty dress shoes protruded from beside the pumps, toes pointed upward. Someone lay on the ground. A head popped up from behind the other pump, shrouded beneath the tree, and its hair — long thick spikes, tightly knotted and stiff as though thickly pasted, sprouting from its scalp in every direction — merged into the leaves above.

"Hey." The word rasped almost as a laugh across the empty driveway of the station, strained yet carefree. The head ducked back down, and a throaty snarl broke the air. "Get him."

"Yeah!" the other shouted, in sport. Two thin men in suits emerged and rushed toward him. Midas whirled to run. He didn't know which direction to go other than sprint for the light of the street lamps. He passed one, dodged cans, bottles, overturned garbage bins and ran through puddles of rainwater.

Their rapid heels clicked on the sidewalk behind. They grunted from their throats and snorted like wild boars. A stench overcame him, not of garbage or rotting meat or anxious sweat. Something he'd never smelled. Something much worse.

To the left across the street was a set of stairs rising between condo townhouses. He ran there, to the false safety of height, which he knew gave nothing.

Midas slipped and heard them laughing and howling behind. His knee hit the stone edge of the curb as one of the beasts hooted in victory. He rose and looked behind across the dark street as they rushed to him through the cones of light. Dark smudges of mud or paint streaked across the blue-suited one's face and disappeared into a mane of hair. Eyes bloodshot, body wiry, too gaunt and pale from a life of sitting at a desk making calls and doing deals, roaming Rinth, thinking or scheming in an office, possibly forever haunted by the living weight of saying whatever they needed to get the deal. The other running behind was chunkier, in a dark-brown suit, hair splayed up like it had sustained an electric shock and a face blasted with soot from a fire.

They might have been wearing Hallowe'en costumes, like the youth of the day who never stopped, not satisfied with merely one night in their rebellious defiance of a world in decay, of an offensive self-destruction they resented so much they'd donned fantastical costumes. This was why he'd harboured a long worry for them. They were vulnerable to this violence.

But they weren't youth at all. Though tattered, ripped and even burned in places, the suits were tailored, expensive threads, once sophisticated and worn by intelligent working adults.

Midas's knees crumbled and he fell again at the base of the stairs. Click, click, went their hard-heeled shoes, running faster and panting like hungry animals. He rose and ran again, up between the townhouses through the narrow passage of stairs to what he didn't know, for everything was spinning.

He took the stairs three at a time and gained more ground on them. Their yells receded as he rounded a corner. At last he reached an open grassy courtyard surrounded by townhomes, each with their own garden, ornate fence and coloured door. He ran across the yard to a door and banged on it.

"Help me," he screamed.

Doubt grew. Their hooting and hollers echoed across the courtyard.

Midas ran to the next door, jumped over a small bush, stumbled up four steps and banged upon the obstinate wood. The courtyard stayed still.

The two suited figures appeared across the lawn in the shadows at the top of the stairs, and they bared their teeth.

One snarled.

Midas whirled his head around, back and forth, looking for a way out, something to put between them and him.

Directing his eyes at Midas, one said, "We have something for you."

The blue suit's mouth opened to a gaping round hole lined with sharp teeth, his eyes went wide with delight and he barked out something akin to laughter. He calmed then and said, "And you have something for us. You!"

They both barked laughter again, a sudden rat-tat-tatting, a twisted mocking humour that ended in a grim gaze. Then they sprinted for him.

Townhouses, a never-ending line of them, blurred along their short lawns as he ran, putting foot before heavy foot and pressed forward. The vast gardened lawn in the courtyard was no way to go; he would trip and they would come upon him, grab him with their claws and gnaw at him with their chiselled teeth.

The clicks came faster, louder.

At the opposite end of the courtyard, he came upon a set of stairs descending into the ground, fenced by a set of criss-crossed bars. It would lead to a basement area of the condo complex and had a doorway at its base that either still worked — or not. The door had a window through which came a dull, low light. He hesitated. A dead end meant his death. It would be a kind of ravaging.

Midas gasped, and heard them behind his back. He leapt to the bottom of the stairs, opened the door, bolted through, then slammed it shut.

The indoor parking lot housed cruisers amid empty spots under a low ceiling with dull lights, some of which worked, others burned out. Across the expanse of asphalt sat the exit of the garage, not far.

A loud bump came from behind him. He turned. Their faces were pressed against the smudged glass of the window.

"We're coming for you, Midas," they panted.

They know my name.

They smashed their hands against the window, their bruised and pale faces pressed up against it, and they howled.

"We know all what you did, Midas," one wailed, and his howling sounded just slightly distant behind the fragile, uncertain barrier. "We're changing, Midas. All of us. No one is going anywhere. It's just happening."

He stood and stared through the glass. Dirty fists, fingers with long nails and a hand with warts slammed against the window. They pounded at the glass and the blue suit stretched his neck out, his mouth rounded into a tense "Oh!" and he barked it.

Midas stood frozen like an animal in the wild before its worst terror.

He looked at their suits. The kids would dress up something like this: characters they invented, combining elements of one thing with another. What this costume represented he couldn't tell. They must have been at a hallower party, high on something. But they were too old for that. He knew he should run like hell, lucky for this chance. Instead, Midas stole a long second to look closer through the window at them. On one's lapel he saw a symbol of a trident.

Their muffled shouts reverberated and he tripped backward, falling almost on his buttocks but recovering to kneel on the asphalt. The lock was stuck, for now. His knees scraped the cement, and his bloodied palms pushed himself up as he dug the balls of his feet down hard to propel forward and away.

Midas sprinted with all his might, the garage door automatically opened as he approached and he ran down Queen Street for what must have been ten minutes. No one followed. He stopped finally, panting in the muggy air. And his thoughts began to coalesce. How could they have said his name? They couldn't know him. Could they?

He ran to Night, feet heavier than lead until Night's door rose ten feet before him, made of black wood and studded with triangular spikes.

Midas stopped and stared at the imposing height of the door, rising and wide like the front entrance to a castle. He heaved oxygen in and out as he steadied himself from the long desperate sprint. He'd arrived and now had to collect his thoughts on what he'd say to Zora. He'd have to tell her what was going on. He had to, because he had no one else. She was just a lonesome customer. A customer, yes, but not just. Maybe his one last friend.

Midas pulled the heavy door open and walked into a large square anteroom full of colourful furniture — two high-backed red-cushioned chairs, a deep green sofa, wide Persian rugs, large oil paintings whose dark blues and browns he couldn't discern, all lit by lanterns and flaming torches.

A guard, over six feet and muscular, wearing heavy jeans and a plate of ornate armour around his chest — a not uncommon garment these days, reminiscent of his own hobby: looking back at the past with artifacts as solace to the present — stepped forth from a shadow and stared at the sweat beading upon Midas's forehead.

"I'm only here to speak to Zora," Midas said to the guard, trying to contain his frantic breath. "Can she come out to talk? Just for a minute."

"She hasn't been here in a few days. She missed her shift yesterday."

Midas's heart jumped. "When was she last here?"

The guard squinted at him. "What's your name? I haven't seen you before." He reached for his belt where Midas noticed a long pistol.

The front door behind Midas had been sliding shut on its hinges and now clicked shut. Beyond the room and past red beaded curtains at the far side, distant music beat over hollers and cheers and a furious bass. He wiped the sweat from his brow.

"Just let me speak to her manager," he said. "I have to talk to him. Just for a second. Please — I'm a friend of hers. I don't come here ever. Don't worry. I'm not trouble."

Midas didn't see the guard lunge, but suddenly he was facing the wall and something harsh and thick like a knee dug into his back. The guard banged at Midas's pockets in a rough search, ruffled his hair hard as though something, incredibly, might be hidden in there and squeezed his ankles. Then he was lifted and whirled around, feet in the air, and he landed upon an armchair.

Midas gasped at the attack. Tried to keep his cool. He was, after all, at one of the most infamous and dangerous dining and night clubs in the city.

"Stay here."

The gleeful hollering from behind the curtain kept on over the music. He imagined the faces of the fighters in the pit and wondered if they were as gaunt and mean as the two monstrous men from the gas pumps. Or if they were as afraid as Midas, in shock at what they were made to do. And the faces of the audience, how they were not gaunt at all, and whether they bore those cruel grins from an hour ago and barked, "Oh!" like a popping rat-tat-tatting machine gun and yelled, "Yeah!"

"How can I help you?" A woman in dress pants, high heels and a high-collared blouse stood at the curtain, beads bunched up in her fists, with striking hair that reached up into a high round tower.

"I'm sorry to bother you," he said. "I'm looking for Zora. We were going to meet."

Her eyes were stern and disapproving.

"I'm a local businessman. I own a café."

"You were going to meet. Lots of people do that here." She laughed and exchanged a glance with the guard.

"Is she here?" he asked.

"Honey, I don't tell people other people's business." She released the curtain from her fists and crossed her arms.

"I get that, but this is dangerous. I mean, she might be in trouble and I'm trying to help her. Can you just…"

The hollers from behind the curtain burst into victorious cheers and the drumbeats soared.

"What the hell is going on in there?" He looked at the dark-red curtain, and more sweat dripped from his head. "Look, I need some water."

"Get him water," she said. Beneath her stern eyes she kept a small bent smile, a little like Zora's, and she nodded like she knew something deserving sarcasm. "It's a contest," she said. "Never been?"

"Never. Heard a few things, though." The woman bore a calm aura, and he needed it. He let himself soak it in a bit. "Zora and I are friends."

"She's not here. She missed her shift last night. We're worried about her too."

"So she's truly not here? No idea where she went?"

"She left after her shift early on Hallowe'en. Upset. Her ex was in, earlier that night, looking to get hooked up."

"He was here?"

"Ah, honey, so you know of him." She said it with some regret. "Come on inside, I'll get you a drink."

They walked through the beaded curtain and the hallway beyond opened to a cavernous room several storeys high. Lights spotted the darkness that spanned upward, illuminating balconies and a wide bridge across. To the right a bright light gleamed from a sunken floor, like an amphitheatre, in which crowded a raucous audience. Their fists pounded the air, they jostled one another and exchanged money.

He followed her to the other side of the huge floor and sat at the long bar made of reddish-black marble with jeering, goblin-like faces set into its length.

"That's her station at the end."

There above the bar hung a mezzanine floor. Although it sat in darkness Midas sensed movement. Lazy people lying within basins. From where he sat he saw hands flopped over the edges of steaming tubs. Beneath the mezzanine overhang, red-cushioned booths with heavy oak tables and burning incense lined the wall.

"Nice spot, I guess."

"Thank you. It's not an easy place to manage."

Midas gazed into the flames of a fire pit and beyond toward the amphitheatre. Again, the violent barks haunted him, no different from the human cock fight below.

She snapped her fingers and took his chin, turning his face to her. "Return to me," she said, releasing him. "I'm Shanti." She held out her hand.

Midas said his name and held her fingers, hesitated, then kissed them. They were long and polished with burgundy.

This sort of chivalrous greeting was not too common. Nor was it unusual.

She frowned again. "When did you last see her? What did she say?"

"Saturday afternoon." He gulped half his drink. "Then she messaged that she had something to give me."

"Ah, yes. She told me about that. I was keeping it for her." Shanti walked around the bar, leaned down and handed him a long object wrapped in cloth.

Midas held it and slid the cloth off. "This is unique." He recognized the blue stone from somewhere in Peru. "Did she say where she found it?"

He'd never seen such a sculpture. The face stared at him through pulsing waves of water. It was so convincing, this deep oceanic place in which the mermaid hovered. Midas felt embarrassed at holding her waist, the contradiction of her silky smoothness made of sharply edged scales, and laid her carefully upon the cloth on the bar.

"No," said Shanti. "Isn't it lovely? Her ex — he's such a strange one — seemed to take interest in it and then she left it with me. When the news came of the violence, she was a little upset. She said her ex went to work there that night after his visit. She's a good person, you know. Even cares about assholes."

Midas hoped the ex was dead and gone by now. But that would not be right. "Why does he come? Harassing her? She's never said anything."

"He keeps coming, off and on. She thought he'd just stop. She's tough, thought she could handle him. She'd turn her back, sometimes respond and chat a bit but always to get rid of him. And it's not just her he's here for. Seems he keeps looking for stuff," she said. "Bad stuff, like drugs or weapons."

"Weapons? What kind of weapons?"

"I don't ask. He looks rich, always well groomed. He speaks like he's got education. But he works like a bum and he creeps around looking for nasty shit. I have no idea if he ever got what he came for.

Zora would say she didn't know. But people do what they want and that's the way it goes. Who am I to judge?"

She was too tolerant of this — as he seemed to be, with the situation he'd found himself in with Hippias — and despite his ongoing dismay, none of it surprised him. He went back into a clouded moment of resurging trauma, to what had just happened down the street when those awful men in tattered suits said, "We know all that you did, Midas."

"But he bought weapons?"

"I said, no idea." Her voice was hard. "All I know is, last time he asked her to the cruise this Friday."

"What cruise?"

"Haven't you heard about it?" she said, disapproving and teasing at once.

"Well I don't know," he said. "There's a lot of parties to keep up with."

Shanti bent her head back and laughed with powerful lungs.

"It's marketed as bigger and better than the Hallowe'en Ball," she said. "Which wasn't even a real ball. Just a party. The cruise, I'll probably go." Shanti kept up her smile, sipped her drink a little and set it on the bar. She probably owned the place, too. She'd never let on. "You're in business. It'll be one of the best networking events of the season. Why aren't you going?"

"How can Hallowe'en go on for a week?" he said. "Things were never like this." He pointed at the amphitheatre.

"A week?" She shook her head, laughing softly. "More like a few weeks or a month. And then the hallowers. Don't tell me those kids don't come by your shop?"

"I've seen violence in my life. But it's almost becoming normal. Things weren't like this before."

"You're right. We're the same vintage, I'd bet," she said. "Things change."

"They're not supposed to change this way. It's not right."

"Change is natural, honey. Everyone — including me — has to be poised to take advantage, adapt along with it and profit." She sipped and snapped her fingers at the bartender for another. "How are you going to help that poor girl?" Shanti continued. "She's a sweetheart. Too good for this stuff. She's good with the customers and tough, though. I like her. But that Ball was trouble, and so is her creepy ex. Then again," she shrugged and let out a long thoughtful chuckle from deep in her lungs. "Lots of creeps around here. You're right, it's almost becoming normal."

So Zora had a stalker. A new layer of anger settled in on top of everything else. A stalker looking for weapons. Or something.

"I have no idea how I'm going to help her." Midas finished his drink.

"Do you need anything? Weapons, drugs, a contact? You came to the right place, honey. If you're this smart, maybe you can actually make a difference. Save her skin."

As though offering drugs and weapons was normal. He'd been seeing this for years, growing in normalcy, and still he wasn't used to it.

Two more drinks were set upon the bar.

"Thanks. I better head back."

"Honey, go to the cruise. If you make no headway til then, go there. It's a tinderbox waiting to explode. Don't ask me what, but I can't imagine it being unhelpful to your mission."

"What's my mission?"

She smiled and said, "I've met lots of people. I'd say you sit between two very different worlds right now. Maybe you need a real Hallowe'en party, honey."

He smiled and met her eyes. They clinked glasses.

"Are you on Rinth with her?" she asked.

He nodded and sipped his drink, she sipped hers.

"I like you," she said. "And I see you like her, so feel free to swing by in a few days again. I'll get you another one of those drinks, honey."

She caressed his cheek and kissed it farewell. She walked into the milling crowd, her long back straight, bare spine between muscle with a V-shaped split.

"If you get anything helpful, you can come by my café too," he called.

She paused and turned around.

"Freehouse on Dundas."

She raised an elegant eyebrow. "Oh, really?"

"Yeah, that's me."

Midas wrapped the mermaid statuette tighter within the cloth and walked out, sorry this was ending because now he was back inside of himself with the encroaching visions of those terrible Hallowers and the mocking laugh they barked with round, taut mouths. He passed the guard and said as he walked away, "None of this is right."

ELEVEN

The bells tinkled as Zora walked into the café, her back straight and long ponytail waving from side to side. Midas was standing by the sink behind the espresso bar, head down as he continued to polish a glass he'd been rubbing obsessively with a cloth, still numb from lack of sleep and the lingering of what happened last night.

She leaned against the espresso bar and set her booted foot upon the base of a stool.

"Midas," she said. She came for one purpose, to tell him she was a good person despite the hell she found herself in. Just five minutes, that's all she wanted, to connect with this good man, before she had to keep going deeper into the embroiled madness. Maybe a little selfish, she admitted to herself as she walked in, but she needed the nourishment of the goodness he inspired.

Looking up from the glass, Midas's heart finally lifted. It was Zora. She had a way of simply saying his name with a settled grin. But the grin wasn't there. And he quickly lost his own smile. She looked haggard, maybe as exhausted as he felt although that didn't seem possible.

"Thank fuckin' God," he said, although it came out like a weak gasp. Gathering himself, he asked, "Where were you, Zora? I thought you cut me off Rinth." He felt a pang shoot through his nerves. At least she was here.

"What are you talking about?" she said. Zora could tell he was deeply bothered by something — so far, it was just silly — and then she felt a wave of guilt. While Midas was trying to contact her, she was dealing with Peacock's message: *Go, Sweetness. Get in front of Augustine. You're avoiding the inevitable. Sober up, you can't hide from us, we know where you are … always … we know, Sweetness.*

Zora had shivered, pouring her glass half full again as she felt herself acquiescing. Peacock was right: She had to stop and get on with it. And now she saw the impact on Midas. *Oh my God. Poor guy thinks I blocked him.*

All she wanted to do was give him a thing she'd found, just contribute to his collection. If it could be cleaned up, it really was strikingly beautiful. But so much craziness had gotten in the way. So now she wanted to give him the one thing that mattered most.

"I didn't ghost you," she said. "My account was frozen." That didn't quite hit the nail on the head, she thought with chagrin, but she'd figure out how to say it soon enough.

She pulled her hand-Probe from her pocket and clicked his number to show him. It beeped and his Probe on the espresso bar beeped back.

"See? We're back on. It wasn't me," she said, and wanted to blurt out the whole story. Zora resisted despite her urge to tell him everything. Telling the truth meant everything to her. Except when you're wiretapped by the terrifying Division Q that's listening, hunting for incriminating comments. Who knows, she thought, maybe they weren't only after Augustine and whatever he was doing. They could be out for anyone else, too. Indiscriminately ready to pounce. And that might at some point include Midas. Inevitably, they'd be overinclusive.

Midas put the cup down upon the counter. Part of him didn't believe her.

"Why was your account frozen?" he asked. "By who? Was it Augustine?" Finally — a glimmer of relief came and he embraced the idea that a jealous Augustine had invaded her account.

"What? No. Not Augustine. Listen! I just came to tell you, no matter what happens, I'm not a bad person," she said in a rush. "Please remember that. Something is going to happen. Just believe in me, Midas. Please."

But how selfish is this? I shouldn't be here. I'm putting him in danger.

"What are you talking about? That sounds a bit melodramatic," he said, but felt a little better now that he knew she hadn't blocked him. And she was here. He didn't have to wallow in last night's terror. He could talk to her, recover his soul from the stony coldness that had totally taken over. He tried to feel glad, to connect with his friend and get past the persistent shock of recent days. His problems weren't hers and he had to collect himself. Now that she was here and safe, he needed to tell her.

"I'm in over my head, Midas."

Those words didn't sink in for him. "Believe me, it's not you who's in over your head," he said. "It's me. I'm getting sucked into a drug trade, for God's sake. Lazuli's gone berserk or is dead by now or who knows what, and a psycho businessman thinks he can recruit me into his network."

Zora looked completely confused. He did, indeed, sound like he was in over his head.

Midas sighed and tried to make it simpler by starting from the beginning. "Do you remember that annoying salesman who's been calling for weeks?"

"No."

"The guy with the funny red bowler hat." Midas walked to the roaster room for one of Hippias's bags. "I showed you his photo a couple of weeks ago, when he was calling non-stop. Turns out he's with Advance, a big company that wants to move drugs." He came back and put a bag on the espresso bar and beans spilled. He had to get this out. To share with her. That relief would be better than the anger and the fear. "These are from him. There are drugs inside. I only agreed to store them at first, but his fucking deal keeps changing and now I don't even know what this shit is anymore. I mean, first he said there were drugs hidden in the beans, and then he says the beans themselves are somehow genetically modified to act like a kind of psychedelic, and then he also says there's this special bag…"

Zora only half-heard him. Worried at what he'd been going through, this worry nevertheless remained stuck as a nascent flash, a scorching concern to be sure but for now a quick burn, for no matter what else she knew she wouldn't be able to really talk to him with this wiretap in her hair. She had to get rid of it. "Don't do this," she said. And then, in the searing confusion of her own worries she realized she'd heard him say *drugs*.

"Don't store those drugs," she asserted.

He stood straighter, feeling a glimmer of anger and renewed energy. "Then last night I went to look for you and wound up getting chased by some crazed hallowers. They must have been high on something — God knows what — because they were nuts."

Midas listened intently for her answer, as he pushed back the stubborn memory of his scraping knees on pavement and the penetrating barks of those men in tattered suits. And Ira's fantastical claim about bad magic. It was raw and all wrong but he needed to confront it, because the fear and anger could bring him back from the shock and numbness.

"Looking for me?" she said. Instead of waiting for an answer, she barrelled on, unable to help herself. "You wouldn't understand. I've been through a really tough time."

"You've been through a tough time?" After the café had emptied and Ira had disappeared, he couldn't escape his memory of the chase. "Did you hear me say I was chased last night by some crazy hallowers?"

Zora tried to concentrate on what he was saying, to stop self-obsessing, as difficult as that was in the circumstances. She was here to connect, and she reminded herself that connection requires listening and responding.

"Were they drug dealers too? See what happens?"

That didn't come out right, she thought. But she was tense, and evidently for his own reasons so was he.

"No, I ran off. But listen. Everything is wrong. I sense it. It's all around us. Something's happening. Those guys who chased me weren't just dressed up. It was like they were actually—" He heard his voice rise, frantic, and the fear surged again with a distant numbness in the background. That horrifying freeze that sucks the life from you and robs you of your confidence. But more words were the only way out, so he continued. "I get that people sometimes are mugged but you should have seen their faces." Midas put his fists into his pockets to stop the shaking. He couldn't start his next sentence for its absurdity, and he gripped the sink again. "They barked like dogs." He felt sickened.

He looked at Zora to see if she heard him, yearning for it, but she seemed still lost in her own worries.

"I have no control over it anymore. Over anything," she said.

Shut up, you stupid spy, she thought.

"What did you say?" He leaned forward over the espresso bar. In the dim light, he thought she said something else.

Oh my God, they can hear us. I've got to get rid of this damn wiretap.

Midas strained as he studied her. Her intelligent, sharp and always empathic face twisted with angst. She was in pain.

"You look scared. Did someone hurt you?" He imagined pounding Augustine to the ground. That scrawny prick's bloodied face would be stupefied with the blows, the dumb arrogance set frozen forever on the top of his neck as he looked up from the ground.

"No. Just a lot of yelling." She rubbed her aching sinuses. "It wasn't Augustine, Midas." *I fucked up. I shouldn't be here.*

"Who was yelling at you? Why?"

"Not at me. Just yelling. Just a bad shift at Night. That's all." She spoke quickly to get the lie over with and turned to the back room. She needed to cover the wiretap in a rug or with something to mute it just long enough to explain her plight. Then, when she was done this awful job, everything would return to normal. *Smother the damn thing in there, just for a moment.*

Midas hated that she worked at Night. They tortured the fighters in the amphitheatre and made them beat one another to death. Perhaps that's who chased him last night. Two of them escaped, mad from abuse, and found a place to rest briefly behind the old defunct gas pumps at the gas station where they woke as he passed by.

"They were like monsters," he said.

"What?" she asked. That was a strange way to put it, but then they weren't talking on the same page. "Wait — just keep quiet for a second."

Stuck in his thoughts of last night, Midas gripped the sink, turned the tap on and splashed a little water on his face.

Zora strained to see where in the shadows of the back room she might put the wiretap clip, what receptacle might mute the device. There were too many random things back there: a globe, old books, a mandolin — that wouldn't work, she'd never get it back out unless she kicked it open — and a tall chair made of ornately carved wood with a stupid throned head on top. A surge of frustration overwhelmed her again because this junk yard was a waste of time. Then she bumped into the beanbag chair. She took the clip from her hair and shoved it into the top, with the tip out so she could retrieve it. It would probably muffle their voices, but she couldn't be sure. It still needed to be covered.

She ran her hands through her hair, freed of the piece, and yet still the tension building in her as she scanned the room was only rising higher. This was risky. Finally she gave up and, exasperated, hurried over to Midas behind the espresso bar and grabbed his shirt. "Give me a napkin! A bunch of them."

He stepped back, still stuck and waiting for the mocking bark from that round, taut mouth of the man in the ripped-up suit.

She let go, confused and not understanding why Midas wasn't answering. Why was he just standing there? She pulled him around, tried to collect her thoughts and rid herself of the frustration taking hold because she was here to connect with him if only briefly. To remind him they were good people in this wicked, raging sea of badness.

But Midas could only stare at her mouth moving, unable to comprehend the sounds.

The door bells tinkled and they both looked over. Midas saw the blue hair of the dog and expected to see Caesar, but Madame Blue was alone. She padded heavily upon the wooden floor, shoulders more relaxed today, and those pinpoints of black eyes zeroed into his. Their distant, swirling purple wisps conveyed a yearning familiarity, and this was puzzling. She walked to the end of the espresso bar and sat on her heavy haunches.

Zora watched the dog then get up and walk, plodding at a patient pace within the espresso bar to finally stop in front of the shelf beside the sink. That's when she noticed the mermaid statuette lying there, half out of the cloth wrapping.

"How's this possible?" she said, feeling a little stunned. She'd given it to Shanti for safekeeping.

Midas was staring at the dog. "What are you doing here?" he asked, as though it would answer.

Zora turned at his words. How strange that a dog would walk in by itself. She had heard of blue hair on dogs, but nothing like this. "Do you know this animal?"

As she spoke, she sensed Midas was very distracted by the dog. He gazed at it with an unwavering focus and spoke to a space between the dog and Zora, preoccupied with the animal, like new parents are with children. They can't keep a conversation with the runts running amok.

The dog rose to put its front paws on the edge of the sink and reached for the statuette unsuccessfully, then sat back down on its haunches.

Midas met the dog's gaze. *She wants the statuette.* The dog looked more delicate than before, with her canine smile along her long jaw as she panted the heat away, and her round intense eyes that conveyed something with their soft swirling inside.

Midas, I came to tell you something. It fell out. Or escaped. Along with the rest of the Seeping.

Midas shook his head. This should be *his* thought, except it felt distant, disconnected from the words he would fashion in his own mind for himself. It was like a surprise appearance, like someone arriving upon you all of a sudden from around the corner on the street.

Madame Blue stood up again on her hind legs and pushed Midas against the shelf. The statuette fell into the sink.

"Back, dog," said Zora. "Whose dog is this, Midas?"

Zora looked at its face for signs of rabies. There were none. The shimmering blue fur was healthy, even vibrant. The dog ignored her entirely while its old eyes flicked from the sink to Midas and back.

Zora's interference might have annoyed him but not now. This other presence was too preoccupying. He looked into the dog's intense gaze, entered those purple whirlpools and had another thought far beyond Zora's distant words: *And now, a representation that can act as a key. And a lock. Let me show you. See there in the sink? The mermaid. She'll act as a key. But she's not. She just wants in — or rather, out — away from there. It's the Seeping, do you see?* Madame Blue's short arching eyebrows moved up and down. *On her side, she's very much like me, here. We guard our sides. See?* The long tail wagged with an excited spurt.

"What did you say?" he asked, looking at Zora.

She looked at him.

"What do you mean 'guard our sides'?" he asked Zora as he strove to refocus. "First, you want napkins, and now you're talking about keys and locks?"

The stress from the past several days converged as a heavy pressure grew in his head; he stumbled to a drawer and found his small bottle of rum. He closed the drawer and left it. He was probably too tired and the stress was just overwhelming. It would pass.

"Are you drunk?" Zora asked. She grabbed his chin and forced him around. Midas complied but his eyes went back to the dog. "High?" she demanded, feeling bad for the force she put upon him. "What drug did that salesman ask you to trade? Did you take any?"

Her alarm heightened. She should watch what she asked him. The wiretap, despite being partly buried, might still pose a danger to dear Midas who, oblivious to the peril, was making self-incriminating comments. As irrelevant as they should be to Division Q's investigation, still, some drugs were illegal. And Hippias's beans sounded to her as criminal as criminal could be.

"You're the one who's not making any sense," he said, pulling away from her. "I think. Or I'm just not hearing you right, somehow."

"Midas, return to me," she implored. "You haven't slept?"

Zora's question dissipated like mist into the recesses of consciousness as Madame Blue stood upon her haunches at the sink and reached a paw inside. She clawed at the fallen statuette. In the distance, Midas heard the voice again. Now it became an airy sound, like a breeze blowing through the tops of trees. A deep jolt happened, somewhere deep in his head like something that shouldn't have happened until it became sensible words, acceptable and safe: *This is it. See her? Recognize her, Midas? Take very good care of this key. And she's breaking the rules. Trying to escape. Don't let her make the Seeping a Happening. Not good. Not good at all.* The tail wagged a little.

He picked up the mermaid statuette, held it in front of the dog and asked, "You want this? Why?"

This isn't working, Zora thought, as he waved the statuette between her and the dog. He was having troubles of his own, and her heart sank as she realized he didn't have enough in him to hear hers.

"Please, Midas," Zora said and choked back a sob. "Ignore the mutt and put that thing down. I found it in the gutter nearby. That's all. Put it down and listen to me."

"No," he said, and his eyes widened. Everything was so confusing right now. His heart raced as he wondered whether he accidentally had some of that bad coffee. He pressed on, desperate to figure this out and said to her, "You just said it was important. Didn't you? Aren't you saying two different things to me? You're talking about a dream and a key and to take fucking care of it."

Because none of what was happening in this moment made any sense. He had to end the nonsense and sort this out.

"What? I didn't say any of that. Sober up." Zora felt a freezing beneath her skin again. He wasn't drunk at all.

He shook, flushed and his face red, about to burst and maybe do violence somehow but that couldn't be. That wasn't the Midas she knew. It was just the stress he was under, or so she hoped, rather than having imbibed an unknown drug, and she had little space in her own head to understand it.

"Okay fine, calm down, Midas," she said slowly, cautiously trying to settle him. "Let's back up. Tell me about this salesman you were talking about."

Her words were now making sense and seemed to return to their conversation. So Midas took a deep breath. "Hippias. He's a big guy with that company, Advance. Wears a trench coat, an oversized suit and a red bowler hat," he said, glad for the moment that she was speaking normally again. "Always smiling."

"And why would he ever want you to deal his drugs? Can't he just sell you coffee? He should know that's what you sell. You're not set up for the drug trade, Midas."

"Everyone seems to want a piece of me." He half turned to her, fists and shoulders tense. "I can't afford it. And I've done nothing wrong other than try to do business better. Now they keep hunting me down. They won't let me go." He fell back against the sink, deflated.

Madame Blue pawed at his knee and reached for the statuette. Midas gripped it tighter and pulled it out of her reach. "Easy there, missy."

The dog's tail wagged again, and he thought he saw its eyebrows wiggle up and down, little half-arches almost winking above its pitch-black orbs. *Pay her no mind, Midas.*

The words hardened inside his head, even as they tumbled like loose leaves from branches in the cold wind in there. *This is impossible*, Midas thought. *It's actually talking to me.*

The blue dog wagged its tail rapidly and its eyebrows arched again, up and down. *She's seeing things she thinks are important. What you see is worse. She sees only the first edge of what is coming. Midas: Don't let the beast in. And Caesar isn't my master. It's I who guided him here, for a purpose — to do my duty, to keep the mermaid away. Now, give me the statuette. I can show you.*

Now he was certain these weren't his thoughts. This dog was speaking to him — *in his head.* Talking about a key and a beast and this mermaid statuette that was apparently some kind of being or at least a representation of one — and a bad one — who existed somewhere else and was trying to come here. Or was it a key? How could a statuette be a key? And it fell out of something? Midas's head was spinning. This all made no sense.

Midas gasped, knowing he was unravelling. He tried to maintain some mental discipline, to tell himself things that he knew were true: *Dogs don't speak, especially not telepathically.*

But his mind kept swirling around the strange things he was hearing. There was a beast somewhere, and it was bad, and the Seeping — whatever that was — meant something bad would happen. Guarding sides, not letting others in.

"Oh shit," he croaked, exhausted.

The tail wagged. *And I sense you've been struggling with a quest of your own. This I can help you with, see? Follow me. Don't worry. Or yes, worry! Remember it's just a representation, for now. Midas: Let it stay there. Just one thing you and I need to do to make it stay there. See?*

Madame Blue tapped her nails on the floor, energized with the earnest confidence evident behind the long canine grin that came and went as she panted. *I need to show you. There's a Seeping happening and she — that underwater beast — is letting Caesar and his gang try to fulfill it. With this, we can halt their wicked project.*

Midas clamped both hands over his ears. "What," he yelled, "are you saying to me?"

Zora stepped back, putting up her hands in defence as the memory of the chiselled face slamming the table and the thin lady with the hot bad breath and giggles returned. And the cold metal clasps behind her back.

"Okay wait, Midas," she said, forcing the terrible image away and wondering what drug Hippias had stored here. Surely he'd popped one of those pills. "Calm down. Here, let me get you some water. Or a drink. Where's that bottle?" She thought she had caught a glimpse of it as he had opened and shut one of his drawers so quickly in his strange panic. On her way to work, when he was closing, she would often stop by and they'd have a couple of shots. She'd have two, he'd have one.

She inched around him and the dog to look under the espresso bar, scanning the shelves and needing some space from the dog. The animal kept staring at Midas, back tense in expectation and tail wagging as it pawed at the mermaid.

"You're a Seeing Eye dog, that's it," Midas said to Madame Blue, even though he knew Caesar could see perfectly well. He couldn't resist asking, "What is this about Seeping?"

For Midas, the distant, airy words were themselves like a dream. They hung in the middle of his head and rolled along in a breeze. He sensed, knowing it was false, Zora merging with the dog as the words went from her mouth — the only human who could be speaking — to his head, yet the blue dog's eyes put them there: the words. But they weren't words, they were thoughts, and they should have been his thoughts, but they weren't.

"Midas, you're yelling," Zora said, and stepped back again.

His bleary gaze shifted from her to the dog and to the shadows of the back room behind her. He seemed empty, shell-shocked. Talking to himself.

"Midas, stop talking to the dog. It's a dog."

His gaze remained unfocused. She wanted to grab his shoulders, maybe wrap her arms around him, but the dog sat like a rock between them and stared at him, pawing.

Midas, do you see? I knew it — she's preoccupied by her own reality. Listen to me, the words crystallizing from the breeze in his mind and the swirling purple-black eyes. *The Seeping is happening and that's a pathway for it, hanging there in the guise of a painting on the pillar. What's inside it must never be realized here. We must seal it shut. Creed — Caesar and his gang — are wrong. They think it's a different place brimming with riches.*

"My painting? You're trying to tell me my painting is a doorway? To what? Some kind of riches?" It couldn't possibly be true. Lazuli and Caesar, whoever else, couldn't be right.

"Midas, my God," said Zora. "What? I didn't say that."

She should go. He might say something worse. The freezing crept slowly along the inside length of her arms and under her scalp, and it kept her there. Her feet melded into the floor. She couldn't move.

The blue dog jumped up to Midas, eager to fetch the statuette in his hand.

No. Midas heard the words in his head clearly. *Not a door. No, no, no! Who'd fit through? That's a squeezing, not a Seeping!* Madame Blue barked with a sudden happy delight at the humour of it. *And not a simple event, but a happening. All around. Not quite a pathway, but in the guise of a pathway. Yes, she would arrive here, over the bend in the forces. And she already has, a little, if only in this lifeless form. The thing in your hand. Now, she wants all in. All, Midas, see? And I can't let her. Because if she succeeds, then you all go. The Seeping will affect everyone, and everyone will become like them, those on the other side. Unleashed.* The pitch-black orbs bore into his as the contented canine grin dissipated into a forlorn sadness. *All of you. Down and bad. Bad, bad, bad*, and her tail hung limp.

"Like how? Like we become monsters? Dealing drugs, letting people die like poor wonderful Zora here — and like me too, letting people die just for my own money?" He thought of the men who chased him with bruising down their faces, spiked hair and tattered suits, who howled and barked like mad dogs. Was that what the Seeping caused?

The blue dog reached its open jaw to the statuette in his hand. Midas pulled away as the words coalesced in his mind: *Boy, you speak in such hyperbole. Symbolism, maybe? Yes, I see.*

Monsters. Yes, call them that if you want. Now, give me the key. I need to hold it as it gets close. I can navigate the path, the way of the Seeping. Same as keeping everyone out, from either side. Only me, you see? Let me show you. Because we have a job to do.

Zora was staring at him. "Midas, I don't know what you're talking about, but you need to listen to me. Division Q came for me after the terrorists hit. They detained me. Questioned me. They're blaming my stupid ex for being involved. Maybe even being a leader in it. You know Augustine is part of a revolutionary cell," she went on, her voice rising. "Well Division Q wants them out of the way. Even if he's not responsible for the massacre, they want me to frame him." Midas didn't seem to be listening. He was staring down at the dog.

Zora was shaking, desperate that he understand. "And now Augustine wants me to film a business meeting on the Hallowe'en cruise on Saturday. To broadcast it over Rinth. The deal is for some kind of technology. It's some kind of government conspiracy. Augustine thinks when people hear about it, it'll incite them into action..." She looked at him, but Midas was still looking at the dog. "Are you even listening to me?" she screamed.

He stepped back, alarmed.

"Midas, I came here because I'm scared and you're the only one who makes sense right now. Or, you were supposed to be that person." Zora sobbed and put her face in her hands, hoping he would come back to her. She continued in a low voice, "I'm so sorry, Midas. They're serious. I'm going to have to do something, so please remember me for the person you believe me to be. I'm not a bad person..."

But he wasn't coming around, and a wave of emptiness overwhelmed her. She knew she was being cryptic, but she kept saying this for lack of choice. She'd said enough; getting involved in framing someone, recording a corrupt business deal, inciting violence, it was all wrong. She shouldn't be doing any of it and she hated it. Exasperated and spent, she turned and walked to the back room toward the beanbag chair.

This caught his attention. "Don't go back there," said Midas. He loosened his hold on the statuette and the dog took it from him. She trotted ahead of him, toward the back room, and leapt deftly onto the stage with surprising speed, then into the shadows beside Zora.

Midas half ran to follow the dog and stopped at Zora's side.

Zora grabbed his arm. "Don't say anything," she whispered. "We're too close to the beanbag chair. I should leave. Just stay away until I finish my job. Then you'll be safe."

Midas had no idea what Zora was talking about. He was fixated on Madame Blue, who was staring at the painting on the pillar. "You've gotta be kidding me," he said to the dog. "It's a goddamn painting."

Zora looked at the painting with them for a moment. It was the same curious artwork that Ira hated so much, now taken out of the main café, out of sight. Not understanding why Midas thought the dog took interest in it, her attention returned to the urgency of the round blob of a beanbag chair with the incriminating tool she'd shoved into it.

Madame Blue stood, shoulders tense and paws dug into the rugged floor, before the painting. Her still, canine face bent to the canvas with determined, piercing intensity.

The words solidified from that distant treetop breeze in his mind: *I came with Caesar because it was inevitable that he would find the painting. I came to have him use the key, and he would then remain trapped. In there with that beast. Stuck and immovable. In a muck. You see? Only able to move slowly, stuck in the painting's bad magic.* The blue dog's aged visage recovered its affable appearance with the long happy smile. *So you see, I need your help. Would you? Yes, you would. This quest will suit you well, do you see? I will arrive with him tomorrow.*

"How can you say this to me?" Midas said to Madame Blue. "Why don't you go in there? Why do I have to be involved?"

Come near it, peer in. It can work now. You see? It's in alignment with us. Look closer.

Midas leaned forward and inspected the painting. The market square calmed under a sunset with spotty, dark clouds threatening storm, the warm air hung heavy and the trading slowed. Merchants were packing up, filling carts with wares, dragging cages full of rabbits and chickens and tying sparsely-filled sacks. Produce and goods sat strewn around dismantled stalls, ready to be piled and loaded. It reminded him of the back room's litter of random, messy artifacts. Now, it was dusk.

Clenching the mermaid statuette in her jaw, Madame Blue gave him another contented long smile and wriggled her arched eyebrows in a playful tease as she clicked along the back room's floor past rolled carpets, the chests, the standing globe and a silver C saxophone to arrive at the base of the Incan throne. She placed the mermaid behind it.

"You keep saying it's not a pathway," Midas said, peering into the darkness to see where Madame Blue had dropped the mermaid. "Not a door. But that can't be right. And how can one painting have this much influence? Like why me, why it?"

Madame Blue clipped along the floorboards back to Midas and looked up at him. *No, no, no, I said it's not a door. It's one of many breaks in our fabric. Caesar is wrong. Only the guardians walk between what happens there and what happens here. For everyone else, it's a change, something that happens, and it works by Seeping. In your heads. So you can't get out of it. The change, it gets stuck in there. In an awful, foul new being. You become new. Not going anywhere. Here to stay. Bad, Midas. See?* Her tail wagged and she shook her shoulders as though to shed something abhorrent. *Bad.*

He tried to sharpen himself, despite being now convinced and terrified it was the dog who spoke, not Zora. Or maybe he'd accidentally taken some of Hippias's strange coffee. "You want me to push him into a fucking painting?" he said weakly. "No."

Zora looked at the painting, at Midas's strained face and around the jumbled chaos of wares and articles strewn across the back room. "Honey, you need to calm down. Please focus on reality. You're living some kind of nightmare right now and I need you to listen to what I have to say."

Midas, your friend has her problems, but Caesar will return and we must be ready. You see?

The words were too coherent to be mere air and a headache. "What happens to him then?" he asked Madame Blue.

"Midas." He knew it was Zora who spoke.

"You need to leave, Zora," he said to her quietly, absorbed in the painting. Zora followed his gaze.

Into its canvas, he looked up beyond the tall walls of the market square, past the town's port and into the sea. Sunset spread a dark orange hue across the waters. At its farthest reach brewed dense rain clouds. From the far horizon, an imposing ship of wood, decks, masts and huge billowing sails crashed toward them — and him.

Zora sobbed, stopped it with her hand and looked into the canvas of the strange painting she remembered vaguely from her first day meeting Midas, and then turned away, dropped lightly off the stage and walked to the door, where she turned back to him. "It's like we can't talk to each other." She blinked tears from her eyes. "Everything is wrong. Please remember that I'm not a bad person. That's all I came to say."

Midas barely noticed as Zora walked under the tinkling bells and out of his café. He stared at the painting for a long time before returning to the bar. His mind was whirling. It didn't settle until he realized the dog was gone. He felt the beginnings of a profound self-doubt: Had the dog ever in fact been there, or had he been overcome by a figment of his traumatized imagination? But Zora had seen the dog too. She just hadn't heard it. This was too much. Midas resisted panic and insisted to himself that the impossible had to have an explanation, somewhere. He returned to the front of the café, took a deep breath, and saw the small card on the shelf. Caesar's card. He sat alone at the espresso bar beside the machine and balanced the card between his fingers.

He resisted Caesar's last words, and yet the writing on the card's backside detailed the time and location of the strange meeting Creed would evidently hold: tonight, and not far from him, in a beautifully manicured garden behind the residence of a wealthy household. And the resistance folded into an urge to discover. He needed to know. Lazuli had said enough.

TWELVE

As Zora walked into the strong winds on Cherry Street through what they called Shantytown, she thought about Midas. How he'd talked to a dog and ignored her. How overwhelmed he was from stress, or did he do those drugs from the man with the red bowler hat? She wished she could have stayed, grabbed him by the shoulders and held him close. Made him listen. But he was in no shape to hear her then. He would have to remember what she said, after the dog was gone. Once he'd sobered up.

Forked lightning crackled from far across Lake Ontario, and the winds came in erratic bursts, so strong that Zora slipped on the muddy road and almost fell. She paused and waited for the thunder to follow. The rains would soon come again too. They'd been fierce while she sat in the streetcar as it glided eastbound on Queen Street. And then suddenly they stopped. This stop and start was becoming more the norm, but it still unsettled her. Like it did everyone. Tonight, no one was out.

Dense with occupiers, crammed with shacks of salvaged wood and corrugated metal siphoning power from the grid, the peninsula had a long history of violence. Zora had heard legends where, decades ago, police brought people to these abandoned roads and beat confessions from them. Or just to intimidate. Once, it had been a quasi-industrial brown land, a place for ships to dock, and there was a beach at the end. Now, with the influx of impoverished squatters, there was a community. Zora had written about their perseverance with admiration only a month ago in a sarcastic piece she now regretted, though at the time she felt she'd simply implored them to put their knives down, stop robbing one another, and band together.

Tonight the sky darkened and the narrow muddy road still gathered water from the recent rains in potholes and long cracks.

She arrived at Cisco's blue door and knocked. The wind gusted so hard her fist lost its way into the air. She leaned forward and banged again just as it opened.

"Zora." He hugged her and she embraced his wiry frame. His skin always struck her as painfully white and probably too damaged, having cracked long ago, dirt irretrievably etched into its edges. His long, once fair hair spread thinly upon his skull.

Cisco grinned with his wrinkled eyes. "Get on in. That rain's bad."

She walked into a narrow room sparsely furnished with an aged sagging couch, a chipped bench and a stool. One lamp lit the room by an exit that led to a barren kitchen. At the end of the room sat a desk cluttered with Probes piled amid tangled computer wires, headphones and a wide screen balanced on a fragile stand.

Zora ducked under a misplaced wooden beam from the ceiling and stepped over a broken piece of corrugated metal protruding from the wall. For a moment in this smart chaos she felt relief.

"Nice place, Cisco," she said.

Her attempt at humour came too naturally, and she caught herself. Because now things were different between them. Seeking an incriminating comment from Augustine was one thing. Conversing with Cisco, given his affiliation with the revolutionary cell, was another. It wasn't poor Cisco's fault, such a kind old drunk, a real revolutionary fighting the good fight for decades long before the others ever came. And he could truly fight. He had stories and a penchant for telling it like it is.

"Want a drink?" he asked. A half-empty bottle of gin sat on his desk.

"Yeah, I'm going to need one. Please." She sat on the stool to avoid the couch and brushed her hand through her hair to straighten it after the wind.

He went to the kitchen when her Probe vibrated. Zora flipped it open and as she read the words being typed, the freezing beneath her skin crept back: *Friendly reminder, Sweetness… Cisco's under investigation, too. Keep him drinking. More info…*

Zora shuddered.

She'd have to watch her words with him, and watch his words too. Yet the cell seemed by now to be the wrong target, given Augustine's bizarre tangential rant that was not so much tangential but in fact revealed what was central to him. She hoped this meant Cisco should be safely incapable of uttering an incriminating comment.

He returned with a full tumbler of scotch and a half ice cube.

"Thanks." She drank. "So this … device for recording you're going to give me … Is this going to hurt? And I need to know — in the eye or by the eye? I think he said by the eye."

Cisco sat at his desk and swivelled the old chair to face her. He put the gin on the floor between them and nodded at it.

"Naw," he said with a dismissive wave of his hand. "I got a good guy for this." He gave her a long look with his sharp, warm eyes. "Don't worry, kid. The piece we have for you is skin only. It's a good model but not expensive. Other wiretaps now — the ones for long jobs — get surgically implanted in the eye. It's what the market offers now, kid. But don't worry, I got you a minor version, goes in the lid. The left one, so you know. Eventually, it'll disappear. Your body just absorbs it in a few days." His voice was characteristically gravelly. He used to say it was from yelling when he fought gangs in the outskirts as a state agent. "Guess you shit it out in the end," he said.

"How deep? How can it be invisible if it's a camera?" she asked, and drank long.

He paused and sipped while holding his gaze at her. "Hidden in the eyebrow, under the skin. It shouldn't hurt." He filled his glass and leaned back to place it between them. "Isn't that nice? I can't imagine getting something placed inside the eyeball. God, that'd suck. Don't worry, kid. Be strong. I'm not going to hurt you."

She refilled her glass. "Let's get this over with."

He watched as she downed her drink. "We gotta head down just a few streets to a tattoo parlour."

She stood and expected him to get up, but he continued to sit and sip. Cisco looked her up and down with a worried frown.

"I never seen you so stressed, Zora. I know this is hard. But it's just gonna be a conversation. You're only gonna sit there at a party surrounded by hundreds of people and two men will make a deal. No funny business despite what Augustine might have implied. The prick."

Her mind raced, divided, seeking a solution to what she should be doing right now instead of what she was doing right now.

Through the window, thick bolts of lightning zigzagged across the sky, so big that two of them lit the entire neighbourhood, in one brief second revealing hundreds of shacks cobbled together with their uneven, crooked roofs. Rain smashed down, then suddenly stopped. Rainwater still dripped down her neck, and she squeezed her ponytail again.

The wiretap wasn't there. Zora rushed her hand back to the right side of her head, behind and around her ear where they'd stuck it.

Oh my God I forgot it in the beanbag chair at Midas's. A seizing freeze rushed through her, just beneath the surface of her skin. They said they'd come for her if they learned she'd rid herself of it. They'd be able to track it. They'd have to start at the café. She had to get back.

Stunned at her foolish mistake and needing to move, she walked down the narrow hall to the kitchen. It was barren, with few dishes and empty cupboards, some of which had no doors. One lone lightbulb dangled from a string in the middle of the room above a tall table with two bar stools. As she slowly walked back through the hallway to Cisco, thinking about the ramifications of this new reality, another blast of rain crashed against the fragile dwelling, and the ceiling — made of wooden beams with metal overtop like the rest of the shacks — shook as though rattled fiercely by a giant overhead.

It didn't faze her. She'd just learned something wonderful.

I'm free of it for now. Cisco's safe. They won't hear anything he says.

She sat down on the stool by Cisco, relieved. This would be quick, then she'd go back to the café right away to get the forgotten device.

"Cisco, I need to know something." She breathed a loud gust out of her anxious mouth and her hand inched to the bottle. "Augustine said you noticed something was wrong at the Hallowe'en Ball. So you left." She paused. "Did that happen? I'm in thicker now, Cisco. Let me in on this."

He stared at her intently, like a tiger in the forest, quiet, still, two eyes on a face through a break in the leaves.

"Shit, Zora, yeah, I saw some strange costumes." His eyes softened and lost focus as he went back to that place. "Must've been five or more by the top of the stairwell. They wore suits. What kind of costume is that, I thought. Tattered all over with holes and rips like they'd been to hell and back. And their faces were bruised, all bony and pale too. Thought it was make-up at first, walked by closer and if it was, then damn well done. Their hair was all spiked and wild and hardened. Saw a long curved knife inside one suit jacket hooked to one of their belts."

He looked up at her from his seat. She leaned down to the bottle, filled her glass again and gave the bottle to him. Winds picked up outside and rain again slammed down in a sudden rush. The pounding drops swiftly became an unrelenting torrent, and the winds hit the windows with a massive slap. The lamp in the corner flickered under the force.

"So that was enough to take off and abandon your mission, no matter how important it was?" she asked.

He nodded as he tipped the glass back into his mouth. "Pretty brutal, isn't it? Had to go, though. We're not fighters, kid. We got one mission only, and that's to get information to the higher-ups.

Anyway, the thing that's going down right now is this deal and we got to record it. You're really important now, Zora. We need to know, and they need to stay alive, so they can lead us to the teleport."

She listened. *Teleport.*

"Imagine that, Zora: a teleport machine. And we think there's a few of 'em. No one, absolutely no one, can die til that machine is found. Because it'll lead us to the others. And it's gotta stay out of the wrong hands. Augustine told you, didn't he? I mean, honestly, you got to know some context or you'll miss an important part of the conversation you're recording, right? People in the business can say all they want about eyeballs and necessity and biological instinct, but I don't believe any of that hocus pocus. You got to know what you want. Come on, surely he let you in on it." He sipped more slowly now and stared at her.

"You've got to be fucking kidding me," she said.

"Pretty wild, eh?" he said. "Game changer. The more we found out about this over the past few weeks, Augustine's been pleased as hell."

"Why wouldn't he tell me? Wait — this isn't possible."

Cisco laughed without humour to the floor as he shook his head. "Believe it or not. Well, hell, maybe they won't talk about that. Maybe we're all wrong, led down a garden path and instead they'll talk about something else. Something more mundane."

"But you're sure."

"Yeah, Zora. I mean honestly, something incredible is afoot. Take that Hallowe'en massacre and the kidnappings. If it's not a teleport, it's something else."

Zora leaned forward and rubbed her forehead as a wave of exhaustion became an emerging panic because Division Q either knew this already, and that meant something, or they didn't, and that meant they would do something once they found out.

She remembered they'd asked about a machine.

A vehicle. Oh no.

Zora knew Cisco told his truth, a stressful truth, and she pressed him.

"How can you be sure? How did you find out?"

Cisco filled his half-full glass with a disappointed smile. "I can't think of one thing Augustine brought in that we didn't pretty much already know. Other than his contact who gave us the tip weeks back."

"What do you mean?" She tried to contain her voice, pitching, then shaking.

"Aw, dear, he's a useless snob. Best thing he ever did was meet you, I swear." Cisco's warm eyes smiled at her and he leaned back. "Hey — want his job? I can do that. Probably safer than what you're doing now, hell, in that bar."

"Never, I'm not a spy." Cisco laughed his long low drawl of a laugh. As though he didn't believe her. This doubt made her nervous, and she took another drink to calm her ragged nerves. It was okay to do this, she told herself. She was free of a wiretap here. There was no harm to be done, for now.

He stood, surprisingly nimble for someone his age, and walked the short distance to his large Probe and tapped the keyboard. The screen lit up and as he moved tangled wires that had fallen from the upper shelf — itself a mess of books, old hand-Probes, dirty glasses and a box of bullets — he typed a password to get into a specific site.

"How did you meet Augustine?" she asked.

He laughed and walked past her, dipping low to pass under the crooked beam toward the door. "Goldie introduced us. I was teaching her how to do our work for a couple years already. She's been security at Power for a long time. The company with all that dirty energy, ya know, the shit magma. The greedy assholes who've crowded out all the other good ones. Goldie's access to their knowledge base is invaluable. Augustine, she said, was an outside consultant to them on whatever the hell he thinks he knows. Something legal but not quite legal." He laughed again. "If you know what I mean."

"Not all lawyers are lawyers," she said, unable to help herself.

"He's a shit lawyer like he's a shit spy," he said as he pulled on his boots, glass beside him on the floor. "I swear, I'd fire him and get you in, if you want. And it's kind of fun."

"So how bad is he, then? Like, why keep him around?" she asked.

"Aw, he's just a little dick. It's me who you got to worry about. I'm the badass." He laughed and winked at her as he finished his drink with one long gulp. "Let me show you something here before we get going."

The screen, a large stand-alone attached to his Probe, flashed fast random designs of blue and red. Simple geometric shapes that built on top of one another, layering to make a three-dimensional thing that resembled a tunnel of shape on shape. It moved, and she felt like she was walking, or gliding, deeper into it.

"Don't worry, kid. This isn't the teleport," he joked. "Watch this."

The ever-building and deepening tunnel of geometric shapes sped up into a fury as if they dove through a tornado's funnel until it suddenly opened to reveal a boardroom on the screen. Long polished table, chairs neatly surrounding it, half full of people in suits, and none of them looked healthy to Zora. Long bedraggled hair, gaunt and thin, so gaunt that shadows were cast across their faces. Behind one length of the boardroom table there spanned a wide open wall of window exposing the city of Toronto, its CN Tower and the downtown financial core with its jagged skyline, office towers that pierced up, red magma-based smoke climbing from their rooftops higher into the sky. On the far wall at the end hung a flag with an intricately woven drawing, a wall hanging of fine thread, of a mermaid holding a trident.

Augustine sat to the side, and his mouth moved. They couldn't hear anything; the whole video was like a silent movie albeit in colour. He was speaking with them, gesticulating with animation as they listened and periodically responded. When they did, they appeared angry. They'd lean over and point an accusing finger, pound the table with a fist or cut the air with a hand as though to declare that was enough.

"We followed him once, hacked into this. Wasn't easy," said Cisco. "Caught him talking on his own to these guys. They're bad. Real bad." He shook his head slowly. "That shithead came to us and said he'd found out some things about the teleport, but he didn't mention the activation key. That's big. It sounds like it opens the teleport."

Zora knew they — the cell — researched and investigated all kinds of things, some strange and some more ordinary, if there was such a thing as ordinary anymore.

"We couldn't tell for sure what the activation key looks like. The audio was shit, so I put this video here on silent for you. Whole meeting sounds like a garburator. I only heard the word *blue*. Blue activates it — whatever fuckin' thing the blue thing is. I heard enough. How mad they were. Ferocious to get that fuckin' blue thing." He leaned back in his chair and let out a quick laugh that died as soon as it came out. "And they have no fuckin' idea what it looks like, far as I could tell."

Then he sank further into his chair and sighed as he blinked his wrinkled eyes and shook a tired head. Like he'd almost given up, too spent from his life. Zora couldn't imagine lasting as long as he had in this world the way it was. And he was someone who'd lived through the worst of it. The last massive turning point into chaos and wreckage. Now they all sat here on Earth, together waiting for the end.

"That self-serving little fucker forgot to tell us that. Been off on a frolic of his own, it seems," he said.

"When was this shot?"

"A week ago. I mean, Zora, we've all been watching this stuff for months now: lots of companies — us, other rebel groups and organizations trying to be do-gooders and save the world and all that shit — and states, governments, investigators, police forces, all that. It's the talk of the town, everyone's watching everyone!"

He slapped his hand on the desk and laughed out loud. The screen shook and almost fell off its hinge.

"Anyway, at the end of the day I have no idea, Zora. The whole thing's a shit show. But we gotta find out. Get the fuckin' thing and make sure no one else gets it." Cisco nodded and reached to pat her shoulder with his strong hand. "I'm sorry, dear. Step by step. We'll get

there. Now let's make it through this next part and you'll get paid."
He put on his broad-shouldered duster coat and put a pistol in a
holster strapped against his back.

Zora knew Augustine was a self-serving manipulator. She could
always tell. That's why she had broken up with him. Her confidence
grew somewhat at the prospect that he was getting closer to being
guilty. But of course guilty of something quite different than Division
Q's allegation. Deep within, too, she harboured a daring, almost
inaccessible thought about the kids and how she could, in some
fantastical heroic sweep, turn all this around for them.

"Let's go, Cisco," she said and walked under the beam toward the
door.

He opened the door and wind slammed it to the wall. Rain poured
in a sheet, paused, and came again with another gust of wind. They
walked, pushing themselves through the hard wind, along the
muddied cobbled streets that curved and wound in a confusing web
beneath rare lights. On this walk she noticed the thorough neglect the
city had inflicted upon this neighbourhood. The people had built
most of the roads, attached electrical wire to most of their ramshackle
homes to access the power grid, creating a messy overhead chaos. At
night, the storm would slam ferociously, its menacing roar pounding
unpredictably, then quieten, only to return again, but when they'd
never know. The weather had become a torture in recent years, and
Zora could only expect this. But in Shantytown it felt worse.
Sometimes she slipped on the loose stones and Cisco would catch her.
Zora cursed, resenting his dexterity and her bad boots.

Zora wanted to ask more questions but her whole purpose, it felt,
was lost in this new darkness. It would all end, this hell, she thought.
She'd been wrong to get involved with the arrogant bastard
Augustine. *A revolution is theirs, not mine. I'm not a revolutionary.
I'm not a rebel. I'm not a writer. I'm not political. I'm an artist, and a
bad one.*

She tried to keep up with Cisco, walking just behind. His strides
steady and his flashlight strong with its beam, he knew his direction.

The potholes, mud and running rivulets from the rain slowed Zora and frustrated her. Here she was, trudging beneath a storm that could easily kill them both — this was common, people collapsing and dying in the winds and rains and, of course, the sunshine — and all because she made a mistake. A wrong turning in life. If only she cared less, spoke out less, she'd be safer. Now she was walking through Shantytown about to have a recording device implanted above her eye.

Holy fuck. Zora repeated this over and over again as they walked down muddy streets, turned corners through narrow walkways amongst the homes and finally to the end where gaped an expanse of utter blackness. No lights, no electrical wires, no houses, no streets. Just a dipping ditch downward and a wretched field full, she imagined, of abandoned wreckage, junk made of sharp metal, broken glass, more deep mud. He was taking her into a field in the middle of nowhere.

Zora said nothing and tried her best to follow.

She walked with no real choice anymore. Cisco held her hand and guided her down the short slope into the blackness and the field. It might have been the lake, for all she knew. It was cold, soaked with rain spattering upon them, and the ground crunched beneath their boots. They navigated thorns and invisible industrial junk that surprised her, likely him too, like a massive tire they had to clamber through or a long board they had to balance their way across over a patch of stinking water. Crunching, pushing through tangled brambles like nothing else had ever grown around here, they trod over dead land littered with rocks, although she couldn't see them — likely not real rocks but busted pieces of granite and stone, the tossed remnants of ruined, long-gone buildings.

At some point, Cisco shone the narrow beam of light into the dark rain to reveal dim, pale aspects of an old barn. Wide empty windows gaped along the top, and nailed boards criss-crossed along the bottom. Zora imagined a wet mountain of hay inside that might shift with the mice and rats.

Cisco's beam lit up a trap door leading into the ground beside the barn.

He banged on the door. He pulled and pushed hard and banged again, until a green light flashed at the handle. He heaved it open to an orangey-red light, the familiar colour of burning magma, and a descending stairwell.

"Get in there," he hollered over the wind and rain.

They descended slowly. At the bottom of the short stairwell, two corridors branched out, one lit by the same burning light, the other one as dark as the streets and fields above, a tube full of nothingness.

"No," she said. "You're not going to choose that one."

"Trust me, dear."

He walked into the dark tunnel, whose walls she sensed were dirt and floor, rough concrete.

"Cisco, this isn't a tattoo parlour."

She wondered why he'd said that. Must've been to make her feel better. It had worked, she had to hand it to him.

He pointed his flashlight fully into the tunnel. No one there, just a long empty tunnel. They walked a little longer, deeper into it, and he said, "Backdoor route, kid. Believe me, it's no barn either."

The blackness in the narrow corridor ceded to more dark-orange light to the right.

He said, "You asked me quite a bit about Augustine."

"I went to his place yesterday. Cisco, I don't like him. I don't like the idea of doing something for him. He lied to me."

"Why?"

"I don't know. That's why I'm asking you things."

"I meant why else don't you like him?" he said. "I know he lied to you."

"What did he lie to me about?"

Cisco laughed and stopped. They were not far from the lit room. Shadows moved from either side of the corridor's end. Her heart raced and she imagined a scalpel, chains and threats. But that shouldn't be, she told herself. Cisco was here.

"The teleport, kid. You should have known. I don't get why he wouldn't tell you that." He leaned his hand against the wall as though resting, thinking and staring at the distant light.

"Are you sure it's a teleport?" she asked, not expecting an answer.

He huffed a short laugh. "Yeah, pretty sure. Sounds like something like that. We know there definitely were teleports, but I don't know what it looks like. So far as I know, no one does. We think it was rough technology and prone to fail. We don't want it to fail. Not this time."

"What do you mean? What failed?"

Her skin prickled. She couldn't help asking.

"This gets murky," he said. He sounded hesitant and she felt the heavy scent of gin blow out of his mouth. "Experiments and pilot programs were held. Not sure for how long or with how many devices. Probably not too many because most of the records on them have been buried. Hell, it was decades ago. They disappeared: destroyed or lost or hidden — but by who? Maybe people were killed, the facts deleted and scrubbed out. Maybe something really useful is firewalled in a databank somewhere. Rumours that only parts of people got through — and that's pretty bad, depending on the part — and you'd never get it back, right?"

Zora's throat froze.

"Something else, too," he said quietly. "Heard some didn't show up on the other side. Not even a part." He stared at the light and in the shadow of the dark tunnel his scruffy jaw was grimly set. "And it messed with your senses, they say. Merely having it nearby. All it did was sit there and sometimes you'd get pretty confused." His voice had a resentful grate. "Maybe it was the interference and vibrations and stuff like that."

"That's enough, Cisco," she said, forcing the words out through her frozen throat.

"Not only that. Also did more digging on the activation key and put two and two together. It was real unstable. The closer the key got, sometimes it just started opening up. All around you. That's when they shut the clunker down. You couldn't have people and stuff getting whisked off all of a sudden, unawares, to who knows whereat, eh? Just because they were nearby, eh?"

"Cisco, this is so disturbing." *So this is what seeking the truth does*, she thought. *Makes you want to run.*

"Let's just do this."

"Yeah, but you got to know who's who in that meeting too, not just what it's about," he went on. "Two guys, I'm sure he told you. If not, Augustine's a real idiot. Zora, know this: A government guy, part of a rebellious, clandestine group in the bureaucracy that has a mission to do something drastic to clean this town up. No doubt more than that. So since that's never going to fly, maybe just make a statement to society. Well intentioned, I think. How in God's hell they can do that, well, they're fucked. This meeting should tell us a bit about what they think they can do. That alone is useful. They'll make an arrangement with a company that's got more resources."

He grinned and his white teeth glinted in the orange light from the room at the end of the tunnel.

"Here's the thing. There's not just two guys but three because it's a competition for the Minister's power. Two companies want his business. Ya get it? State's not dead quite yet, my dear." Cisco laughed softly and began to walk with her hand in his. "One represents a popular and well-heeled group called Advance. They're into entertainment shit: fancy food, parties, clubs, events, booze and drugs. Sure, they trade in sex, but stay generally clear of weapons other than their play in the private policing biz. Beyond that, relative to their competitor, not that bad, but yes bad. They cut the corners and make big enough moral sacrifices to make their money.

"Then there's Creed. Those are the bad guys Augustine met with I showed you. The ones in the wrecked-up suits and that trident symbol, all that. This group is more like a network, and not sure I'd call them a company, not really. And they're new. We don't like them."

He looked into the dark orange light and the shadows flicked. "Augustine's contact found himself working for them and was having problems. So the lad tipped us off. Don't know where the poor kid ended up. He's totally gone."

"Okay, I get it," she said. "Let's go. I'm nervous. I want this done."

Cisco didn't seem to have heard her. "Creed is evil," he continued. "I don't know where they come from or who leads them but they're the worst abomination of a business I've ever known. It's like a new evolution of something, almost a cult. They take the psychotic element of making money to a dark place. And above all: They must not ever, ever, never, get their hands on this machinery."

"Okay," she said. She could barely speak with her peaking anxiety. Too close to it, embroiled and central, it was dizzying and she just needed to act, get this done and then get the next part done. "I get it. I'll find the three guys and see what they say. Let's just get this operation over with." She held his elbow and turned to the light.

He held back, too powerful for her to pull farther. Still, Zora yanked him harder, defying the vertigo coming at her. She pushed her anxiety down.

"Trick is to know what they want to do with the teleport," he said. "Obviously, anyone would want it. But why now? Did their plans hatch before, without knowing its whereabouts, or get formed once they discovered it? And where the hell is it? We don't know yet. And above all, which company is going to get the deal."

He breathed tense gin into the dark tunnel through the orange shadow.

"Oh my God, buddy, this is getting worse and worse with every word. Can't I just have a wiretap and a bad business deal?"

"What's the fucking deal," Cisco said, grim and determined, yet carefree to speak the truth.

Zora imagined what he might have said next that would have killed him if she'd had a wiretap strapped to her head. And she was about to get another one, this time on the inside.

"Let's go." She pulled again at his elbow.

They faced each other, his kind eyes to hers. He squeezed her hand a little. She squeezed back, a little harder.

"Made your brain foggy," he said to himself, and shook his head. "Kind of wonder where some of the disappeared went. If they'll ever come back. But don't worry. We'll get it."

He held her hand and they walked through the archway at the corridor's end. She turned to the three people in a long room and saw an operating table set up at a forty-five-degree angle and a simple desk with tools laid upon it. A wide lamp beside it shone a big bright light, creating a lone cone within the stretching shadows of the room. Throughout and farther to the right, the room's expanse lengthened deep into indiscernible darkness, though closer to her by that cone of light lay several rows of low beds under the ceiling's glowing orange tubes. White sheets covered still bodies, sometimes shifting in their sleep, while two nurses walked among them, leaning in to whisper with a drop of water and a pill. Zora didn't say what she thought: *What the hell is this?* She shook and tried to slow her panicked breathing. *My eye, no, my eye, my eye, no, no.* Every muscle in her body seized in terror. *This is about to happen to me. No choice. It's too late. Too far in now.*

Cisco touched her shoulder and said, "Everything's going to be okay, kid. Those people asleep are here for something else. These two will take care of you."

She remembered when they first met and the wrinkled smile around his piercing black eyes. Like pinpoints, with such kind wisdom buried inside.

A man in a white coat walked toward her with a needle. A nurse guided Zora to lie upon the angled table. To her right hung a bag of clear liquid by a hook. All the cortisol in her coalesced in a paralyzing frenzy. The man said with a stiff smile and vacant eyes, "Hello, Madame. Be calm. So, what do you do for a living? You remind me of somebody."

THIRTEEN

It took at least forty minutes to get north of Bloor to the house where Creed would be meeting. Once a mansion with balconies, wide windows, and spires atop two towers at either end, the huge expanse was now split into two homes. Midas thought of what the poor neighbour was doing or to where they'd fled during this bothersome gathering, if only to escape the avant-garde music emanating from the backyard, to seek relief from the high tones, erratic rhythms and operatic soaring of someone costumed, no doubt, in something bombastic.

Midas walked around the side of the house, struggling to see where things were in the early evening November darkness. Through the spired black gate and toward the noise in the back, he touched the brick wall of the grand old house to keep his balance and stepped forward with care. The loud mix of chattering voices, clanking barbeque action, popping bottles, laughter and music of a boisterous yard party surged into the air as he arrived at the back.

To his side as he entered the long garden, two women talked over glasses of wine.

"Isn't he brilliant?" one said.

"Yes, so prescient. And surrounds himself with beauty in a world bereft of it. What a wonderful garden he's had set up."

She stared at her friend over her eyeglasses.

"Such intriguing ideas, by this Creed," the other said, averting her eyes. "And he even has children serving us. Where's that ugly one with the wine?" She turned to a nearby guest. "Call it over, honey."

Midas continued across a ground-level deck and noticed at the end of the garden a podium set up on the grass. People mingled in clumps, sipping wine and grabbing hors d'oeuvres, jabbering around him, their words mostly meaningless but for an odd comment, recognizable perhaps because he had to pause sometimes as he weaved through to the other side of the yard. The bright colours of the costumes they wore unsteadied him. The guests were dressed up, somewhat in line with the season but not overly costumed, instead sporting a garnish such as a cane with a black bowler, a witch's crooked hat, a silver glove and jacket — all just enough to disorient him.

This is ridiculous, he thought. At least no clowns.

"What's that?" said a voice to his left as he walked by a barbeque steaming with steaks. The man who spoke, thankfully wearing simple designer jeans, jacket and dress shoes, turned to face Midas, his deep red nose thankfully blending in with the perspiring stress on his face that he strove to compose. "In the tree there. What is that?"

The tall spindly lady to whom the man directed his question shifted behind her tall glass, blurred by its white bubbles, and cast glances around the curious aspects throughout the garden. Midas followed her darting eyes. Beyond sculpted bushes, carefully planted flowers and sprawling vegetables, the leaves of trees had fallen from their tangled arms, all of which were packed densely together and revealed a surprising variety of animals lounging in their midst: lizards basking in the heat, multi-coloured parrots and, in a tall cage nearby, a macaw. A pond to the far right contained a very still crocodile, beside which stood a man who threw small furry creatures that struggled in vain against his chainmail gloves as he tossed them in to feed the beast. It would leap and eat them swiftly, splash water upon the nearby tittering guests, then calm into total quiet. It didn't care.

"What do you think he meant with that message earlier?" said a voice to his right. As Midas turned, he stopped to steady himself again, ignoring the target of the question's tiresome contribution to the apparently subtle Hallowe'en spirit going on — a short yellow cape and a black domino mask — because in the next tree within a twisted tangle of branches sat perched another, much larger bird. He couldn't tell what species it was — not a hawk or an eagle, but something with no feathers and tall, like a penguin, but thin and bony. The skin, thick and grey, had hardened, pointed bolts protruding at odd angles, and its tall wings nestled tightly behind its back. Midas blinked from this distance at the black claws protruding from their tips.

Midas squinted to focus his sight. *Did this guy bring his zoo with him?* he thought, struggling to find some sarcastic humour for himself, his urge to learn anything further about this strange business network swiftly dissipating.

Midas turned, needing to walk away, but not before he heard the guest's response: "Does it matter? I'm here to get my dessert, if you know what I mean."

"I need to know because I came to make a connection," the companion replied — a man dressed in a suit of deep purple and a head of long black hair — "I need this. Do you understand how important this could be to us? We have businesses to run."

A youth costumed as a court jester walked to the trio next to them, a little further on from the tangled tree, thankfully, and offered a plate of wine and cheese. They grabbed two glasses each and ignored the cheese. The youth proceeded into the crowd.

"What a cute boy," said one of the women.

"Not cute," said another. "Just another hallower."

"But no," said the third. "They're ahead of their time, aren't they? How that crew — I know what you're thinking — how they were only, for so long, just a rebellious youth movement, but look how people have changed." Her voice rose, vibrant and full. "They've influenced up, haven't they?" And she laughed, and the laughter became infectious and they all laughed.

"And we're even better off now, aren't we? I mean, these ones — those ones over there — just embrace the movement. The Hallowers. The real ones now, with a capital *H*. The adults. And by this point I wonder who co-opted whom — did the kids start something and the working world adopted part of it, or did the kids make a laugh out of what we've been doing?"

"But they're not as creative as the young folk. Those kids really know how to dress up."

"Is it a movement?" asked another who stood from her chair, holding a large glass of vodka. "Is it Creed or the Hallowers, as in, the big ones?"

At this, laughter flowed among the circle of guests and they all paused to sip their drinks.

"I thought Creed owned them."

"Owned? I didn't know you could do that now."

Laughter again.

"Well, it's not exactly that and anyway, things have changed so much and only in the last year, haven't they? So quickly. And Creed, I'd say, is on course. That's why I'm here. Get in early, people."

Midas moved on, feeling a little dizzy. He needed to get out of here, away from their offensive talk.

Then the clumps of attendees shifted as they turned to the podium. Midas felt uneasy and wanted to back up against the imposing dark gate, but it was too far so he turned to the other side of the house. He would remain for a brief moment, just to hear Caesar out. Because still he felt he had to substantiate something — anything — of what Lazuli had said.

There, by the quiet side of the house in the evening shadows of an expansive tree, was a bench, a spent barbeque and another gate. No one was there. Just wide leaves from a heavy tree, thick brush and flowers, a small empty pond and, lying beneath a wooden bench, a blue dog.

Madame Blue slid around the back of it to sit upon her haunches, all in one fluid movement. No one noticed, he thought, as he glanced around his back at the crowd densifying before the podium where

Caesar stood, hands on its edges, chin up and gazing above their heads with his bug-like sunglasses.

Midas sat on the bench beside Madame Blue who sat on the ground at the base of the tree. He met her black orbs, their swirling purple galaxies, and the distant air breezed again through his head. First, a long calm wind through treetops, but then it gained speed. He thought he heard the rain of a storm.

And indeed, the purple wisps therein whirled in an especial fury. The dog's long smile turned hostile and it bared its canines, dripping saliva. A light growl, and he tensed at the sound.

Midas, he heard in his head. *You're coming to understand what we need to do.* And the tail wagged while the eyebrows arched up and down again.

That seems more friendly, Midas thought.

Caesar spoke to the crowd. "Welcome to Creed, my friends…" Midas turned back to Madame Blue, shook his head as though to signal to wait a moment to hear Caesar, but her black orbs hardened. They gripped his eyes like a vice. He couldn't move, not without inciting another growl. Her canines protruded and the long jaw was not smiling.

"Lazuli spoke of a passage that leads somewhere, maybe to another world," Midas said, as quietly as he could. "And I was just chased by zombies. So what the hell is this — this painting?"

The air rustled in another fury and the rapids in the back of his head crashed over rocks, down a cliff and coalesced into words: *Caesar is wrong, wrong. Midas, I told you. It's a Seeping. In your heads. The change, it gets stuck in there. See — you need to understand what happened. Are you ready?* Her eyebrows arched, just slightly, and her tail slapped the floor.

Midas stopped himself, reached for a glass of wine from a nearby platter, glanced at the crocodile and nodded. "Okay. You better be telling me the truth. Because I don't have time for bullshit."

Madame Blue's eyes tore deep into his and the arching eyebrows crossed. There was no growl, but the jaws bared and dripped, and the rapids raged under a quickening wind.

They see what they want to see. Yes, that painting is not mundane. But it is no wormhole. No rich world in a faraway place. If you went there — as I intend for him, seal his fate — you'd get stuck inside a painting. A place, yes, but it's not real. It's a piece of art. Bad art, yes, but Lazuli is wrong, and Caesar is wrong. They look and quest for their legend, not knowing what it really is, only casting it in a myth, fuel to their innate greed.

Madame Blue's eyes almost lit up, deep within them signs of exploding stars spinning across the vastness of space, such a delighted dog. She almost barked a bout of laughter then stopped herself.

So we move swiftly, before they find out. The push has to be a surprise, doesn't it?

"I'm not pushing anyone into an abyss," said Midas, whispering under his breath with frustration. With each word, he hit the bench with his fist. "I will not do this."

Madame Blue's teeth lengthened out of her long mouth and her eyes swirled into his, hooking them with something until the orbs calmed.

Caesar's words continued on the other side of the yard: "Follow us and our path … We will take you to a place you've never imagined … More wealth than your wildest dreams…"

Midas, you see? Listen and learn. It sounds incredible. But nothing like what you people have been doing. Her words were a wind. *Such toil, so long, such a waste.*

The blue dog bristled as her shoulders bunched and her growl grew. People looked, and Midas put up his hand to quiet her and her eyes met his, knowing what was happening in there deep within his troubled mind.

The painting and its cousins came first. They enable the Seeping and that simply brings out — accentuates — your inner self.

She wagged her tail, just an inch, and bore further into his eyes as she flexed her shoulders with surprising muscle.

"Look, when you first came to me you called yourself and that mermaid basically guardians. That you guarded your respective sides.

Now you're saying this shit comes from inside of us? Not influenced from another world? The Seeping, if that's what you mean?"

Madame Blue's shoulders tensed. She leapt up to put her paws on his knees and leaned her face toward him. Bystanders glanced at them, some smiled at how cute it might appear, and Midas felt the claws dig into his thighs through his pants.

The wind blew through treetops with a fierce gust. *I have used words that you'd recognize to understand the complex concept. Those on the other side of the canvas bear a kind of evil will, but they don't live like here — another dimension. Something dark seethes inside and it Seeps out, more because of that underwater witch, because she leapt out to this side as a representation of herself.* The claws softened and the canine smile almost returned. *And then you exacerbated the Seeping by your foibles, your taking, so it's time to make this right.*

Midas shook his head. This was not his fault. "Don't pull that on me. Look — Lazuli said he gave you to them. I didn't know what he could be talking about. How did he find you? If you're in charge as you say you are, tell me that."

The blue dog's eyes glanced, brows lightly up, casting from side to side, and her long mouth opened again to pant the heat off as she seemed to think this through. *I knew the painting was in that ship. It needed a safer home. And I knew what was bound to happen. And then you took it.*

Midas clenched and almost grabbed the dog by the scruff of its neck. "I didn't take anything. Well, I did, but … we made up. He called it garbage." He stopped talking then, stopped making excuses.

The treetops wavered in the wind with the dog's words: *Midas, stop this. What's done is done. We both have a job now. Because she wants so much more. And Caesar has fallen under her influence.*

Midas reached for Madame Blue, drawn into her, and yet felt the impulse to challenge her claim, one last time: "You think? Well, fuck that." Midas leaned back on the bench and slapped his palms to his forehead: "What you say defies the laws of physics. It's incoherent. People aren't naturally Hallowers. It's a bit rich to think they can change like that. Which means Lazuli is right. Which means Caesar is right. That there is another world. That it's a portal, a wormhole, whatever. A thing of quantum physics. So tell me: What's over there, and what is coming?"

Her soft, canine smile hardened again, dipping into a light growl. Her eyes flashed. *This is the lie. They want what they can't have. So they impose an illusion, and look what Caesar's doing to these people. It starts as a lie to himself.*

"Then where does it — or they, if there are a bunch of them, because I heard you, you said *cousins* — come from? Why? What the hell is it other than a painting?"

Nearby guests turned away from Caesar's speech and looked back at him. Midas sat on the bench, trying to appear normal as though he was not talking with a dog, and hushed his voice.

People made the paintings. Caesar and Creed are tempting you. It's all a lie, and when someone creates something so terrible, things get confusing, don't they?

Madame Blue's dark growl turned light again, as though she'd arrived at a sarcastic joke.

"What?" he almost shouted, then quietened himself as two suited men from across the yard with spiked long hair and gaunt faces turned to gaze at him. "How many are there? What are they — evil magic or something else? And if they're something else, is there something on the other side? Because if they are, then there has to be. And I can tell you this," his rattling whisper rose again, "there's no way a bunch of skinny, suited assholes seemingly burned to a crisp and contorted like they're demons can show up around us if it's just a damned haunted painting."

The breeze in his head rustled with an irate fury and coalesced into a distant sound of rocky rapids.

I implore you. Their theory will always appeal. Remember: someone — or some people — at once or through time, made these.

"Made what?" Midas yelled, angry at Madame Blue's cryptic comments that ignored what was actually happening around them.

Hallowers were becoming real. A culmination, like Lazuli had said, of something bad and innate within everyone. Yet if this painting were the root cause or pathway, as Lazuli and Caesar called it, it couldn't possibly spit out Hallowers if it were just a simple painting. But it wasn't a simple painting. It was Seeping something. And there were more of them, presumably all over the place.

And then trapped some part of themselves within.

Midas calmed himself quickly, his heart slowed and he looked into her swirling orbs one more time. "How could it — or they — influence at such a distance? While locked away like that? The bad changes in our world have been happening for a long time. Amongst everyone. Far away from that shipwreck."

Suspend your disbelief. A set of ideas, a will, to be sure. Ah! Her blue tail wagged and black orbs softened. *That's what's confusing you. You can't see yet that a will is there. The ideas inside it are Seeping out — the ideas and values, Midas — maybe you can understand that?*

"Okay," he said, voice hushed and harsh from the disbelief that he was speaking to a dog, about this, "if people made these things, then why are you here? Who made a magic blue dog? Ever thought to answer that?"

Madame Blue growled lightly yet continued her insistent message: *When the ancient ship that was lodged in the sandbars and rocks off the coast of a port town was disrupted, yes, there was an upset. Then, you took the painting away. That was another upset. And then, yet another happened. It fell off the wall, Midas. And she leapt out. And now, she must be stopped. She became a representation on this side of it, our side, just like there are representations everywhere here of other things that are there, and so too there of things that are here. What comes out, must go back in too. And he's the one who must go back in — to stop it, and more — with her, that mermaid statuette, and there they will stay. And then this nonsense of Seeping can slow down again to its proper, natural flow.*

"There's a lot left unsaid here," said Midas.

Madame Blue's words rushed with the fury of a powerful storm. *Caesar thinks he can unleash and access the terrible will contained within this thing. But he doesn't understand. Be careful what you wish for, see? And when we put him in, let it suck him in, then he'll be stuck in a muck. A still-life, frozen and forced to move at a snail's pace. Forever. Because paintings don't die of old age.*

Forever, Midas.

Her last two words echoed in his head. Midas sat back on the bench, exhausted and spent. He drank the rest of the wine, looked at Madame Blue and said, tentatively and only for now, "All right."

He had to know more. And then he could always leave. Run far from here.

The two men with their ragged hair, tattered suits and gaunt faces with a bruised streak stared at them from across the lawn. "So we seal it shut, then. What do you need from me?"

Her canine mouth spread into another grin, and she panted with her intent eyes. *Just welcome us into your café. Talk to Caesar. I'll bring him forth and in he shall go, and so back shall the beast. Push, push him in. Forever he shall go. And Midas* — the breeze through leaves slowed, then rose again — *beware the statuette key. The closer it gets, it could open. Things are unstable then.*

Midas might have kept the argument going but the two suited Hallowers approached over the grass. The cortisol in his bloodstream jacked. So he stood and walked through the gate nearby and ignored the grating voice at the microphone speaking words he couldn't attend to, feeling with frustration that Madame Blue hadn't answered enough.

Midas paused at the end of the street, on Yonge. Cruisers shot by, gliding on their magmatic fury. He pulled out his hand-Probe and messaged Zora. He couldn't help it. He had to share this with the one person he had left who made sense. That the painting Ira hated was a portal to another dimension, activated by the statuette, that it might kill you and was probably already killing us all because we're all innately bad and that's why it's happening, even though the blue dog didn't say it quite like that.

Ashamed at his rant, he sent it anyway knowing his shame for sending it was less than the shame of the truth.

In her apartment not too far away, Zora, tired and readying for sleep after a difficult time in Shantytown, read his message. She blinked from her own exhaustion and focused her eyes on his words...

And somewhere across the city, the Hallowers screeched with delight. Their victorious howls rose into the farthest reaches of the sky. Finally, they knew where it was.

FOURTEEN

The dark rain hammered the roads outside and buffeted the bay window. Ira had disappeared an hour ago — without saying goodbye — and the last customer had walked out the door into the wet, windy Thursday night. Midas turned out all but one of the lights and paused. It had been busy, and despite Ira's mild drinking, and somehow despite Midas's bumbling, they had kept it together.

He wished he hadn't messaged Zora the night before, after he left the garden party. He knew he sounded like he was losing his connection to reality. How could a painting in fact be a portal to another world or dimension, as Madame Blue claimed?

How could a statuette of a mermaid not only serve as the key to open such a fantastical portal but also represent — in fact, be a version of — herself on the other side of this portal. Apparently trying to bust her way in here. And apparently she'd been succeeding because the Hallowers grew in influence amongst them all. Before he resigned to losing his mind, he resisted: no, he'd seen them. They'd chased him. There had to be a reason why this was happening, he thought, almost gagging with the stress. He held his hand to his mouth — if it was in fact happening and he wasn't completely losing it.

He leapt up onto the stage area of the back room, intending to stand before the painting hanging on the inner left pillar. There, he would contemplate it and finally come to terms with what it really was. But up there in the darkness of the back room he felt a chill and something he imagined behind him and above, as he turned to face his café. The back room's high-domed ceiling cooled and tugged at his spine. As though something lingered up there out of sight, watching over his ragtag collection of artifacts strewn across the floor. It yanked, invisibly and without touch, at the base of his brain. Unsettled yet fighting back the fear, he stood and wondered as he regarded his café. Was it a portal, a device, a pathway, as Creed said? Or was Blue right: a seething, Seeping thing created by badness that lived somehow, like an homage to Rinth's tech, infused with the fraud and taking innate in people, its own sticking muck? Or for God's sake, why not just a goddamn painting?

A customer entered and stood at the espresso machine.

"I'm closing, sir," said Midas in an irritated tone. But then he sighed and leapt down from the stage to get to the machine. "Thanks for coming in, though. What can I get you?"

The customer wore a dark-brown suit with a blue shirt and yellow tie and a wide-brimmed hat covered his face. He was tall, slim and hunched over. "Just a coffee."

"It'll have to be to go." Midas poured coffee into a disposable cup. "Sorry." He gave it to the man and walked away toward the roaster room, expecting him to leave.

The man lingered by the door, sipped beneath his fedora and stared out the window. Midas watched him from the end of the espresso bar, annoyed.

Another customer walked in, also thin and tall, wearing a navy-blue suit. He went to one of the sofa chairs facing the bay window and sat down. He too wore a fedora.

Exhausted, Midas tried to sharpen up, to think clearly in spite of the resurging memory of the mugging: tightly wound-up lips of the beast who burst out the mad clown sound in a twisted mix of rage and exuberant joy and pushed its face against the glass in the parking lot's window, eyes wide, just before he scraped his knees and got up to run like hell.

"What do you have here?" asked the man in the navy-blue suit from his seat.

"A café." Midas forced the words out. "I gotta close up here, guys."

One sat and the other stood, still as stone, one staring out the bay window, the other past Midas into the back room, faces invisible beneath the rims of their fedoras. Midas watched. His skin itched in the November air.

Midas wished Hippias had sent some of his undercover guards by now. Hippias had promised but it hadn't even been a week. He went to the roaster room, pulled out his Probe and wrote Hippias. *Something's happening, how about another delivery. Stuff's great.* He returned to the café and stood by the pillar.

"Mind if we take a look around the place?" said the one in the brown suit by the espresso bar.

They looked at him from the other side of a mess of tables and chairs. Midas put his back against the stage as his mind froze with the one repeating thought that reminded him how right Hippias was. He was a sitting duck. "Yeah, I do."

"Make it easy on yourself, Midas."

The brown suit had a tear at the wrist and the lapel had a small hole, as from a burnt cigarette.

Midas looked at the front door. "I've got nothing," he said. "Just a bunch of junk. What do you want?"

The blue-suited man tipped his fedora and laughed with no happiness.

"The new way forward," said the brown-suited man.

Midas stepped onto the stage and stood beside the left pillar.

"I'll get it for you. Just tell me."

"Let's play a game," said the blue-suited man. The more they spoke, Midas heard their voices take on a grating tone, like a loud coarse whisper.

"You want to play a game?" said Midas. "So you don't know what you want?" From some well of energy, he found defiance. "How can that be? How can you want something and not know what it is?"

"We'll say a piece of what we want," said the blue-suited man. "And you guess what you have that matches what we want." He moved through the chairs swiftly, shoving them out of his way. The three of them formed a triangle in the café with Midas at the back room, the brown suit to his right and the blue suit to his left.

"What has a wide flat surface?" asked the blue-suited man. A lock of stiff black hair sprung from his fedora.

Midas could barely hear the words through the man's rasping voice. He felt it might be his fatigue, or just the stress, but something else was wrong. He sensed a presence in the air all around — a soft noise — and as his cortisol levels jacked once more he thought this sounded like Madame Blue. But she wasn't here. Still, this was not anxiety. He knew that feeling from a stressful life, long-lived. This, instead, was visceral yet external to him and he couldn't place it.

"What the hell," said Midas amid the muted, vague noise converging from behind and either side. He looked out the bay window for a streetcar but the street was empty. The distant buzzing was smoother than one of those machines, like water flowing over the rapids of a river.

"What gives the illusion of three dimensions but is only two?" said the brown suit. Both now stood at the edge of the stage near his feet.

"A movie," said Midas. He checked the front door again for any sign of Hippias and his delivery people. A long shot, he knew.

They snickered between themselves. One doubled over and slapped his knee.

"What reveals some place far, far away?"

Midas stood at the side of the left stone pillar, bracing his foot at its base in a defence of his back room. "A telescope." He heard his word as a croak. He knew he didn't have to do this, talk to them.

"What has such beauty it lures you in?" One of them leaned over the stage on his elbows and glared up.

He answered, "A woman." His lungs were heavy. "I think."

He heard laughter again.

Midas wrapped two fingers around the lower corner of the painting's silver frame to steady himself. It held strong and sure, and something then tugged distantly in his perception that this corner of the painting no longer protruded. It seemed to bend, following the curve of the pillar.

A heavy haze crowded his head and his thoughts felt distant from himself, lurking behind the confusing background noise. It felt like a bubble had formed around him, and it muffled their cackling voices. It stuck him under the surface of rapids within a river's coursing water and they laughed above from the shore.

He could barely stay standing under this bizarre and offensive pressure and found himself leaning toward the painting. Desperate for Madame Blue impossibly to be right, he might go in and escape and it seemed strangely possible. As though the boundary between him and here, that and there, didn't exist like it did before. He sensed a vague fluidity between here and there.

Madame Blue had spoken of instability when the mermaid statuette approached closer to the painting. The noisy haze he perceived, the statuette only a few feet away, hidden so close, was seeming to peel the portal open. A bit here, a pause. A bit more there, a pause.

He turned toward the painting, stared into it. The marketplace was bustling and storm clouds were brewing on the sea's horizon, far past the ship to the edge of the ocean where dense sheets of dark rain fell. The ship was closer than before but still distant. Meanwhile, oblivious to the incoming tempest, merchants and buyers haggled over their goods and wares: fattened fowl, salted fish, colourful fabrics and tools. Clowns and musicians performed, as did here and there a mime, illusionist or acrobat.

Midas surrendered, too weak and frozen, to its fine, rendered detail until he came upon a round pool encased within a raised platform made of blue and red brick. Beside the pool was a man tied to a pole, mouth gagged.

This was new. Then the blood left Midas. He felt like a heavy, empty husk.

It was Ira.

Midas gripped the frame of the painting. The image was clear and true. Ira's face twisted in frozen horror and the drawing, though still, was so well done it seemed to move. Ira writhed desperately to free his hands as his head tilted toward the pool. Every muscle in his body recoiled from the water, denying it with his terror.

Midas fell to his knees. Unless a cruel joke by Ira himself painting himself in, the detail was too perfect.

The blue suit rasped, "What's back there? You looking at something, out of the way in the shadows? Nice stuff, it seems. Antiques?" He tipped the wide rim of his hat up and long spikes of hair flipped out to hang from the back.

Midas looked for his Probe.

But he wasn't quick enough. The men converged in a fluid, raging rush.

"Get away," Midas tried to say but he couldn't hear himself.

Their bony hands came at him as they lunged, grunting in unison with deep, rasping throats, their faces stone frozen but for one mean, animalistic intent: to take from him. Midas turned and grabbed the silver frame again, pulling to dislodge it from the pillar. He would throw it at them, destroy it and them together. But though he yanked at the painting, it remained bent, fused into the stone. He fell upon the hard floor as their power overcame him with blows to his head and back.

Their pale faces snarled above him, accentuated by dark smudges across their bony cheeks, and one of their wide-brimmed hats rolled past as a hard fist slammed merciless and sure.

******

How long had he been unconscious? Midas heard them rummaging around the café. Precious artifacts tossed from shelves, drawers dumped of their contents and dishes crashed to the floor. Midas blinked yet saw only black. Then he sensed cloth wrapped around his head. He tried to take it off but couldn't reach it. His hands were tied behind his back.

Turning on his shoulder, he bumped into the sharp edges of a block of stone. He knew he must be lying within an uneven gap between the wall's concave edge and the rectangular base of the Incan throne. Midas rolled upright on his knees and shook his head, desperate to rid himself of the cloth. He felt they would kill him next, soon, and there could only be one way out. He had to see. So he bent to the sharp edges of the Incan throne and rubbed at the thing over his head. The blinding cloth fell to the floor. It was a bean sack.

Something crashed on the other side of the throne. He cowered beneath the height of the throne's wooden back. They were closer, kicking things in the back room, and he pushed himself, mostly in vain, beneath the throne's chair through its back legs. One of them grunted and something crunched and cracked. Dim light flickered and showed lanky shadows upon the wall before him, of fedoras pacing, peering and lurking, their long crooked fingers in search of something.

He swallowed and choked.

Sandino's typewriter was lifted into the air and thrown to the ground.

How dare they? thought Midas, and they kicked over a shelf of twentieth-century books. Their shadowed figures picked them up and shook them for something that wasn't there.

As their dress shoes clicked the floor, he knew they didn't know what they were looking for.

The pistol he'd produced the last time was now in the roaster room, and he clenched in regret and fear until he recalled that around the corner of the throne sat a trunk from Buenos Aires in which might be, if he remembered right, a dagger from an old bayonet. These artifacts were too old, but he had to fight. All he needed was to free his hands.

"Where is it?" one of the suited men growled.

From his hidden position behind the throne, he saw upon the wall before him a bent humanoid silhouette.

The other one replied from farther away, "Boss — or somebody — said it's a blue woman. That's what he wanted?"

The shadow peering over Midas turned its head sharply back and snapped, "No. A statue." The fedora swivelled back to Midas. Then the Hallower bent over and guffawed. This uproar ended abruptly. "Shut up and look for the fucking statue!"

Midas sunk lower.

This one kicked the front of the throne where Midas remained crunched in a ball. "It's too big, dammit. And it's not even a statue."

"Yes, it is," croaked the other. "See — there's a head and a face carved into the top of the back. It's like a throne. Get a pick and we'll bring it in chunks."

"No, you idiot. It's supposed to fit into the thing. That's too big."

Midas wrapped his arms around his knees and tried to shrink. There, in the dim light from a lone antique lamp in the back room, amid flickering shadows on the wall and beneath the silhouette, a slender, scaled tail was sticking out from under the throne's base. The mermaid. Midas used his toe to gently slide it under the throne.

The brown-suited one leapt up from across the stage and said, "What about this? Isn't this a statue?"

His voice sounded charred.

The blue-suited one snapped, "Not a parrot. Haven't you ever seen a mermaid? The mermaid holding our beloved trident. Ignorant."

The wooden parrot was thrown into the café proper with reckless abandon.

Midas's shaking overcame him as he knew there was nowhere to go. He felt the tail with his heel and tried to slide it back, but it lodged against something. Then the silhouette's long bony hands came down in a blurry arc. He was heaved up and yanked into the lamp's light. Bent on his knees, he blinked and blood dripped down his cheek.

The strong bony hands held Midas's head and shoved him to face the wreckage of the café beyond the stage. His eyes bulged and he shook at the tossed chairs broken into pieces, the overturned tables, the smashed wall shelves with their artifacts scattered and, within the espresso bar, a wreckage of glass shards. A sword stood erect in the middle of the bar, stabbed into its surface.

The blue-suited one, his splayed hair bouncing with excited fury, shook Midas's head again, spewing bloodied spittle out of his groaning mouth. The blue-suited man's bruised and pale face leaned close to Midas and hacked from something burnt in his lungs. The breath smelled wretched and unrecognizable, some awful mix between an old pit of sewage and rotting flesh.

"Where is it?"

"Ask him what he knows," growled the other one. "How to use the portal."

"We need the magic statue first, you idiot, to open it up."

Midas blinked against the red swelling in his eye. One of them gripped the back of his neck and shook his head again. He said with broken breath, "I don't know."

The brown-suited one kicked a hard shoe into his stomach. Midas coughed and groaned, "Ira."

He turned away from the ruins and looked to his right, across the bookshelf fallen on the floor, a broken globe and a crushed mandolin, to the pillar and the painting now seemingly fused into its curvature. "Get him out," said Midas.

"What are you talking about?" said the blue suit. He made a string of noises, part laugh and part grunt, and leered into Midas.

"There against the pillar," said Midas, and he felt a surge of weak rage. "Get Ira out of that painting."

Midas choked and spat blood to the floor. He continued to blink furiously to clear the blurred vision but to no avail. Something was wrong in his head and blinking wouldn't cure it of the oppressive weight that made everything disparate and fuzzy. It was different than a concussion. Something was happening outside of himself. He thought they ought to feel it too. "I can think," he insisted to himself in a swollen-mouthed mumble. "I know I can."

They hooted gales of laughter.

The blue-suited one held Midas's ankles and pulled him over to the painting. Midas pulled his face up from the splintered floorboards as he was dragged. "You can think, can you? So is this it? This is your beloved painting, the portal then, is it? And your stupid friend, where is he?"

"Who cares," growled the other one.

"Ah, then tell us how to get your stupid friend out because we need the statuette," he growled. "So where is it?"

"That's what the boss said."

Midas squinted at the painting for Ira. *This is all my fault*, he thought. "I thought I could do both," he said to himself through swollen lips.

"Do both?" They laughed. "What is this guy talking about?" A dress shoe hit his thigh, and again his buttocks.

Surprising himself with a kernel of anger and strength, Midas said, "Do good and make money, you fucking asshole. Get Ira out of there."

The blue-suited one bent down to Midas in one sudden movement, and Midas shirked as he imagined the mouth to shape like a taut "Oh!" and bark like a mad dog.

Brown suit, who maintained a glimmer of human poise, laughed with gleeful mockery. "Ah, I see what you mean now, don't I? Do both. Go into the other side, fetch a prize, and come out intact? Steal from the Devil and get away with it? What a good pirate you are!"

They laughed again.

"I can't," Midas sobbed. "How can you get him out?"

"We need the key." They dragged him farther along the splintered floor and set him to kneel before the painting. The blue suit shook Midas and yelled into his ear with a long scream that dug and wrenched at any integrity. "Where is it? Tell us, and we'll help your little friend."

The brown suit added, "Always dicey, mate. Maybe you got to go in and get him."

The other one snapped, "Shut up. I'm not going in."

Midas choked, desperate to get Ira out.

He felt no choice but to keep going, one last chance to get Ira out of that haunted abomination. "It's under the wooden throne there, against the wall. A statuette of a blue mermaid. Please get him out."

They doubled over with laughter and their victorious hooting filled the domed room.

Soon they held the mermaid statuette, hooting and jumping up and down with fierce glee. "It's true, it's true! Just like they said! She's beautiful! Test it. Make sure we have everything."

They approached the painting. With trepidation, they held it close to the canvas.

Midas shut his eyes, but that only created more pain inside his blurry hell. The hazy sensation thickened, and now he could barely hear as the heaviness in his head coalesced into a fuzzy noise. It was more than their grating voices, different than a strained streetcar outside; this background interference became clearer to him, still distant but rushing closer and louder, water crashing in rapids, and it drowned their meaningless words into sounds shaped only by tongue and intonation.

He curled up to kneel, bowed to the floor.

"It's opening," one of them yelled.

A bright white light flashed, and Midas squeezed his eyes shut as the ever-present noise at once surged louder, merging the hazy weight in his head with the watery crashing that grew into a raging roar while the air shook and the floorboards rattled.

Through this massive disruption, something around them growled: a large, low, lingering warning from the depths of a beast's throat. Midas pushed his cheek into the dusty floorboards, a desperate and useless act, as though he could sink into the floor and disappear.

It was coming.

"Nicolae," said a sullen voice.

Panicked, the blue suit shoved the statuette into the candelabra on the frame of the painting. A loud clap, a wave of unstoppable air reverberated over them, and just before total darkness descended, a mass of blue fur leapt over Midas.

Screams — and then the watery crashing noise muffled them. Midas pulled his face up from the splintered floorboards and sensed a dark blur of desperate scrambling. They ran past him, and one pale face lunged near his in the dark as it fell to its knees, then kept running. Yellow eyes widened in alarm lingered, almost begging to him just before it fled into the blackness.

Midas came to his feet to run, tripped and fell to his back, crashed against a steel drum and, ignoring the wound its sharp edge cut across his arm, manoeuvred to stand.

Chairs flew across the room, tables overturned, coffee urns scattered, more dishes crashed and their shards sprayed through the darkness. Midas squeezed his eyes shut again, yelling, "No, no, no, stop it."

"Take it, don't lose it," he heard one yell through the unbearable watery roar. Then came frantic scuffling, hitting and dodging, weight shifted and heaved upon other weight through shouts and grunts. Beneath the overwhelming roar of this giant, raging waterfall, Midas heard growls that became, as the roar subsided, dispersed and sharp and soon settled into the intermittent barks of a dog.

The clicks of their heels clattered on the floor all the way to the closing door. The barks slowed and gave way to panting. A light flickered on from the lamp across the café and grew stronger.

Midas rose. Most of the artifacts from the walls had fallen, glass was everywhere and the café was in ruin. The painting was gone.

By the espresso machine near the door lay Madame Blue, panting softly.

Midas came to her side and fell to his knees. He smelled the bloodied fur and followed the red line along her back to a knife protruding between the shoulders.

Madame Blue raised her head and panted in quick starts through the mermaid statuette she gripped firmly in her jaws. The breathing calmed.

Inside the haze in his head, a breeze blew through treetops, and beyond it the distant familiarity of unseen tumbling rapids: *Oh Midas, what you can do!* She panted, and her long grin along the canine jaw came back, wavered and tried to come back again.

"Wait, I don't understand."

The short furry eyebrows lifted into the arch, and they wiggled up and down. He gripped her shoulder, felt wet blood and retreated. *Friend.* And the words coalescing in his mind through the windy breeze said, *Have you got rid of your monsters? Those are for the bogeyman. Aren't they, see?* She let the statuette fall upon the floor and rested her head.

Midas leaned closer to her eyes. "What do you mean? They're real. They were just here now. You're not saying everything. Why?"

Madame Blue lifted her head. The words she said in his mind hovered, soundless yet with a calm timbre: *The Seeping is worsening. Big change afoot, bringing out the worst in your people. And now, Creed has it. They stole it. You must do something.*

Midas recoiled and fell back against the espresso bar. They took the painting. Now they had Ira too. "But I need to know at last what this painting actually is," he said, desperate to understand what was happening.

Her black eyes squinted at him. *Haven't believed me yet, Midas? You still think it's about sides? A portal that leads to another world? That's not how this works. It's a painting. Remember: A person made this.*

"This is a nightmare," he protested. "How can you do this? What are you?"

In his mind he heard the soft words echo: *Here she is.* She brushed the statuette with her jaw to him. *Like me but different. Opposite to us, a representation. You must ensure the fate of this thing follows the path I intended: to go back and stay. Banish the representation, Midas.*

"Banish? What do you mean?" he said. "And why me? Why does this have to happen to me?"

He inched closer toward the dog. She winced, and a shiver ran down her back. He imagined what might be on the other side, of whatever this was. What else it held of such allure as to attract all this intense attention.

"What do you mean that's not how this works? Of course that's how it works. There are worlds. There are people. There is good. There is evil. How else is it supposed to work? You haven't been answering my questions."

Madame Blue panted and wagged her tail, but she couldn't raise her face up enough to look at him.

"It's just a painting," he sobbed, desperate for it to be so, and for Ira's image to have been merely painted in as a cruel joke. "Please. If it were what you've been claiming all this time, they would have robbed me from day one." *And I don't want to do this.*

The tail patted the bloodied floor and the eyebrows arched over closing eyes.

They didn't know. They've been seeking the legend of a phenomenon the shape of which they didn't yet know. They've only believed that there existed in this world a portal to a land of riches. To be exploited. Whose influence could be brought here — these are the Hallowers. By the time you and Lazuli spoke, he was gone. A full-blown Hallower.

Midas rotated the blue statuette with his wrist. The perfect scales made the stone seem silky. Her angular face beheld something in deep, dark waters and she looked upward, possibly gladdened, to a dim ray of light far to the surface.

"So how did they find out?" He froze with a slow horror. He'd said nothing, other than to Zora. The blue dog lay silent with no answer. It dawned on him he had no choice anymore, certainly not to run away. He had to do something.

"How the hell am I supposed to do this?"

Madame Blue shivered. *As you approach, the key rifts it open bit by bit. It's been doing that already — always unstable the closer it gets.*

Take Caesar there. Hold the mermaid statuette tight. Then throw him to her, her real self on the other side. And the statuette must remain there. Seal it all shut. Above all, you need to hold it, reach into it, for it to get through.

"I thought you — or you and that thing over there — were the only things, or ones, who could do this. Travel through, like walk through a portal. You won't be there?"

It's in better alignment than I thought. You should be able to, with this key.

Midas choked. "What if Caesar doesn't follow? What if I can't?"

Don't fret about going in — just lure him. Leave them both there.

"What if I fall in or slip over with them? What's the way back?"

Madame Blue's breathing slowed. He sensed in his mind her words and fatigued thoughts receding. *You'll have to trick him.*

Midas tried to imagine what the place looked like. Full of riches or empty desolation. What norms she spoke of, what comforts, what they traded, what they did to one another. What Caesar and the others in Creed quested on the other side that drove them to such fury.

"What about Ira?" Was he stuck in a painting made of evil magic or was he in another world, living and able to be saved?

Appeal to Caesar's greed. Make him want to go there and see things for himself.

"What if?" he whispered, wondering. What if Madame Blue was wrong — or lying? He rubbed his forehead. Even at death, she couldn't explain this thing clearly. Midas sat cross-legged and gripped his knees tightly with his arms wrapped around to slow his shaking.

He shut his eyes, like he had when the robbers approached the painting with this very statuette, trying in vain to shut out the madness. Here he was, believing himself to be in telepathic conversation with a being who claimed to guard a gateway to some terrible and forbidden place with a kind of evil influence. Whether a place in the normal sense as Caesar and Creed believed, or another dimension as Madame Blue claimed, this absurdity couldn't be true, and yet he'd seen it. Hallowers chased and robbed him, massacred people at the Hallowe'en Ball. They stole it. So something about this madness was true. Was it absurd to believe Madame Blue so much that he'd follow her bidding and act?

That couldn't be the only question. Was it equally absurd how they — everyone, not just him but across the city, the world — came into this situation? A massacre. Caesar had arrived, taken Lazuli. Creed was real. Zora herself had become drawn back into a worsening vortex of revolutionary intrigue, spying and danger. The world's climate far past the breaking point with a mad reliance on one source of power — the dirtiest of them all, ever; voracious companies intent on unbounded growth in a finite world; power vacuums filled by criminal gangs and companies where the difference between right and wrong was lost or abandoned. All of these things happened for their reasons and each of those reasons was fuelled by lies and greed. So yes, he concluded, this was real enough. It wasn't happening in his lone head, and all he needed was this crystallization into one concept, an answer to his self-doubt. No, what was crazy was fraud. Not him or Madame Blue. The burnt suits, Creed, their shitty choices getting worse by the day together with all the rampant fraud. Now that fraud had reached a terrible zenith, and he couldn't bear to imagine what lay beyond that. Other than whatever was on the other side of that painting.

So despite the madness and confusion, incredibly, it circled back around to make sense. In this moment beside a dying blue creature, having lost his café to marauders in business suits seemingly burnt in hell, Midas decided the most rational act he could accomplish was to follow Madame Blue's direction. As incredible as it was, Midas knew the inconceivability was surrounded by outrageous reality. So he could only see this as an opportunity to fight back, do his part. Make a true, final attempt to protect that which he loved most dearly: the idea that you can make money and do good at the same time.

He'd find the painting and, as he regarded her beautiful face suspended deep in heavy sea water (elsewhere, he now accepted, on the other side), he vowed he would force the pathway shut with this tool in his hand. Stop the Seeping.

The blue dog's eyes went pitch black, set in her still face of furred skin, bone and jaw.

He looked up through the bay window to the hot navy dawn light, the stars and round moon. He moaned and the blue dog glanced at him from the sides of her vacant eyes just before she closed them for the last time.

FIFTEEN

In the Friday morning pre-dawn light, Zora hesitated as she stood before the bay window of the café. It might have been minutes that she stared into the darkness before the silhouettes of furniture took their shape. She was too early but needed to see him one more time, if only to warn him, and possibly to get that wiretap back and gone from here.

But the door slid open as she approached. It wasn't locked.

Zora entered tentatively. Only the dark-navy light of dawn let her see the shapes in the café. Her boots stepped upon shards of glass and porcelain on the floor, and she bumped into a table, a chair, its upside-down legs that reached into the air. She almost slipped upon what felt like a sheet of tiny round balls, like beans, and grabbed the espresso bar. Zora stood and listened, watching the shapes take form.

"Midas?"

Then everything appeared to her in the dim shadow to be wrong.

She visualized him while the robbers kicked tables, threw chairs, smashed dishware, slashed coffee bags, and she choked. The back room, shrouded in deeper shadow, looked like a black hole beyond the columns and archway that framed it. Fallen from the stage into the café proper lay the globe of the earth hung off axis in its frame, pockmarked by the holes of a boot, crushed instruments with splayed strings; throughout the café, overturned tables and splintered dishes showed a determined level of violence. Ripped paintings, wall hangings and cracked photographs dangled along the wall. A ragged length of leather lay at her feet beside the strewn balls of the beanbag chair, and a long knife stood stabbed into the counter.

"Midas!" she called. Then to herself, "Who did this?"

That pit with its high-domed ceiling gaped back at her, invisible, and the whole place was empty. He must have fled. Or they took him.

Zora leaned over the espresso bar and squinted into its narrow corridor. Midas's Probe lay on the floor by the sink amid shards of smashed cups and saucers, screen cracked and turned backwards on itself like a snapped branch.

Every organ inside of her quaked. *Unless he did this. He was angry last time. He was losing his grip on reality. In trauma from the mugging. Or was he also high on those fucking drugs from Hippias. A man who's worse than Midas knows. The man with the other company Cisco called Advance.*

She peered through the shadows at the mangled shelves along the far wall and back to the stool beside her where a line of drying blood trailed along the floor into a morass of overturned tables and chairs.

In the stillness she resisted the recurring memory of the cold clamps on her wrists, the spindly beaked lady and her taunting giggles. In the same second the other obvious question — whose blood was this — rushed through her and she bent as she followed the blood line. It ended a short distance away where a tuft of blue fur remained caught in the splinters of a broken sculpture of a multi-coloured parrot.

She knelt to pick up the eyes, painted red on intricately carved wood. Zora stared at the parrot, its red, yellow and black paint, and held the beady eyes in her hand. *Red, yellow and black.* And for a moment she drifted back to that place and the cruel giggling in her right ear...

The week's violence crashed in and now the violence had come to poor Midas. *What about the fucking blood?* she remembered screaming at the long line of her own thick, bloodied drool while her right eye ached, unable to open.

Augustine's mockery returned: *Do you write with a typewriter, Zora? Did you get it from your silly friend?* He'd laughed at her when he described the wiretap device to be implanted in or by her eye. And what Cisco said: *It's what the market offers now, kid.* No one would use an old, antiquated version for a job as important as this, with the stakes so high. No one would use a hair clip. Certainly not Division Q.

The freezing crept back along the insides of her skin. Peacock had messaged her at Cisco's while the wiretap clip was still in that beanbag chair. So they'd known she was there somehow. Peacock had read Midas's message, then. She'd also seen Zora staring out the window when it was supposed to be a clip behind her ear. To record, not see. *Stop staring out the window, Sweetness...* At the time, the strange woman sounded like she only knew Zora had been procrastinating, languishing in distress.

Her mind raced, piecing things together. The clip had been left here in the beanbag chair, but Peacock had messaged her after, while at Cisco's, knowing what she was doing. Watching her. Through her own eyes as she read her Probe, and had taken hold of her Rinth account.

"Midas?" she tried to yell into the blackness of the back room, but her voice was a croaking whisper, oppressed by the shock of what she now realized.

The wiretap in her hair was a ruse. Division Q must have implanted another one. She touched her right eye and remembered the pain she had there for days after the interrogation.

Everything crashed and tumbled down. They had heard everything, including all of Midas's rambling, drug dealing, affiliation with a bad company, and if there was anything buried in his words that held even a sliver of meaning to them, then Division Q might come.

And maybe they already had. Because of her. Because of the wiretap in her right eye.

I need to leave. Keep him safe from me. And she ran out the door, along Dundas westbound to home wondering whether it was true.

When she arrived at her small apartment fifteen minutes later, Zora grabbed the cold vodka bottle and dumped it into a tumbler, gulped, and poured again. The willow tree outside, barren of leaves, hung like the sad witch she had met on Hallowe'en. She threw her hand-Probe onto the kitchen table and stared at it with eyes she now began to despise.

Zora rushed to her bedroom, found a scarf, wrapped it around the right side of her head to cover that eye and wrote to Midas on her Probe: *I'm in trouble. I have to do something. Stay away from Hippias. Competing with Creed for something powerful. Everyone's hunting for it. Advance is bad.*

She reconsidered, doubting it all again, even the very existence of the absurd revolutionary cell with Augustine and Cisco, and for the first time she cared nothing for her life. All was lost, and her eyes with their unbelievable wiretaps had to go. That was the only answer and way out. The drawer had a knife she found herself holding in the air by the vodka she had emptied into her glass. A big one.

One more message to poor Midas, she thought, because this one mattered the most.

She wrote with the Probe on the table facing the ceiling at a distance from her. *Sorry if I wasn't able to listen to you. It's just trauma. Does stuff to you. You're okay. I'm the one dealing with the fraud artists in business suits. Get out of town. Go with Ira.*

She sent it, and soon the Probe blinked with the offensive giggling words of Peacock: *You're taking another break? Too many breaks. We know what Midas means to you. He's safe for now. Nice and safe. Get to the cruise or we get him. Get to the cruise.*

Any lingering doubt in the horror that she'd been wiretapped in both eyes now vanished. Surgically altered, invaded, cast adrift as bait. A piece yanked periodically by the force at the other end of a long string. Watch the meeting, Augustine said. For reasons. So did Cisco. For different reasons. Get his confession, Division Q said. She couldn't help but wonder: Who else was listening? What were they looking for?

None of this made sense to her. She descended, a deep loss tugged her down, spiralling, and wouldn't let go.

Zora threw the Probe at the window where it only cracked the glass. She lunged for the big knife and brought it near her eye. Tear them both out for once and for all and end it. No one would see anything ever again and she'd be nice and dead. She stood there with knife in hand and it felt steady, proud to do this one final act.

But they'd only kill Midas if she dug her bugged eyes out. They'd find him easily and they'd murder the children. Zora decided. No choice, no sorrow allowed, so she put the knife down. Somehow, she'd find a way.

SIXTEEN

"Meet me at Night, then."

The hologram's smooth lines flickered as Hippias's image disappeared. Hours earlier, Midas had woken in the back room and read Zora's cryptic — but enlightening — message.

He couldn't resist messaging Zora back. *You don't understand. It's a portal to another world full of evil. Might even be hell. Stay away from the café. It's been trashed. All gone. I have a job to do. Wherever you are, go home.*

He felt dragged back to his disturbed dream from last night, the one about his café in shadow while a thin humanoid stood outside under dim moonlight beyond the bay window, staring in.

Midas told himself bitterly that, really, there was nothing left for him to do.

He'd spent the morning and early afternoon with the door locked, sweeping glass shards and picking up pieces of fallen paraphernalia, putting them in piles, and then abandoned that ridiculous project to wander the streets until he decided at last that the only thing to do was confront Hippias, for at this moment he was the only way Midas might locate Caesar and, potentially, the painting. Midas walked out to the street wearing his leather jacket despite the beating afternoon sun, only because the mermaid statuette fit in the long inner pocket. As he strode eastward on Dundas Street to the edge of the downtown core, his steps became stronger and his mind clearer. In twenty minutes he arrived at Night.

Inside, the cavernous hall seemed smaller than before. At early afternoon, the amphitheatre was thankfully quiet, and the fire pits reminded him of campfires with their low flickering flames. Midas navigated through the thin crowd along the bar to Zora's area and at its end, beyond the line of drinkers, sat Hippias in a booth beneath the mezzanine hunched over a plate of food with a tall decanter of red wine. Two torches lit the table and above billowed red steam from baths behind the mezzanine's high ornate railing.

"Ah! Midas, so pleased!"

His mouth full, Hippias reached hastily for his wine glass. It was half empty, so he dumped the decanter in until it filled, splashing splotches across the white tablecloth and onto the meatballs on his plate. He gulped to clear the way to speak. Midas coughed lightly on the distinctive fumes.

"Don't mind those, my friend," he said, still chewing as a lump lingered within a cheek, "the tubs. And that lovely red steam. That's slider." He almost grinned. "You've heard of slider, haven't you? Quite the shocker of a drug. We at Advance once traded it but things happened, you know, and liability began to creep up so we moved on. Sometimes, customers just cost you too much, right? When they die it gets a bit heavy, don't you think? After all, who wants to have such sordid fun as to dip into that viscous liquid, get zapped by its electrodes and be brought to the brink of death so close at the precipice you'd just about fall deep into the void, and then what? What do they see? Is it so fascinating, really, to take a sneak peek at what is to come for you at the end? Is it heaven or hell, I suppose some are curious to know. What I never understood was the feeling — you know? — of getting high at that bleakness. But then, who's to say, maybe the sight itself of God or the Devil gives such a fun tickle you just can't stop."

He chuckled, shoved another meatball into his mouth and swigged a gulp of wine. "My friend," Hippias surged on, "where were we when we last spoke?" His face was ruddy and sweating, and the cheeks bulged, fattened with the squishing meat.

"The lucrative success of the drug trade," said Midas, waving a busy waiter over. "Pint," he said, and barely looked at the man in tuxedo, who gave a curt nod. "And then there was the break-in," he said, feeling stronger and determined. "They destroyed the place."

The red wine from the chalice set still into Hippias's lips dripped down his chin and Midas caught his eyes shift left to right, blurred behind the wide glass.

"Yes, my goodness, so you mentioned," Hippias said softly.

The music grew louder from the DJ's balcony several floors above.

They stared at one another until the pint came. Midas tried to sip and not drink too much. "So," he said. "You know Caesar."

Hippias faced his meatballs, rammed a fork into the largest of them and squeezed it into his mouth. He paused, munching fiercely, then lunged for his chalice and finished it. The meat's juices and the red wine dribbled from his mouth, and he dabbed them with a white napkin.

"I've heard of him," said Hippias. "Somewhat of a psychopath. And now you've been robbed and ransacked, my friend. I feel awful, just terrible. Do you think he did it?"

"Robbed, eh?" said Midas. "That means violence plus theft. I just said they trashed it."

"But you told me they took something." Hippias filled his chalice with more wine.

This might be true. He'd been distracted, shaken and a little hazy still when Hippias called.

"All right, so do you know where he is? I need to find him."

From the other side of the wide chalice, Hippias's eyes magnified as he drank long from the cup. "If that horrible man is in town, then we're in trouble," he said.

Midas waved the waiter back for a bourbon. "Do you know where he is or not?" He heard his frustrated sigh almost become a growl, a bolder than usual reaction that had repeated itself lately and he stopped it.

More drinks came. The waiter extended a silver platter with a gin and tonic and a tall scotch. Midas shrugged and accepted.

"Oh, my," said Hippias. "I forgot to say lemon." He took a deep sip. "But I needed this."

"Focus," said Midas.

Hippias put the gin down. "Yes, my friend, it's completely fine. I forgive your impatience."

"Don't forgive me," said Midas, and he finished his scotch. "Where is Caesar?"

Hippias swirled the gin and continued, rushed, and said, "Dear friend, we want to do business with you. You know as well as we that coffee is a precious, rare resource. And coupled with water in such short supply, what a waste! Or is it? It's like caviar, or even oil. And we drink it, don't we?" His eyes gleamed in their wide, expectant way and sweat beads trickled. "And some stay away from the slider up there, isn't that so?" He waved his hand above to the wisps of red mist. "Because these drinks in our hands are safer and precious too. So we turn to these, and to pills, powders and fumes, to intoxicate and entertain."

"Yeah, that's your business, right?" said Midas. He recognized Hippias's tone, his disingenuous attempt at deflection. "You guys are disgusting. Make me sick."

"No, Midas, we won't. We aren't. We can turn it all around. Think of the good you do. A wondrous function to the community, as you know!"

Midas gestured to the waiter. "Two more, on him."

Hippias clasped his hands upon the table and smiled. "Your café brings people together for healthy debate and exchange of ideas, my friend. Which brings us to why we meet. Midas, Advance has agreed, after long and strenuous negotiations this afternoon — on my part — exclusively — to finance the rebuilding of your troubled café. Yes, that is how much I believe in you."

Hippias refilled his chalice with more wine and said with a sudden gravity, "But here's the unfortunate rub. My friend, they don't loan out money at risk for free. As you appreciate, this is just how it works. They want collateral. And thinking of a few of your more valuable items in there…" Hippias rolled his eyes with an exasperated sigh, a shrug and a little grin.

"What happened to interest," said Midas.

"I know what you're thinking." Hippias poised a finger in the air. "I felt, my goodness, how could they do this? Then I realized it can be seen as just this: your loan to them. I mean, they take collateral but you know more than they. That there's no risk. Right? Hey? And sure, there's the interest on all of this. But at least you capture loads of value back. And you're the one with the chattels. Right?"

He chuckled and leaned back, eyes intent on Midas. A new trickle of sweat held on the chin and then ran down his neck. "It's called leverage." He winked. "Really, it's just about point of view."

The haze from the previous night began to creep back into Midas again so he sought his drink. As the curve of the glass touched his lips and they spread across its edge, dipping into the warm liquid, he remembered the days of deal making when the money, laughter and vigour flowed. He bent in to his glass again, just enough for a quick taste.

"What does Advance really want? Why me and why store drugs?"

"We want the same thing, my friend, believe me," said Hippias. He wiped his mouth, reddening the napkin with tomato sauce. "Midas, what did they take? You seemed especially distraught this afternoon. I know you had valuable chattels throughout, all the product of such hard work, your years of creative search. So admirable." Hippias raised his glass to the air between them, beckoning Midas to reciprocate. "To rebuilding. Yes?"

Midas drank his glass empty and placed it down hard, refusing to answer his question for nothing in exchange. "And where is Caesar?"

"Not sure. We keep an eye out but he flits around, ever evasive, and yet ubiquitous." The cup went down and he leaned forward in earnest. "I'm curious, Midas. In what way would he be interested in you? If you'd reflect a while longer on this, I might be able to help. Knowing a man's interests leads you to understand his deeper motivations. Remember: positions are what we say, interests are what we want — ha! I was about to say *need*, but that's not so; we have everything now anyway — and motivations are, well, motivations. The darker side, the hunger. That's how you sell, yes? We both know this. So how can we meet his needs, truly?"

Hippias swirled the little wine left and blinked, satisfied.

Midas called for another round but the waiter was gone. He made a little growl and breathed to calm down.

"I'll take care of this," Hippias said with a calming palm in the air. "I know the manager."

"Listen," said Midas, irritated at Hippias's distracting comments. "I hear your company is up to no good. And by the way, I'd bet it's got something to do with Creed. If it does, then you're either working with them or against them. And you've got to know where they are."

"Oh my dear, no!" said Hippias, eyes widening with alarm.

Midas's anger boiled up within him and despite his drawing on a well-exercised discipline, his frustration became almost overwhelming. A growl came back to the base of his throat and his fist clenched. He pointed his finger at Hippias across the table. "Why would I continue this deal with you? You want me on board? Sure, fine, and I need you on board too."

"Midas, when you called earlier and told me about their deplorable behaviour, I felt so sad. But you're getting paranoid. Creed is evil, as I told you. Pure evil. We have never seen anything like this. It's not just a business but a cult, or even, if you will, a phenomenon. Midas, please tell me, what did they take?"

"They wrecked everything." Midas searched Hippias's gleaming face.

"Come now, Midas. We have power at Advance and are positioned to put Creed in its place. Join us. We can only help you if we know what they want."

A moment of quiet came.

"Tell me where Caesar is."

"Please, truly, Midas, I have no idea." Frustration appeared in his voice for the first time. "Let's work this through together now, shall we?" Hippias reflected. "They invaded your café, chased you and destroyed it. They wear suits, my good man. They weren't mere street ruffians. So this was no random act. What they wanted must have significance. Did you find any peculiar item whilst on your travels over the years they might be interested in? Such a thing that might seem to be, you know, the elephant in the room?" Hippias reached for his fork and jabbed it into the remaining meatball.

So, they were not in cahoots, Caesar and Hippias. He truly didn't know what they stole. Nonetheless, the salesman had to know something. And he wanted to know what they stole. "Tell me why you kept changing the deal," he said. "Why you're now trying to sell them as doped-up coffee beans? And what about the one special bag? — And I'll think about your question."

Face as red as his wine, Hippias blurred his face behind the wide chalice before putting it down, and he exclaimed, "Ah, well, secret's out!" His hands flung into the air in surrender and he rolled his eyes. "Here is the new proposition, dear friend. Are you ready? We're moving some poison. Just a bit — I reference the very one you just did. You'll recall it was labelled *Tea Party*? And very targeted. I'm telling you the truth. Only a select number of people are to be eliminated. One of them should be Caesar, by the way, but my client, the little rogue group, didn't expect him to show up so swiftly."

He paused with his presumptuous finger poised in the air once again. "Midas. I implore you. Now, you get a premium for the risk. It's just a little poison. Appreciate, please, that they're bad and deserve it. And rest assured, we aren't absolutely obligated to host it at your fine café."

Midas opened his mouth to protest. There was no way he'd let such a nightmare happen in Freehouse.

"Mind you," Hippias said. "It'd be convenient. And besides, the effect takes a while because it operates by infection and gradually builds into a multi-system failure. No one will know the cause. They'll be long home when they die of, well, who knows what, hey? Why, even Shanti here, the owner of this nasty establishment, isn't as foolish as to preside over an immediate, incriminating death. She'd do the same thing if she were in the same situation. And we shall pay you. In fact, we are paying you, aren't we?"

Midas couldn't believe what he was hearing. First, this salesman wants to sell him coffee, then he wants to hide packets of some kind of drug in the bags to move through the underground market, then he changes the deal so *all* the beans are drugged up in some mild way — Advance couldn't help itself but make addicts out of its customers — and now there's a special bag of killer beans and a plot. From the otherworldly horror of Creed to the insidious corruption of Advance, bad business just doesn't stop, he thought, exasperated. Maybe he wasn't losing his grip on reality after all. His hand went to his drink but he stopped, determined to refocus on what he needed. "If you've been watching Caesar, as you've already admitted, then I'd like you to tell me where he is."

Hippias's eyes pinned on Midas through the flickering flames of the torches.

"Aha, a quid pro quo, then? My, you're as good as they said." He admired the chalice's empty chamber. They both looked around the hall, aware of the growing clamour.

"They're the same. The goblet and this hall."

"Sure," said Midas. Both empty, hungry to be full. "Answer my question, please."

"Well, who goes first?"

"I'm not accepting your poison. Keep your money," said Midas. This bluff was dangerous. Hippias might walk away and then he wouldn't find Caesar.

Hippias waved a hand in the air above his head while Midas winced with irritation until he felt firm, dark fingers on his shoulder, manicured in bright blue.

"Hi honey, I missed you." Shanti breathed into his neck.

"Good evening, Madame," said Hippias. His eyes darted to his decanter, nearing empty.

She snapped her fingers and a waiter came, took the decanter away and she said, "What did you think, you'd only get one bottle? And thank you for the security. The camera over here was well positioned." Shanti leaned over Midas's shoulders from behind with her arm wrapped around his chest. "It helps manage the slider business up there."

Hippias smiled. "You're such a wonderful hostess, Madame. I trust if you saw anything else, you would tell us."

She said across the table, yet still into Midas's ear, "So did you display that mermaid nicely, maybe on a shelf? I think she got it for you because it reminds her of herself. Don't you think, honey?"

"Nice to see you again, Shanti," he said. "But this guy and I have something to settle." He leaned across the table. "Where's Caesar, Hippias?"

"Isn't she irresistible, dear friend?" Hippias laughed and wiped his brow with a clean napkin. "Now, you two seem to know each other. Madame, in case you're in the market, I can assure you this one is a good man. A real keeper."

He gave Midas a wink.

"We have a friend in common," Shanti said. "Zora, one of my best. Honey, she's missed two shifts. Seen her?"

Midas felt the blood rise to his head, and Hippias's face fell.

"Oh, my goodness," he said, and leaned to Midas. "Whatever happened? You're friends? Do you need help finding her? What does she look like?"

Midas wanted his drink refilled more than ever.

"This was her station, I believe? Shall we see the video from her last shift, so I can source this?" said Hippias. "I'll send it to my people. I told you we have security divisions and, well, one in particular notorious for absolutely excellent work. We'll put a call out for her. Done. On the streets and such, wherever we have a gig in town. Anything I can do to help."

Hippias clapped his hands with glee.

As irritating as Hippias was with his incessant distractions and obstinate refusal to answer the one question Midas needed answered, he couldn't help but feel pleased with this development. Finding Zora was in fact more important.

"Shanti, please, would you?" said Hippias.

She snapped her fingers and a waiter produced a small Probe screen. A moment later they stared at Zora. The camera angle showed the length of the smooth black stone bar, the gnarled creatures protruding from its sharp edges and a tentative exchange between her and Augustine over a long blue object mostly wrapped in heavy cloth.

Hippias hummed and from the back of his throat came a squeaking sound. "Ah, there we are."

Midas touched the statuette in his pocket and looked into Hippias's smiling eyes. He could see how even if the salesman made you feel frustrated, he was otherwise positive and welcoming. "What? You recognize her?" Midas asked.

"No, I'm saying we now know whom to look for." He relaxed. "Goodness, you're jittery, aren't you? Only trying to help out, my friend. After all, despite some of our ripples with bean varieties, we're business partners now, aren't we?'

"Fair enough," said Midas. It wasn't fair but he might as well pretend.

"In any event, back to business. What did they rob you of, dear friend?"

Midas contained his irritated shaking as Shanti wrapped her arms around his chest.

"Midas. He can find her," she said.

"Then find her," he said to Hippias, and glared.

Hippias shook his head with sorrow and chuckled. "Oh no, dear friend. That's not how this works. This is business. That means a quid pro quo. Yes, I can find her. And Shanti here can help. But I need to know what they stole."

Midas felt like choking. Hippias was wearing him down. "Why? What's happening to Zora has nothing to do with me and my problems."

"Motivations, Midas, remember? A mere clue. Every little bit helps. What's the worry?"

Hippias looked down at his plate, saddened and resigned.

Shanti sighed, "Oh no, honey."

Finally, Midas said, "A painting. A very, very valuable painting. Big deal. So where's Caesar?"

"Midas, my friend. Here I'm finding your girl for free, and…"

"You're leveraging my entire business and its chattels when all I own is a broken junkyard."

Hippias clutched his chalice. "Tell me about the painting."

"It's big."

Hippias turned up to the balcony above and laughed at the red mist wafting out into the air. "That's not what I meant. Of what is the painting? What does it depict?"

"A seaside town with a ship at the horizon. A funny marketplace with clowns and acrobats, merchants. Sometimes. That's it, though. It's weird."

Hippias nodded. "We'll get it back. Won't we? We'll get all the money back. You from Advance, and Advance from Creed. And yes, knowing it was such a valuable painting assists. Oh, Shanti," he said in a rush and snapped his face up to her. "What say you?"

She sighed and stood straighter. "How in hell would I know where a man who steals a painting would be?" She leaned her head back and laughed.

Hippias winked. "Want to take a guess?"

Midas held back another low growl and gripped his glass. "This is useless," he said. "In fact, you're useless."

"How about an art exhibit?" Hippias suggested, playful and oblivious to Midas's frustration.

Midas slammed his glass upon the table. "Forget it. Just find Zora." He stood, extracting himself from Shanti's embrace. "I'll burn the café. It's already ruined. If you want something, you can make something out of the ashes."

He began to walk away, past Shanti, who reached for his arm.

"Wait," she said. "Just go to the cruise. If this guy you're looking for is in business, he'll be there. More likely there than here, or anywhere else."

"Yes, brilliant," Hippias exclaimed and snapped his fingers. "I knew it."

At this, Midas almost slugged the incorrigible ass with his fist, now an infuriated clench at his side.

"And if not, then, well," she said, blinking slowly, "bring your buddy back here and we'll give him a truth serum. I can help with that." And she cast a sarcastic smile at Hippias, who briefly paled.

Hippias twirled the last of the wine in his chalice and gazed into it, admiring the viscosity upon the glass. "Aren't you afraid of missing him? Midas, perhaps you should reconsider. You and I really need to attend." He leaned over his plate, gravely concerned.

The energy left Midas. "Why did I even come here?" he said and faced the faraway beads covering the exit across the hall.

"For good reason," Hippias said. "We had to problem solve together, didn't we? And, well, sometimes we have to take a risk, so thank you, dear friend. If it's the cruise — thank you, Shanti, so very much for your wise suggestion — well then, I think I know how to find him on that ship. And believe you me, won't it be a crowded mess! So now, we prepare."

Midas stared into him, suspicious and wanting to believe that Hippias knew the whereabouts of Caesar.

"You shall swiftly repair your café and, imagine, you'll have even more to store and move than one measly bag of red Tea Party beans." Hippias smiled broadly. "All for a good cause." He grabbed the bottle of red wine, filled his chalice to the brim and held it in the air between them. "To Caesar. The fool."

Midas picked up his glass for this bitter toast.

"And I shall take you there," said Hippias with an exultant grin. "A suite on board that ship, wherein specific deals get done, or so I hear, and through the guards we shall go. You and me, partner."

"Right," said Midas. "Don't forget to find Zora too."

SEVENTEEN

The horns boomed across the churning lake, the plank rolled back, the gate slammed shut and the ship set sail. Midas felt the statuette in his pocket and complained about the heat, but Hippias reminded him it was another Hallowe'en event so an incongruous warm coat fit right in.

"So where is Caesar?" Midas asked. His recurring doubt settled in again when a heavy gust of wind buffeted the ship. Hippias lost his footing, exclaimed and flailed. One leg slipped over the ship's edge and dangled above the waters. Midas gripped a rope, pushed his foot against a rail and heaved.

"Oh, my." Panicked, Hippias pulled at Midas with his weight. "Oh, please." Midas held on and pulled back, pressing his foot into the rail, and slipped himself. He held on, balancing himself with both feet against the rail as the statuette poked out of his pocket. Despite the harrowing moment, he gripped tighter with the one hand to steady Hippias while pushing the statuette back in deeper with his other hand, then gripped Hippias with both hands again.

Hippias stood, face flushed, and moved ahead along the narrow walkway.

"See up there to the quarterdeck, up another staircase and you'll reach some private suites. Maybe there?" said Hippias.

"I thought you knew where he was."

"I know he's on this cruise, my friend. He's undoubtedly moving around like the rest of us, don't you agree? Roving like crazy. He may settle eventually, but why wouldn't he enjoy the party?"

Then with an unexpected sweep of his arm, Hippias grabbed Midas by the elbow and yanked him around a corner. "Not to worry." He shoved Midas against the wall with surprising strength and peered around. "That gentleman will lead you to Caesar."

A wiry older man with a tall cowboy hat over a worn face walked down the stairwell from the quarterdeck. He stood at the railing and surveyed the partygoers, resisting the powerful winds with steady feet.

Then the winds calmed.

"You follow him," Hippias whispered. "He'll recognize me. I'll hold back and see if Caesar is in one of the rooms. And there's a gambling hall and another lounge below off the main deck. Don't do anything stupid, my friend. Before you make a move, wait for me. We can meet up in half an hour. All right?"

"Where, here?"

"No, too crowded, and we might be getting attention by then." Hippias stroked his chin as he thought. "Oh, why not. The very tip of the bow. It's the only place where we know we'll actually find one another amid this pandemonium."

The cowboy's duster coat billowed and revealed a pistol strapped to his side. He crossed the deck to a descending stairwell.

"How do you know him?"

Hippias hushed him with his finger and shook his sweating head. "You heard about the terrible abductions of poor innocent children, didn't you, Midas? We've been watching him. We think he has them. He's a member of an underground network that might even pass as a gang. He's a bit of a legendary criminal and goes by the name of Cisco."

Cisco, thought Midas, *Zora's friend.*

"Listen," continued Hippias in a rush. "Meet me there in a half hour. Right at the bow. I hope you're not afraid of heights — just hold on tightly. We'll reconvene and assess what's next, my friend."

"Fine," said Midas.

"Here, wear this," said Hippias as he picked up a fedora that one of the partygoers had dropped. He placed it upon Midas's head. "It'll keep you disguised." Hippias found a moment to chuckle and pulled out a black eyepatch from his coat pocket. Winking playfully, he said, "Oh, had to bring something costume-like, you know, to fit in, right?"

Midas turned the corner into a thickening crowd. A couple dressed in blue spandex bumped into him with another bout of wind and waves, ignored him and walked on. Midas shrugged and trailed Cisco along the narrow portside promenade. He kept some distance and relied on the milling crowd, and now his hat, to remain unnoticed.

******

Zora felt her neck and brushed her hair back, damp with sweat. The humid air of another warm day didn't cool this evening, and her anxiety only made her perspiration worse. She'd tried to wear loose-fitting clothing, nice enough for the role she was here to play out but not too nice because it was still so offensive. Her typical light black leather pants, low-cut ankle boots and a white tunic. She strained to see past the dense lineup, all in costume, and behind her along the narrow walkway at the side of the ship. Too many people, she thought. They shuffled, jostled and tried to dance as they inched ahead, shoulder to shoulder, anticipating their entrée on board where a boisterous party had long since started.

Zora walked past the entry point and moved with the flowing crowd, so dense there was nowhere else to go but follow along the promenade and hope for an open area. For her, she needed to find the main deck and its primary bar to locate Augustine.

The ship sat tall and heaved upon the choppy waters of the lake with so many on board. Their dancing pounded in a wild intensity from port to starboard and their reckless numbers, crammed on deck, rocked the boat. Zora felt their shrill intoxication alone might capsize it and then the debauchery would finally end. But it stayed upright, and across the surrounding waves shimmered a pale moon in the dark November night. White sails flapped in the wind while hundreds of masked partygoers laughed and frolicked in their coloured garments, some costumes recognizable, others new. Zora stumbled as their elbows pushed and jostled.

Soon, she came upon an open area with a stairwell to the quarterdeck and a door above. Giggling groups ran up the stairs and tore through it.

"Hey," she said to a couple walking up. Hypervigilant, she noticed they wore simple costumes of blue spandex with the drawing of a trident on the chest. This was interesting. "What's up there?"

They gripped one another and laughed. "Private party suites, sweetheart. Rich guys, you know. Want to join us? We have stuff. All steady."

Zora shook her head. "No thanks. Maybe later. I'm meeting someone."

"Yeah, who? Does he have anything to throw in?" the man asked as he shifted his fedora.

Zora hesitated, lurched with the ship and held the railing. Below, the lake's waters churned as the structure plowed ahead and from this steep view the dancing crowd below on the main deck, as a mass, seemed to pulse.

"Anything?" he asked again from sunken eyes with brown bags, one of which merged with a scar descending down the cheek. "We got a good room invite. Good room. Yeah."

His feet danced in small angles on the wooden deck.

The woman rubbed his back. "Sshhh, honey. Let's keep moving. Gotta get to the king's suite." She giggled. "Get us some slider there."

Zora shuddered. "Who's the king?"

"Some loaded guy. Why, baby, you want to join us slide to the other side for a bit?" The woman held her boyfriend's elbow to steady him.

"Sounds like lots of fun." Zora barely paid attention to her own words as she continued to scan the crowd. These kinds of conversations were the norm at Night, and these two sounded too high. "Lots of those guys around here, right?"

"Hey, do you have this shit or not?" said the man.

"It's not her, baby, it's the king who's got it," said the woman as she stroked his back again.

The couple walked up the stairwell and gripped the banister as they laughed and stumbled.

Augustine had said to meet at the main bar, but there were just bars with too many people and no room to dance, let alone find someone. Winds crept up and the ship sailed across the harbour toward the islands' outer rim as white caps crashed upon themselves and the ship dipped into deeper troughs, sometimes as big as the waves of the sea, beneath the stars shining around the pale moon.

How strange, thought Zora.

On the main deck below, people stumbled more than they danced, reaching for something, often one another, and dropped glasses.

She stumbled along the walkway, bumped by a stream of costumes that surged like salmon zipping upriver, bumping continually against the frantic line going in the other direction, all in a self-made rush with drink in hand and a prop. Flowing by her went a gnarled walking stick in someone's hand, an eye patch, a naked woman clothed only in thin pink strings, a white cone atop a man in a ghostly robe and then behind him, from the writhing mass ahead of her, emerged a beige overcoat above which bobbed a gleaming face with an eye patch beneath a red bowler hat.

"Hi!" he cried, waved and whirled gracefully along the tide. With a helpless glance he rolled his eyes full of fun, and his fingers wiggled in the air above to follow.

She could tell he recognized her, but why? The crowd moved and danced around Zora, bumping, elbowing, toes into other heels, laughing recklessly and spilling drinks, while she inched toward the main deck. Farther down along the stream of people, the red bowler hat rolled easily along. The promenade was narrow and really there was only one way to go — that way, ahead, the path everyone travelled along the side of the ship toward the main deck behind the man with the red bowler hat who gesticulated enthusiastically. She kept on with hesitant steps, remembering Midas's salesman friend. Midas had emphasized the man's red hat and oversized overcoat and constant grin. This must be him.

The red hat disappeared, then bobbed to the surface again and descended a wide stairwell to the main deck where she glimpsed the main bar where Augustine had told her to meet.

Zora needed space desperately, because this was all so suffocating. Closer to the main deck and its expansive bar, she saw no signs of Augustine, and the dizzying noise of the party disoriented her.

"Move ahead," someone snarled. She tripped on someone's heel in front of her, and the person's elbow jabbed back into her to push her away, while someone else stepped onto her feet. Zora refused to jab backward herself, and as a clump of frustrated costumers surged forward at her side, charging through the crowd like a panicked herd of cattle, Zora choked and felt plunged by their force off the promenade and through a wide, open doorway.

There. Pushed out from the furious line and into a large room. Here was air to breathe. A low ceiling, cramped and dimly lit quarters, but the room was long and wide, set throughout with tables, chairs and a long bar at the far end. Music receded as the door behind her closed. People sat hunched around the tables and concentrated on the quieter words of men in tuxedos doling cards.

A large man with a red bowler hat jumped up from a nearby table out of the shadows. "Hippias, so pleased."

Zora started with surprise and recovered. He leaned over from his side of the table set against an open window and extended his strong hand. Wind burst through and he fumbled to salvage his hat.

"How do you know me?" she asked. Perspiration trickled along the back of her neck, and she worried she would appear nervous so she stood by the window. Out there, the waters made agitated white caps under the powerful winds and the lake's dark grey surface seemed to bubble and boil deep into the starlit horizon.

Hippias followed her gaze. "Bad night for a boat party, I should think. Ah, well!" He chuckled and slapped his palm upon the table. "We'll be fine. Too big to sink." He smiled broadly, placed his eyepatch on the table and flicked his hand to attract a waiter's attention. "What would you like?"

"Double cognac, please."

Hippias reiterated her order, saying, "Yes, that's right, you heard her, and I shall have a glass of red wine."

A longer gust hit them. He gripped the table as the ship swayed with the force. Zora sat down.

"I heard of you through our mutual friend, Midas," said Hippias. "I'm sure he's spoken of me. He's quite fond of you. Did you know this?" Hippias laughed and stared into her eyes. "He manages to weave you into our conversations all the time. Clearly a valued customer."

"So what? Did he show you pictures or something?" How could he know about her? *Something's up with this.*

A hint of fear crossed his face as he glanced out the window. "Well, you flashed on his Probe once while he listened to a message you left. You know Rinth after all, so thorough it identified you just as he did." Hippias nodded reassuringly. "It's nothing, my dear, we're all just pieces of data to that thing. I agree with you completely — it's totally intrusive. Best just to ignore it."

He squeezed his eyes with a pursed smile. Like the wind, his words gushed in spurts and might slow with thought.

"Nonetheless, you know salesmen," he continued. "We're detectives at all times, noticing details everywhere, hey? We're really quite excited. Midas is a fine man with a fantastic concept. In fact, he came with me. Brought a rather weak Hallowe'en costume, sadly, having arrived with a ridiculous mermaid toy in his hand, so I said to him," Hippias bubbled laughter as he spoke, "I say, 'Oh, Midas! You're supposed to *be the mermaid* not just carry it. It's a costume party, something some people around here seem to call, oh I don't know, can you say, Hallowe'en?' Ha! Can you believe it? So I found a hat and plopped it on him."

Hippias shook his head as his laughter calmed.

Zora's heart jumped. "What?" she exclaimed. "He's here?"

He's safe.

"Why? Why come here? With you?"

Zora noticed he maintained her gaze. A bit unnerving, she felt. How he'd maintain a flinty eye contact even as he lost himself in his own joke.

"Oh, well, why not? The cruise is, after all, a business networking event, not just a mad party. And we're business associates now. So I thought it fitting to attend with him. You know, do a kind of networking tag team. He speaks to someone, then introduces me … I do the same for him … we meet more people that way, hey?" He smiled broadly again.

"Where is he?" she said quickly, and immediately hushed her rising voice. Zora knew she was not cut out for any of this and she couldn't trust herself — how she'd come across, and what impulsive word would burst out of her mouth under the impossible pressure — but at least she knew Midas was here. Alive and free. Of all the many things coming at her, none of them making much sense, this was the most important fact for now.

Hippias looked almost dismayed for a moment, yet Zora could tell whatever he harboured there was somewhat wooden.

"Unfortunately we've become separated. Big chaos on this boat. Wasn't quite expecting it. In any event, there's one meeting I must have that should remain private. At least, somewhat private."

"And you work with Advance. Yes, I know who you are now." She thought she would have felt fear upon meeting him. For a drug dealer, at least partly so, he came across as a comic buffoon. "So, what private meeting?"

Instinctively, as she said this, Zora rose to leave but his large hand swiftly came upon hers on the table, and he gestured her to sit back down and stay.

He held her gaze with an intense smile. "I'm here to meet that man." He jutted his finger behind her with a dramatic arc of his arm.

Across the room, a tall man in a plain grey suit, white shirt and thin black tie walked toward them.

Oh shit. This is it. This is the meeting. At least, one of them. The one where Advance would compete with Creed — which was nowhere to be seen yet — for possession, or she assumed the purchase, of the teleport.

She scanned the tables and bar for Augustine. She was supposed to have met him first, to get confirmation on the whereabouts of the meeting and identify the subjects. The plan included some introduction. *Didn't it?* And Caesar. She began to panic at the possibility she'd stumbled into the wrong meeting.

The man in the grey suit arrived at their table and sat across from Hippias. He looked at Zora with no smile, then faced Hippias. "Who's she?"

"Yes, of course, Mr. Minister. She's with me."

"Get rid of her."

"Well, of course I see your concern sir, but she works with us. We need her. Very much so, I'm afraid. A very industrious and determined new worker bee, aren't you now, dear?"

"Yeah, sure, I know what I'm doing." Zora felt foolish for saying this. Her brow poured sweat and it stung her eyes. Surely they would turn on her and ask questions, expose her and do something terrible. She scanned the room again for Augustine. "But don't call me that," she said.

Hippias smiled, embarrassed, yet didn't pause. "Sir, again I implore you to focus on us. Advance has the piece. Well, not exactly, but it is within our grasp. Give me the evening, I guarantee. This company is the one you can trust, no other. Not Creed. Certainly not them. We have new information you need to know about that network. A most vile group…"

Everything was going wrong. Zora shifted closer to the windy window to dry the nervous sweat from her brow. Hippias perspired too, and more than her. She almost felt sorry for him, as the rivulets of sweat trickled down his cheeks.

Irritated, the Minister put up an open hand to stop him. "We know Creed, Hippias. We've done our investigations. They're here, like you, to convince us of something. The information we have gathered about them is unsettling. As is their proposition."

Hippias nodded vigorously. This threw droplets of perspiration across the table.

Fighting the soaring panic within her, Zora tried to remain still. The Minister did this well, possibly owing to his bland face that had no feeling other than that required to get something from someone.

"Yes, such information as there is to gather, indeed, good sir. It's out there. The information, I mean. Rinth is wonderful for that, isn't it? And if you can find such data through Rinth, who else is looking at it? And who owns Rinth, anyway?"

The Minister frowned. "You digress."

Hippias glanced at Zora and said, "But they invented the teleports. Rinth is not nothing. Still a powerful going concern, wouldn't you say? I mean, we rely on it, no?"

The Minister turned with irritation to the window and the choppy waters. "True, though it's a shadow of what it once was." "Yes, I agree with you completely," said Hippias. "And their proposition — that of Creed — is horrendous, isn't it? I mean, really, the very thought of their little legend — how silly! — to unleash a hoard of evildoers and worse, can you believe it, to actually *go there* — rampage another world and rape its resources. And to leverage this wonderful potential. Imagine, to teleport. Save transport fuel. Faster communication. More meetings because for goodness sake we need more of those, don't we? And there Creed is, Caesar at the bloody helm, wanting to put this technology to waste on a delusion. Where do you think they're going to go? Somewhere else on Earth, that's where! Only to exploit! That's their explicit value proposition and that's *all* it is."

Zora looked from side to side, capturing it all. Hippias appeared beside himself with a clever mix of exasperation and triumph. Quite the pitch, and he seemed to have a good point, although she wasn't so sure he had a better use for this incredible device. But broadcasting a bad deal that might incite outrage wasn't enough. She still needed to frame Augustine, she told herself with cynicism, and she scanned the room again, which was full of too many random people. The breath went out of her as she decided with finality she no longer cared about that anymore. Children were abducted and being held for ransom. Division Q could kill her if she failed to frame Augustine, and this possibility became, at last, tolerable. It had to be, because it was a red herring. That's not what they were really after. They didn't care about a massacre, about powerful people's ransomed children and the justice that should happen with their rescue, about the blood smeared across that window above the Hallowe'en party. They, and whichever rich asshole had hired them, cared only about finding the teleport. That's all the meeting was ever about and the only thing anyone, whether Division Q, whoever hired them, or the cell, was interested in. As great as Cisco's motives were, no one gave a shit about inciting outrage or revolution upon hearing about a bad deal, and she knew she didn't give a shit about a teleport except to the extent she'd get the kids out of wherever they were.

"Rinth is weak, too," Hippias continued. "The state isn't the only entity suffering in this world." He touched the Minister's forearm. "Don't you worry, Mr. Minister. We at Advance know your group represents a resurgence of the good power in government, and indeed, in society. Unlike those terrorists and certainly as opposed to the evil of Creed. After all, virtually all companies are weak. The essential truth of our time is we are all weak and dying. No one's in charge. The time is now to make a change. And our plan — the Advance proposition — has the hope and focus we all need as a collective." He nodded fiercely with a joy whose incongruence disturbed Zora.

The Minister looked up. "I don't share your uncharitable view of the government's power. You know we stand to make a deal with Advance or with Creed. It's to us that you both come. So Hippias, what is the problem? I thought Advance had located the device and the pills were set to be distributed according to your proposition. Before we can agree to collaborate, we need to see the structure established. There were two counters on our part to this meeting. First, bringing us the second teleport will push Advance over the line to get the deal. We'll finance the support of its use, and we'll arrange the terms of its use. Remember," and he pointed his finger at Hippias across the table, "we still have power. The state isn't dead yet. And second, because we'd arranged this already, those individuals must be eliminated in one well-coordinated moment."

Zora had to admire the bland man's command of what he was about.

Hippias nodded with a feint of wisdom. "Yes, and our primary proposition is to utilize this local project as a prototype. 'The Toronto Prototype', as I've titled my memo. Right now, I've sourced an establishment that wields a fine reputation with the trust of the community. It's perfect. And they do need, shall we say, consequence. The community — you know, society and all that. It's the right thing. I mean, honestly, they're just terrible. What they do. And perhaps we can throw in a few Creed types to the Tea Party, as I like to call it? Not too cheeky, you think?" He paused, pleased. "All part of the plan."

He giggled again and splayed his hands. "Then, we achieve a recalibration, if you will. Or rather, the beginnings of one. In phase two — or perhaps, yes, I admit, it might need to be phase three or even four — we move millions of them, swiftly coordinating, yes, as you say."

How fast he talked, Zora thought. Barrelling onward.

Hippias glanced at her quickly and returned to the Minister. "And with the teleport, imagine our freedom. No longer constrained by border control, we can infect the waters across even the oceans. And then the population can at last be brought under control." He smiled and clasped his hands. "Together we shall save the world."

Zora felt numb. Hippias returned his eyes to her, and it turned into a long hard gaze, unnaturally so. Zora's brow dampened, her hands clammy, and she reached for her drink.

"It's an option," replied the Minister. "Albeit with some delusion of grandeur. Creed has theirs. Convince me yours is better. And tell me where you have the device. We need proof." The Minister leaned back and continued, "We have layers of people who know people, and so on. I have no idea where our teleport is. But we have sure and secure access to it. And it's nowhere close but that's not the point. The point is, bring us the second one and we'll close the deal."

Hippias's eyes went wide. "Oh, no, that's not the issue. Not at all. Well, it went missing, but when we find it…"

"Missing? What?" The Minister moved closer to the window and Hippias shifted along with him. The Minister pointed his finger at Hippias's sweating face. "We need that teleport."

The ship pitched into a deep trough and the crowds gasped. White water sprayed into the air from the lake below and crashed across the decks outside. The room began to fill with people and the noise rose with their chattering.

Zora couldn't help but hear them, the partygoers. Their words and tones remained vague and distant, and wavered from alarm to delight. *Idiots*, she thought. *My God, how can they enjoy this?*

"We shall reclaim it, I assure you," Hippias said. "Creed can only betray you if you turn to them. What are they saying about this? What empty, deceitful promises are they making?"

The Minister leaned back and shook his head. "No, now it is a threat. I came not only to hear you out. I came to hear Creed and Caesar out." His jaw set firm and grim. He bowed his head. "Because I have to. They have children. The children of some fairly powerful people, some of whom are close allies. I can only thank God they're all still alive. And I heard from those bastards again yesterday. Their message was to meet them at this cruise for their pitch, and at the same time we could — in their loathsome words — 'Meet some of the children and seal the deal by these means.'" The Minister's mouth quivered and his voice cracked. "Some of them."

This is insane, thought Zora. *This Minister — part of what Cisco called an errant government group — is actually negotiating with these*

Creed terrorists. With other people's children. Willing to sacrifice them for something powerful? This is sick.

The Minister looked out the round window. The lake resembled a smouldering surface of bubbling grey lava. Its waves capped into violent thin white crests. *It's like I'm in a dark silver hell,* Zora thought. *This is no storm.*

"What are they going to do to those children?" said the Minister with bitterness. "And the twisted part is they make their pitch as though once we agree, under this sick duress, we'll maintain a collaboration. How do people operate like this monster? How can you do violence to someone and then expect them to be your ally?"

Zora realized her mouth was open.

"My goodness, how monstrous indeed," said Hippias. "And hypocritical." He leaned forward. "Isn't that the right word? Or what is it? The right word, I mean?" he mused. "What are they expecting? Ah, is the word, instead, *incongruous*? No, not quite that." Hippias gazed out the window, thinking.

"They're expecting us to tell them where the other teleports are," said the Minister. He exhaled in frustration. "But we have no idea." He straightened his back with an effort. "We're all looking for them. Or for it, if indeed there's only one left." The Minister held back a sob, and Zora suspected he did, in fact, have some humanity left in him. To be overwhelmed by the long, lingering atrocity of Creed, if only for a moment. He composed himself swiftly and found a small anger again to heft back at Hippias: "How did you lose it?"

"Lost sight, Mr. Minister," Hippias corrected. "We never had it in our possession, not really."

The Minister stared hard at him, cold and still as stone. "Who took it, then?" and his voice rasped over the wind.

"We're looking into that very question."

"Get it back, Hippias."

"We shall, I swear, good sir." Hippias forced a somewhat broad smile and nodded. "Oh yes."

The Minister turned to a nearby waiter and asked for a martini. "I suppose even Oxford may be affiliated with Creed by this point. They're influencing everyone. All business. Anyone might have it."

Zora had heard that name before. Oxford was hosting this cruise.

"I see." Hippias scanned the room, and back to Zora. "Where did he say to meet?"

"The bastard wouldn't clarify." The Minister's face reddened. His martini came and he grabbed it from the waiter's hands. "Said he'd find me. I thought you would know. I haven't seen any of his grotesque employees either. The Hallowers."

"I'm sure they're here. Wait and see." Hippias turned to Zora and stared straight into her for what felt like long minutes.

"Now, how would I know?" she said, scared he'd directed his statement at her. "I don't know who they are." *Fuck, I have no nerves. I need a drink.*

"You'll notice them by their costumes." Hippias waved his hand in another arc at the room. "Tailored suits of varying colours and patterns, all tattered and ripped, burned or charred in spots, wild hair, blazing eyes, and a bruise across the face. A bit like they've been to hell and back." Hippias leaned back and found a moment to laugh. "Probably they actually have! Ha!" Then, a stern, affected pause. "Plus, a stench."

He looked grimly out to the wind that slapped the side of the ship with a sudden whack. The chandeliers swung and clinked, drinks spilled and people tittered at the sensation.

The ship maintained its rocky course and the winds slammed again. This time frothing water sprayed through windows. People toppled and fell against furniture, the walls and one another. Voices cried in panic from outside along the decks and promenades. Dishes crashed. The music booming from main deck skipped.

"This is no storm," she said. The lake looked like a sea swelling toward a tsunami. Except that was an exaggerated thought. Zora wondered what was really happening out there. The air was warm, humid and rancid with pollution. Then on the sudden a swift waft of brisk, cool, clean air would rush in through the window. The waters churned as though the winds and temperature changed, and she was sure they were changing. She'd become accustomed to climate change like most people, but she'd never seen anything like this. Waters and winds don't churn like this with a clear night sky. She could see stars past the smog. No clouds.

"Of course it's a storm," said the Minister.

"She has a point, sir. This isn't a storm. Zora here, has been watching everything. Many clues have been found to date, to be sure!" Hippias slapped his hands upon the table in a state of revelry, like he'd just revealed a wonderful joke.

Hippias's face reddened, sweated and gleamed. He might have been anxious. Zora suspected a glimmer of excitement too.

"Oh, Mr. Minister, you know everything's been watched, right? Take this one." And he reached his arm around Zora's shoulders, sidling up close beside her as if they were old friends now. "This is the recording. Everything. Division Q's in our employ, hey? We've always had this covered. And by covered, I mean everything. All of it."

Hippias leaned on the word for emphasis, eager to impress the Minister. Then he turned to her and stared intently into her eyes and winked. "Oh, yes, my friends. We're ahead. Very much ahead of all of this." He winked again, this time with a crooked grin beneath those flinty eyes that bore into hers, and Zora wondered what that soft comment, mostly a whisper only to her, could possibly mean.

The Minister was staring at him, his mouth hanging slightly open.

Hippias slapped his palms together and chuckled. "Yes, Minister, I've had my friends at Division Q watching everything through this wonderful agent. Through her eyeball." He chuckled with satisfaction, proud of his little feat. "Follows everything. Even better than a drone is a human. All you have to do is set things up just right. After all, humans listen, respond. Drones can't do that."

Zora looked out the ship's window to the dark silver hell storming across the changed waters. She could hardly breathe. *No wonder he knew me through this impossible crowd. He works with those fuckers at*

Division Q. In fact, they work for him. So he wasn't such a friendly guy after all. He's a plotting predator.

Zora wanted to lunge for his throat and knock his teeth out. This awful human was responsible for implanting a surveillance device inside her right eye. He'd seen her entire conversation with Augustine, with Cisco, her *other* recording device implanted, why and for whom, and all that Midas had said if any of that mattered. This stranger, this strange man, was a completely evil fucker. And he knew they — the cell — were watching this very conversation. He was doing this on purpose. He didn't give a shit. In fact, he wanted them to hear this for some mysterious reason. He knew what they knew, what they'd known, and now maybe all he had to do was unnerve them, as though he was recklessly gloating.

There was a stunned silence across the table. Then the Minister gave an instrumental nod as though this could be normal. The Minister stared at Hippias while Zora felt stone cold as she descended into self-loathing. She let them do this to her. Recording devices implanted within her eyes, to work for them like a slave. They assumed it was okay, that she'd acquiesce, and the worst part was, she had so far.

"I mean, honestly," Hippias rushed to continue speaking, "after Augustine and his dirty little revolutionary troupe were poking around — mainly Augustine himself, truly off on a frolic of his own — finding out more and more, bit by bit, about Creed and its business, and then Creed's ridiculous legend promising people a land full of fresh, pristine resources to exploit, a portal to get there, well then surely we had to look into it. So suspiciously similar to the teleport, their strange legend. 'Take you to a land flowing with riches without the constraints of our laws and traditions,'" Hippias mocked with an exasperated tone. "Or, what did they say? Our *ethical* constraints. Or someone did, anyway. Not sure who! And all that bunk, no? I suppose we could have plucked him off the street and tortured him, but what would that do? No one knew where it was. Until recently ... with this precious one's good work!"

The Minister held up his palm in the air again to stop Hippias from his incessant rambling and said, "If you're so cunning, then make yourself and your team useful and go find him."

"No, this is impossible," she said quietly. Zora's skin beneath its surface curled again like freezing water. Her predicament was impossible, indeed incredible, yet here she sat, used by these pompous men who sought a deal and to shut out a bad competitor. Being wiretapped to frame Augustine for a fierce private police force was now obviously irrelevant. Beyond that, their brazen nonchalance melted her icy astonishment with a raging fire. They were negotiating with those children's lives. So these fuckers would lose. This, she vowed. Not helpless, either, because she'd learned something, she realized, from an early moment on this cruise. Those kids she'd run across as they went into the *king*'s suite had tridents on their shirts.

"This is ridiculous," she said aloud. "Stop it. I think I know where this Caesar might be."

And where the kids might be. That's all that mattered now.

Hippias smiled more broadly. "Yes?" he said. His eyes darted between hers and the Minister's.

"I ran into some partiers on the stairs to the upper quarterdeck," she said. "They were talking about someone called the king."

"Where?" asked the Minister.

"They pointed to a door at the top," she said. "I couldn't see past. There couldn't be much up there. I mean, this boat is built like an old eighteenth-century ship."

"Almost, but not quite," said Hippias with a happy lilt to his voice. "This beauty still has many luxurious modern features. And I do believe that's where some of the art suites are. You know these pompous show-offs, hey? I thought the auction for charity was a bit much for an event like this. I mean, why? We're just trying to have a party, after all."

The Minister glared at him in a frozen state and his eyes swam red with anger, all while slightly stretched in horror at Hippias's offensive digressions.

Hippias rushed, flustered, "But yes, certainly an homage, this ship, to that which once was. And yes, I do appreciate the spot you reference."

"Everyone does, Hippias," said the Minister. "Every ship like this has a quarterdeck."

Hippias squeezed his eyes shut with mirth and chuckled. "Yes, how silly of me." And he shifted the rim of his crimson hat on the table, pressing on, "And now that we know where the king might be — brilliant, Zora, simply brilliant detective work! See, Mr. Minister? Add to that my own little contribution to our quest for clues — isn't it interesting? So why don't you go there, would you, dear? Just take a quick peak. Find out how full his suite is not with partiers, but business leaders."

His eyes went wide and he snapped his fingers before the Minister's face. "We need to know his influence, don't we, Mr. Minister?" he said nodding vigorously at his own suggestion. "Not many have rooms like that on the boat. Would you? I, for one — goodness, no — certainly can't go."

The waiter walked by with a platter full of martinis. Zora stood quickly and lifted two as the waiter passed. She gave one to the Minister and drank the other in two gulps.

"And you may even see Midas in there," Hippias added.

"Don't talk about him," Zora said swiftly and took another martini. She needed to get out of here, her wiretaps far away from Hippias's non-stop mouth.

"Now that she knows where the king is, this is our best bet. And by the way, I have done business with the man for some time — Midas, I mean; he owns the indie café on Dundas, don't you know. Such a fine fellow! My, indeed, and what a curious coincidence. Who knows."

"Why are you talking about a café..." the Minister asked, frustrated again, but Hippias jumped to speak.

"And to be sure," Hippias pressed, "she must go in, get a good look and return quickly. That's what I mean to say. That she shouldn't stay. She'll get in easily. Regard. See how pretty she is?"

Zora put her face in her hands. Her next step had to be to enter that room. Zora blinked from the Minister to Hippias and his smile, back to the Minister and back way down deep to that cold room with the heavy breathing, the giggles and the strange towering striped hat. The Minister's set jaw wavered and his heavy, sunken eyes met hers as they both thought of the same horrifying image of children trapped and tied up, frozen silent with terror. *Mommy, mommy*, Zora knew them to be saying.

She leaned toward Hippias and grabbed his eyepatch that sat on the table. She put it on, over her left eye. She figured the cell's wiretap was too close to Augustine. He'd fallen into corruption, affiliated with Creed. None of them would be seeing through her eyes this time. "I'll be right back. You fuckers," she said, and walked into the crowd.

EIGHTEEN

The ship lurched. Drinks spilled and the music stopped and started again. Cries of awe and dismay resounded, some playful, enjoying the danger; others gripped against a terrible uncertainty.

"What a storm," Zora heard someone say as she walked along the main deck beneath the night that was still dark and crisp with stars shining. She arrived at the starboard promenade filled with onlookers mystified and curious, and pushed through to the railing to look over. The water sucked and pulled at the ship furiously, as though it passed through rapids.

"Chica, just an eye patch?" said a voice. "Where's your costume?"

Zora turned to face a group of four wearing painted wooden masks that enveloped their heads with sleek elfish features. These must have been heavy to bear, but they remained enthused to keep the party going, as one continued to dance, despite another hiccup to the music when the ship dipped deep to starboard down a sudden trough in the waves. They stood on a wider platform at the base of the same stairwell where Zora had been earlier when she met the couple in spandex with the tridents.

Zora realized she'd come to the party without a real costume.

"Where can I find one?" she said over the music. The rest of their outfits were plain: just jeans and rocker tees. "I like your look. It's to the point."

The elf whose black mask had red stripes like war paint turned to his friends and shrugged. They stood facing her in a semicircle and one gestured for them to leave.

"Wait," said Zora. "I really need one, you know, a mask like you guys. Do you know if there are any extra? Like, for sale or something?"

One of them replied in a muffled voice, "Don't think so. Why, not having enough fun?"

They laughed.

"What's up in there?" Zora pointed to the doors above at the quarterdeck. She tried to calm her impatience, not show her anxiety.

"A few super cool party rooms," said the boy with the red war paint. They laughed. "I got into two of them and one was especially bad. Like the fucking rich guy, but some weird shit was going on in there." The slender, red-painted boy doubled over, laughing. "I just left. Wasn't going so well for me there but wouldn't mind trying again because the man is rich. Stay right here."

He disappeared into the crowd.

Zora's gaze lingered on the mingling costumes, and her anxiety over what she was about to do — enter what she believed to be Caesar's suite — wrenched her gut into a knot. Vertigo briefly came over her as the milling crowd of costumed partiers took on a new impression, stronger than before and more pronounced. A clown mask — mostly white, with red nose and black eyes — turned upon her and howled a string of laughter, then disappeared into the boisterous crowd. Another masked presence — this one, a dark balaclava from whose eyeholes gazed bloodshot green eyes, and when they leered at her more closely, leaning in as though to give greetings, or howl at her as another selfish joke, she saw trickles of real blood dripping from them.

Another group surged past from behind, bumping into her, and she felt a hand reach out and push her out of their way. She stumbled and swore softly, with some disbelief. One of the elves steadied her, and she turned her attention back to them.

These elfish kids seemed friendly.

"Guys, is that the king's suite?"

One of the elfish masks cocked its head. "Why do you want in there?"

Zora couldn't think of a decent lie, but she didn't need to. Another elf piped up.

"He said there's security," said the large elf. "He may not get in, though. The first time in he had to follow some funny-looking people."

"Funny looking?" she asked.

Masks turned to one another as they stood with hands in pockets and shifted their feet.

"Got it," said a muffled voice behind her.

Zora jumped, at which he guffawed. He gave her a lighter mask, just across the eyes, made of green and blue mesh. She'd put it on, over top the eyepatch. She had to keep that on.

"Where did you get that?" she asked with some trepidation. Better to have a more convincing costume, to fit in more but there was something wrong with this kid. Like he might have done something bad to get it.

"Don't ask him," said the big-eared elf.

They laughed and waved the two off as Zora fought another chill at their reaction. She sensed they meant that he'd done something bad — to someone — to get it. How bad could it be, for just a mask?

She and the boyish one with red war paint ascended to the quarterdeck. Beyond that door they descended a few steps and walked down a corridor lined with doors to numerous suites, to the end where stood a tall figure wearing a suit made of expensive navy wool that had suffered some ragged edges and burned holes. From beneath his hat protruded black hair somehow shaped into long thick points.

The elfish boy tentatively approached with Zora right behind. Her heart pounded.

"Hey man, I forgot something," said the kid. He began to reach his hand out to the man's shoulder, and Zora pulled it back. "Just need to get it quickly," he said loudly, almost shouting over the music and standing far too close. "That ok?"

"What?" the man asked.

The boy turned to Zora, whose mask hid her paling face.

"I don't recognize you," the tall man said to her. A bruise streaked down his cheek and his teeth bared just slightly. He stared straight ahead at the door.

Zora opened her mouth, but nothing came out at first. Then, "My costume. I loaned him my, you know, my trident. It's in there. He forgot it." She tried to smile. "We need it back, don't we? I mean, all I have is this mask."

The yellowed sunken eyes of the tall man bore into her. "You can go in and out, quick."

From inside came the sounds of a party: laughter, shouts, a brief argument and old jazz.

"That wasn't so bad," said the boy as they entered a room billowing with red mist. Beyond lay white sofas, high-backed chairs, a furry blue carpet and a glass coffee table. People gathered in dispersed groups, chatting, lying indulgently with one another, drinking and smoking. To the right a bar nestled into an alcove and to the left the floor rose as a platform upon which sat bathtubs. The red mist floated from them, and she almost gagged at the notorious stench of slider.

"Thanks, you should probably go now," she said to the boy, and scanned the room.

"What do you mean? I got you in here." He stood too close with his masked face before hers and squeezed her forearm. "I'm getting you a drink and you're pretty. Too bad you have a mask on."

She pulled away and stepped ahead. "Don't make a scene, kid." Zora blinked, because the red mist waxed and waned and obscured her surveillance, already made difficult by the confusing array of costumes. At the other side, a wide doorway opened into a candlelit area and beside it another door remained closed. The elfish lad went directly to the bar and, oblivious to the glares of the small group of men in suits, snapped his fingers at the bartender. Zora's eyes widened behind her thin mask.

This kid's going to ruin everything.

Zora scanned again through the wafting red mist and found herself checking exclusively for Midas, but all she could see was a crowd of costumed partiers visiting in clumps, drinking and smoking: a man with whiskers extended from his face, another in a grey and black batman outfit with three women draped around him wearing nothing but white tufts on their breasts and between their thighs, someone in a toga, a large man with a heavy purple robe and a crown made of twigs. Zora turned to the hot tubs and their horrible sloshing liquid, the billowing red steam clouding over languid arms that hung from the edges, one hand was open, upright and limp, another dangled and maintained a grip on an icy tumbler of vodka.

Zora looked to either side, through steamy red fog on the left and to the right where a group leaned against the bar, some in tattered suits, black pointed hair, gaunt physiques and bruised faces. They glared and surrounded the elfish boy. Past the tubs, amongst sofas, low-lying tables filled with champagne, cocaine lined up and martinis, behind red mist that waned, sat in the middle of a fluffy white sofa a short round man in a white suit enjoying something that looked like glory while surrounded by about a dozen costumed people milling about. From where she positioned herself, trying to remain obscured by the tubs and the thick, seething mist emanating from them — in a small area between the far wall and the raised floor area on which the tubs sat — his back and the back of the sofa were to her.

Zora stood closer to the wall. She gagged a little, but knew how to handle the slider, having worked beneath it at Night. It wouldn't hurt you if it didn't touch you. As a waft of the red mist waned again, she recognized Augustine sitting beside the round man, speaking in earnest. His mouth spread into a slit of thin yellowed teeth as it moved. He didn't see her, preoccupied as he was with the short rotund man. She gagged some more, and held it back, trying to keep quiet.

She could hear them.

"Except now we hear they don't know where the other so-called teleports are," the round man said with a honey alto voice. Such a calm, silky way to speak. Too silky, sounding dissociated from the meaning of his words. "Except one that sneaky bastard Hippias almost found, then lost, to us?"

He laughed, and continued, "Or the one that weak, small-minded bureaucrat claims he has — somewhere but who knows where?" His steady voice rose with contempt and outrage at the stupidity surrounding him. "How could you let this happen? He's been beating us to the favour of this group of Ministers. We're almost losing the deal. He virtually told us this to our faces when he said that to her: 'We're way ahead.' Isn't that what he said?"

His voice had peaked and pierced the music, the crowd's chattering and clinking of bottles upon glasses paused as they stopped pouring for a brief, alarmed moment.

Augustine rushed to speak, "But we already have it, sir."

"Well where's the bloody key, then?" Caesar screamed, his face crimson red around the black bug-like glasses strapped to his sweating head.

"Wait," Augustine said, visibly shaking as two Hallowers emerged into Zora's view from the thick red mist, standing up from their seats. "I had her wiretapped with the highest quality recording device — within the eye — and so now we know as of yesterday early morning that Division Q's been wiretapping her, with that disgusting Peacock harassing Zora on her Probe just when she's about to stab herself in both eyes. How was I to know, for goodness' sake? And we've pivoted plans swiftly enough, haven't we? I mean, I hacked the cell's wiretap, and routed to the Ministers' Probes. They're linked up and ready to hear us. She's on her way. We heard them send her. We have time yet."

Caesar threw his glass in a fit of rage at a nearby guest, splashing red wine across her seated lap. She made a quiet noise in protest that was quickly quelled by her nervous friends.

"We do not have time!" Caesar screamed. "He is here. I know he has that mermaid statuette on him — Hippias said so. We must keep this momentum going. We need that key. So close, all of it coming together so quickly. Now, Augustine. You've promised me this much and you want in, don't you? To Creed? Do what you said you were going to do. Get that key, *tonight*."

The strange man's voice maintained its honeyed veneer throughout this dispute and despite the sporadic scream or outburst, he carried himself with poise. Back straight, face relatively stoic, although now a pointed finger sticking at Augustine's shocked face.

Zora noticed larger bruises down his cheek and neck, and now figured they weren't bruises but simply marks, as though he'd been poisoned. Somehow damaged. Hair messier, he resembled the Hallowers by the bar as it spiked upward and outward. His suit, expensive and tailored, was more tattered, ripped and burnt.

"The trouble now is, our proxy spy Zora has disabled her eye device. Or did you just turn it off? Sometimes I wonder if you ever really knew what you were doing, hacking that device. Or perhaps your old cell is just too clever for you. Perhaps they realized your betrayal and turned it off," he said, still pointing at Augustine who continued to shake.

Zora felt her eyepatch beneath her mask. So it was true, as she figured. Creed had been watching too, at least since Shantytown. Seeing, hearing everything. And now she was too close. Hearing them speak like this, about her, the thing they'd placed inside, she felt like she might start giving off an alarm.

Caesar reached for a slim knife on the coffee table by his chalice, picked it up and thrust it before Augustine's face to stop right before his eyes. He laughed slowly, in his haunting alto pitch.

Shaking, Augustine tried to hold his own. "Sir, we know she's coming. We just saw her speaking with Hippias and the Minister. So when she's here, we'll not only speak to the others in the Minister's little group, but to Hippias. He's watching too, obviously. He'll have to send Midas. Plus," he added, now almost languid again like he'd been at his apartment days ago, sipping scotch, "they don't believe the mermaid statuette Midas carries does anything." Zora sensed he was forcing renewed confidence in himself. "They think we're clowns."

Caesar's reddening face deepened to a new crimson, and he screamed again, "They'll send the man along with Division Q. You idiot." His voice pierced the air, stunned the party to another momentary stillness that matched his own expressionless face. He burst out again with a curling, cruel mouth beneath anonymous bug-like eyes, "We have no time. We need Midas and that key here on *our* time."

Augustine put his hands up and stood, shaking his head. Then he looked right at Zora.

Zora jumped involuntarily, but it was too late. He pointed at her as the mist cleared and said something she could barely discern as 'She's right here,' through the anxious fog that seized her, made those blurry words into a distant echo.

Hallowers clamped their nailed, powerful, bony hands at her elbows and shoulders from behind. She had no idea they were coming. So frozen with fear she could barely curse herself.

Augustine stood at the edge of the sofa, between her and Caesar. Steeling his eyes, still nervous, he said as strongly as he could, "How long have you been…"

Caesar stood in an exasperated rage, slapping the table and sending all glasses crashing to the floor. "Oh, don't ask her that! She's heard everything already. And so have they."

Augustine quivered beneath his clothes, even as he grinned. His yellow teeth appeared chiselled, almost like fangs here and there. Zora saw that despite his fear of Caesar, his own version of the wickedness innate in Caesar and the other Hallowers gave him some recurring confidence.

"They can see what we're going to do to her, and to the children," Augustine said, savouring his words as he turned to Zora's eyes and spoke directly into them. "With the Ministers waiting for our call we will do two things, if we're not already doing it now. Tell us where the other teleport is. Where the others ones are, if there are any. And above all, Hippias needs to send Midas in. And only him. Don't you? You're working for them, aren't you, Hippias?"

He stood up close to Zora's face as he said it and spoke into her right eye.

Augustine reached for a drink. "They're all one grouping of interests. Now we can leverage all of them at once."

Augustine is right, she thought. Everyone was hearing this. Advance, Division Q, the cell. They'd heard everything all along. Creed was only now trying to catch up. They may have what she assumed was the — or, a — teleport device, and that's a victory. But their enemies were on their way. And Creed had no key yet.

Fuck their bloody keys and plans and machinery, she said to herself deep within. She'd find those kids and get them out of this bullshit mess.

Caesar calmed and said, staring into Zora's eye too, chuckling with his blank face, "Yes, just one child." He looked at Augustine. "Or one at a time. We shall need to stretch this out for a while. The Minister's little group still has utility for us, doesn't it?" He said this to the rest of the room. Snickers came from the Hallowers congregated by the bar and the two who held Zora. "They have more of the teleports, I know it. Scattered about, locked away in buried cocoons for safekeeping. Their dumb little secret. Dumb because they just don't know what they have."

He reached for his chalice on the coffee table and curled his lips at Augustine, his voice rising like he had made a speech before a large audience, and it rang over the music and din of the party.

Red steam billowed, the bar tittered with excitement at this turmoil, at the potential for violence and cruelty, and the playful dancing went on.

Caesar's face went into a stone-like state. Zora saw his stress, despite his eyes remaining as blank as an insect.

"Race is on, isn't it?" said Augustine to the hooting gales from the Hallowers. "We're inevitably positioned to win."

Zora couldn't believe this. They were all as deluded as Midas. She'd been trying to piece this together all evening, since Hallowe'en, while absorbing the horror that she'd been wiretapped in both eyes by two competing companies, both hunting a teleportation machine. Or something else. All in a race for an insane prize.

My God, this can't be happening.

"Whatever the hell you're talking about, you're evil," Zora spat on the floor. Their bony hands clamped harder and put her in a vice. She couldn't speak as a growing, numb awe came over her at what they had seen from her own eyes, in their wiretap — the thing that Cisco had coordinated, lost in his blind ignorance.

Caesar stared between her and Augustine.

"Evil?" he replied. "It's not that. We're Creed. For, first, we must do a fine deed. A grand one, that of bringing the world to its proper fruition. They shall all come over to this side. All of them. And we, to that land, those riches, such freedom. And we need its essence… The Seeping remains too thin. All we have are a few of these snarling Hallowers." He gestured at the men in tattered suits by the bar, who settled down in their snickering. "A mere smattering of their true potential, if only the Seeping could complete itself. Once we've done this, we shall all be Hallowers — and more."

He pointed his finger at Augustine's face again and said with a tight constraint, "Get her in there and get going at it." He waved his hand at the closed door. "The longer this takes, the sooner Division Q could be here. When that happens, I want our new Hallower friends to be flowing through that portal, arriving as they will once we have that key, that gorgeous statuette tucked into his pocket, appearing everywhere and always with us, all ready to take them on."

Augustine sniffed into the air. "Certainly, sir. I assure you, Midas shall arrive in no time."

Caesar's dark bug eyes scrunched into blank fury and he growled to the Hallowers at the bar: "Find Midas. Get him here. Things are changing quickly and we have no time."

Augustine grimaced and nodded at the Hallowers' tightened grip. He bowed his head and said under his breath, "This isn't going to plan."

"Now!" screamed Caesar. His honeyed voice ripped through the silenced room.

How can you all be so lost on one fucking boat? Zora thought she said it, but the ship lurched again. Glasses and bottles crashed to the floor, a crooked painting fell and tubs slid, sending red mist billowing across the room. The Hallowers mustered themselves and walked out the door as the music resumed.

The Hallowers who remained, clustered around, wrapped their arms around her, tied her wrists and dragged her along the floor. Through the closed door at the far end of the room they entered, into a dark, cramped and barren chamber lit by a hanging lantern. A cage in shadow sat in a corner and directly before her on the wall hung a painting with silver framing and two candelabra on the upper corners. Beside it, another narrow door.

Zora recognized the painting from the café and was again struck by its deep texture. The oils seemed to emerge from the canvas: a marketplace in a walled town on a mountainous coast beyond which stretched a sea. But now it was different again. Deep into the night, the trading had long since ceased and within the busy market square frolicked orange and purple clowns with long forked tongues amongst tents surrounded by billowing red smoke burning from fire pits nearby, and people milled about tables laden with wine, fruit and cheeses. Costumed partiers gathered sporting coloured garments, often scantily clad, and whirled in dance, threw their heads back with an open bottle, and in darker areas mauled at one another in fits of drunken passion. She was drawn to a scene in the corner of the market by the far wall where a pole with two ropes dangling from its top leaned over a round pool framed by brick. The frayed ends of the ropes floated upon the water's surface.

So they stole this from Midas. But why? They're so concerned about their lunatic ravings — whatever Seeping meant, a fruition of some kind of plan, or a mad race for a teleport and its activation key — and where's the teleport? They talked like they actually had it.

Then she remembered Midas's message from a few nights ago, right before his place had been trashed.

She heard cries. She wrenched her eyes from the painting to the cage. *My God, no*, because amid blankets huddled a group of children.

NINETEEN

The tall man in the duster coat walked through the jostling crowd with long strides, and Midas struggled to keep up. He bumped into everyone and had to resist looking at them or he would lose sight of his target. Midas almost resented how the man's presence forged a path when the reckless partiers unconsciously backed away.

On the wide promenade near the main deck, the man stopped at a slightly open door, knocked, paused and entered. He kept it mostly closed. Midas approached, concerned he would be noticed, and kept himself flush to the wall outside, somewhat grateful for the others who lingered at the rail across the promenade, hoping he would appear just like them. Except they admired the brewing waters, the bright moon amid the dark shades of the sky and the Toronto islands; in contrast, Midas felt like a conspicuous creep, watching.

Midas tried to see in. Cisco had left the door ajar, and he sat at an angle with his back mostly to it. This gave Midas a wavering view of the duster coat and his broad shoulders, as he leaned his back into the chair, crossed his feet and shifted his broad cowboy hat back from his brow to reveal a worn, aged face etched with a hardened kindness and piercing eyes beneath thick white eyebrows.

Cisco shook his head with dismayed sorrow. "Poor kid. I'm so sorry." He leaned forward and gazed intently into his hand-held

Probe's screen. "Listen to them," Cisco said to himself, thinking something through. Midas tried to see the screen, keeping himself flush against the wall out of sight. This would never work and he felt like a fool. The second Cisco noticed the door hadn't closed, he'd see Midas.

Midas tried to hear what Cisco listened to. The noise of the partygoers around him made it hard to make out the words. All he could hear were the alto tones of Caesar: *Evil? It's not that. We're Creed. For, first, we must bring the world to its proper fruition. They shall all come over to this side. And we, to that land, those riches, such freedom. And we need its essence... The Seeping remains too thin. All we have are a few of these snarling Hallowers.*

From this angle, Midas thought Cisco scowled with anger, judging from his flexing shoulders.

"Shit, this wasn't the deal. Putting a goddamn stop to this."

Midas couldn't help but lean in a little more. He felt absurd and desperate with his face peering around the door frame.

A massive wave smashed upon the ship's side before Midas, and white-frothed water drenched everyone on the promenade. Midas almost lost his footing and grabbed a bar on the wall that held a lifejacket. People screamed, some in fear, others with delight, and some laughed. But Midas felt a fleeting terror as the ship leaned steeply upon the lake's surface. The water came at him from straight ahead, and his feet dangled in the air as he wondered how the ship could ever right itself from that precarious angle, until it heaved back from another disruption in the waters below.

"What is this storm?" Cisco said to himself, despite being alone. "Earth's falling apart. Plain and simple. But this is something else. And now I gotta fix this."

Midas held on to the metal bar, incredulous this could happen so quickly and with such force. As though the ship were crashing into something yet never hitting anything. No one fell overboard; it felt on the verge of sinking, yet, despite the extreme assault on the ship, it stayed erect. This was no storm. The ship withstood an onslaught of some kind, as though they twirled in a vortex, a disruptive, perilous tunnel where the laws of nature no longer applied. And then the chaos of the lake calmed with the same suddenness as it came, and the ship leaned back to an upright position.

Midas grabbed the mermaid statuette in his pocket to confirm it was still there. He stared across the lake, at the bubbling waters beneath the bright full moon, and he sensed again a whispering wind in the back of his mind, the familiar rustling through treetops he'd associated with Madame Blue's talk. This invasive presence in his head was the same as the night they stole the painting. The exact same. When it opened up.

The closer it gets to the portal, the more unstable the opening. A greater rift happens, Madame Blue had said. This made no sense at the time. He'd been frustrated with Blue's opaque descriptions of what awful thing was happening all around them. The least she could have done was make it clear. What was clear to him was one consistent message from Blue: They were creatures, guarding the *gate*, keeping them safely separated. From God knows what. And that one, the mermaid beast, was breaking the rules. Maybe this was part of how she did that, through this sneaking statuette, a kind of representation of herself here. So here he was, marching with a reckless, mindless weapon that could tear the fabric of the universe to expose them all to God knew what that seethed on the other side.

This widening rift was clear to him. He was witnessing it, the closer he walked toward the painting. He shouldn't be here. *We're flipping over to the other side of whatever boundary this is. All my fault. I'm walking us across, and it's a terrible storm.*

Because the skyline was not the city of Toronto. The islands remained spotted with occasional lights from their simple cabins, but behind them over to the mainland shore he saw only blackness. A flash of lightning came, lit up the CN Tower, and the next flash showed only the vast expanse of a dark forest beneath the stars and full moon. He slipped in the swirling water that came and went on the deck. The door opened. Cisco left the room and walked along the promenade.

Midas stood, balanced himself at the railing, and followed Cisco. As he walked, trying again to keep a good distance behind, unnoticed, his gaze kept returning to the lake's expanse and the shore. The sky had cleared to a dark navy-blue early morning with a round moon whose reflection of the far-off sun shone pure like he hadn't seen since childhood. He breathed into his lungs and was filled with new energy, a powerful cool oxygen of which he had no memory. And then the waters churned and raged as ever, sinking into whirling pits, then gushing upwards like miniature volcanic bursts. Rain pounded, blinding him. He grasped the rail as the ship steeped again far to starboard. When it steadied, he looked up and confirmed they'd arrived at the base of the quarterdeck.

A strong hand pounded his shoulder. Cisco stood facing him.

"I think we're crossin' too. We got to stop this shit from going down."

"How do you know this?" Midas screamed back over the raging rain without clouds, lightning without thunder, but a deep rumble beckoned from deep below the surface of the lake.

"To the other side!" Cisco yelled back. "You're getting too close to the fuckin' clunker with that goddamn thing in your pocket." He paused, held the railing nearby and considered, giving Midas a sizing up of a look. "But ya know what? This is a good thing."

Cisco pulled out his long pistol, nodding at Midas with it to follow him to the top of the stairs on the quarterdeck.

Midas went up, feeling again the growing, familiar sensation of cotton in his head. Desperate to rid himself of it, he mustered his anger, for it pushed back the cotton-like fog that always came with the whispering air in treetops, just like when the Hallowers robbed him of the painting that night, that awful invasive sensation of a predatory presence encroaching, up from the base of his spine, and that furiously burrowed into the back of his mind. He grasped the rail as tightly as he could as he went higher to a perilous height amid an uncanny storm that flipped and turned everything upside down.

Behind Cisco, Midas arrived at the top of the stairwell. "Caesar," he said with a growl under his breath.

TWENTY

Zora squinted and counted: There were seven children, all of them.

Thank God.

They held one another, tense on their knees and fixated on her. They made desperate sounds Zora struggled to understand until she realized they were indeed saying, after all, "Mommy, Mommy, please, Mommy." Seeing it wrenched her heart, them calling together to their mothers, none of whom were here.

Long, strong fingers gripped her wrists then ripped her mask and eyepatch off. Zora felt a familiar cold metal wrap around them. Augustine shoved her upon a metal folding chair to face the children. It was just him now. The other Hallowers had left, apparently to find Midas.

"Zora, my sweetheart, not all is as it seems to be. For me, so much became clear thanks to you and your looking around in all the right places. But somehow I doubt you yet understand despite sharing your sight with us all." He laughed. "The irony. Poor Zora. And now you will share it for the one last deed that must be done."

"You're evil," she said, sobbed, and spat on the floor toward him. "All this time, I actually doubted Division Q. Maybe that's what held me back, not fear. But they were right. You work for that damn asshole Caesar. You're guilty, after all."

Inside the cage, the children sat upon blankets and pillows, and empty plates littered the floor around them. Behind the cage through a large round window the lake raged and thin clouds glided beneath a bright full moon.

"We know what it is, sweet Zora — ignore Midas, Hippias and all of them. We did this — I did, rather. Co-opted the revolutionary *cell* as they call themselves. And Cisco, the old drunk, he's been viewing all this, haven't you, my man?"

He called this out straight into her eye. "Been watching all this time? Sometimes? Sometimes not, I'd bet." And he laughed at her, at Cisco. "Well, guess what I've been up to? Learning what Creed was really all about, discovering their legend about a portal to another world full of riches, freed from our moral constraints, freed to take as much as we can. This became clear at the Ball when I discovered its proof, when I encountered the Hallowers congregated just before the massacre. They spoke to me. So convincing, Zora. Can you believe the bounty? Their promise is real. The Hallowers themselves are proof. They are very real. Those were not costumes."

He was yelling with delight. Giddy in hopes she would agree.

Zora regarded in growing horror at his dangerous delusion. It was a delusion that Midas too seemed to share.

"And before, in that crucial moment when the kid in the alley told me about the key. The blue woman made of astounding stone. So close to Creed's legend of their mermaid. Their guardian. Madame Blue's match on the other side. So we are here, filming you — everyone, seeking it. And so are they. They know what it is — the men in suits on the other side of your eye."

Augustine stood between her and the children. They watched, quieter, and waited. One boy stood apart, boldly near the bars while the others huddled beneath blankets in the cage's centre.

The ship dipped to one side and water smashed, foaming white caps, against the window. The ship's wooden frame groaned like a tortured giant under the stress. Dishes and bottles crashed from the main room. The children shrieked and Augustine fell to his knees.

"This can't be," he said under the clamour. The renewed confidence he'd found in this room alone with her, the children, separate from Caesar for this brief moment, disappeared and he became as pale as the moon beyond the window. "How can it be working like this?"

"What's happening?" she yelled at him. It was a storm, she told herself, then self-corrected in the same thought. Something else was happening out there, and to this ship.

Augustine ignored her. He seemed to gain a new strength as he pulled himself to his feet. "Look at the cage," he ordered.

Zora didn't move, but when he reached to force her face toward the cage, she pulled back and turned her head on her own, her eyes focussing on the children. "You're sick," she said over the rising clamour, the ship creaking, then cracking, muted screams far above on deck, distant pounding bass in a persistent party, and the gradual emergence of rushing rapids.

Shit, we're going down.

Augustine held on to one of the bars of the cage that held the children as the boat careened, and he mustered some lonely determination. Then he grabbed Zora's chin, turned her face and stared straight into her eyes. "Mr. Minister, and colleagues, send us the location of the teleports. There is no way someone in government doesn't have access to their whereabouts. And their keys." He lurched with the shifting ship, held up a pistol and looked to her eyes again. "If you do not, these children will die one by one."

"Asshole," Zora screamed over the growing clamour.

He ignored her. "See them? Ha! Let me tell you: She aims her eyes, and always in the right direction. Much better than the old version, yes?" He laughed and held on to the bars as the ship dipped so steeply Zora thought she saw through the window an oceanic whirlpool sucking them into its spinning centre.

"Let them out!" she yelled over the groans of the ship's wood.

No, no, no, no, keep him talking, delay, stop this.

Because he was going to shoot one of those poor kids dead. She looked around the room, back at Augustine and his pistol, desperate to find a way through this.

"See how curious she is too? She looks because she needs to see this. Even as I blow the brains and guts out of one of the children with every moment you remain silent, she'll watch and you will bear witness to your awful choice."

He coughed a rattling fit.

"After all, Sweetheart, you need material, don't you? You're as corrupt as the rest of us."

Zora wanted to beat him senseless with his own pistol. As the ship dunked to the side again and waves slammed against the window, her chair toppled. She yelled, "You fucker!" and tried rolling to her knees but she could only strain her clasped hands behind the chair. "They don't know where the teleports are. Didn't you see the Minister's face? He was telling the truth."

"Look, Zora, look," he yelled. He went to her, stumbled to his knees and struggled for balance as the ship plunged, far down and forward. He set her upright, positioning her to face them again. With him momentarily close, she wrenched her wrists against the metal clasps around them and tried to head butt him. But she choked on swallowed water and he dodged backward.

"Wait," she said, stalling things, yet scrambling to do the right thing. *How can I know what the right thing to do is?* She cried inside herself. No one trained her for this. Nor for anything of what she'd been drawn, tricked and lured into doing. All for what, other than feed these bastards' greed. So she said, "I know where one is. A teleport."

Delay the bullet going into one of those kids.

He rushed to the bars at the cage and held them. "Just watch, stop talking," he said, struggling to stand straight against the bars with the ship's ever more wild careening.

"At the café. You think he only has one?"

She winced inside, regretting the lie. Division Q was listening. They might find Midas again and kill him for it — but then, that fight was for later. This fight needed the kids freed from that cage.

The children were crying, "No, no, no."

She sobbed aloud with a surge of despondence that she managed to defeat and bury. "It's not this painting," she forced herself to say. "They got the wrong one."

"Impossible," Augustine yelled again over the deafening cracks, strains, and then explosive bursts of the embattled ship. Another heavy bump came from the decks above, and the screaming turned frantic at last.

Zora balanced herself on the chair with her freed feet and looked at the children, then forced her eyes to the wet floor and squeezed them shut.

She refused to look at him shooting any one of them. Not to be a party to this extortion of some political bureaucrats, to be the vehicle of killing even one of them. Never to play along.

"Open your eyes, Zora. You know you must. You can't resist."

"I don't have the same temptations as you, you bastard," she yelled at him over the splintering wood, the smashing waves and now the pouring water.

Augustine paused, and pressed, "Then what is it? What does this third portal look like?"

"Free them first," she said.

Augustine shook his head with total doubt, and as the ship dipped deeply again, he fell and soaked himself in water rising over their feet and ankles. His shoulders and hair drenched, now from long drops of water raining down that wet all of them. The floor's planks began to open by inches as the ship cracked under the unbearable pressure from whatever awesome force outside inexorably bore upon it. The water poured down from the ceiling and upon the floor. Everything around them was imploding, exploding, cracking at the seams.

Zora looked past the cage. The window remained closed.

This is no storm, she thought again. Something terrible was happening. But they were crazy to think about a portal to another world.

He grunted, reared his head up and snarled like a rabid mammal. He dragged himself up upon a sofa, turned and tried to stare into her eyes, readying to make another challenge to his audience. "Dear Ministers," he yelled up at her, sustaining an impossible faith in his project in the face of such total destruction crashing around them all. "Give me the teleports."

He almost begged by now, like the children who whimpered beneath the blankets and the small one who wailed.

He half-stood and stared into her eyes deeper and gnashed his chiselled yellow teeth.

"You've become a beast."

With his face down, almost touching the growing pool of water upon the floor, he barked out a mocking laugh.

The ship cracked loudly somewhere and leaned to the left while water poured, people screamed above on deck and the strange, heavy haze wafted inside her head. It was recurring, she noticed, along with the ship's careening and the bursts of the bizarre tempest on the lake. A fuzzy brain fog that waxed and waned, and a distant roar of rapids.

Within the painting, the waves of the ocean beyond the marketplace heaved and sank. The moon was wide and silver and the ship on the horizon leaned at a precarious angle as it descended deep into a cliff-sized trough in the sea.

Augustine pointed his pistol and said, "You've joined the ranks of the Hallowers too, Zora. Lying all over the place. Well done. I will not be stopped."

The ship lurched amid a cacophony of distant screams — now everyone terrified — blistering, burning wood, tumbling furniture and cracking glass. Her chair toppled again, and she slid through the water across the floor.

At the base of the painting, Zora went to her knees, still braced to the back of the chair by handcuffs. "Yes, you will be." Desperate, she slammed her shoulder into the painting's silver frame. It fell over top of her and onto the floor into the water.

******

Zora couldn't see, for the air filled with water pellets raining down. She called to the children through the creaking planks and the crashing and cries from outside. The noise rose into something else, a reverberated vibration, louder and piercing. The children held each other and screamed with her as a heavy sheet of water swept over, engulfed them and muted everything.

She choked, held her breath. They choked, surrounded by water, no longer able to scream, held on.

She remembered the painting had fallen over her, but she felt nothing other than water. From intensely thick rain pellets to blinding sheets and then what felt like waves, it churned around her head as she suddenly felt herself plunging into a narrow depth. She sensed she was now elsewhere, not in a room at all but sinking into a body of water. Bubbles spewed upward, warm and salty. Eyes open in terror, unable to see clearly for the swirling turmoil, she nevertheless quickly sensed this was a pit of some kind, for the soles of her feet rubbed against a wall as she descended, her back slid down along vertical bars, her hands still caught in handcuffs trapping her upon the chair. She writhed, panicking at the total inability to breathe, and upward saw the wriggling legs of children within a circle of light shining from beyond. They kicked as they sought air toward a white round moon in the distant clear night sky, and they swam to the top of the cage which now showed itself to be, as the frothing cleared, suspended within a conical pit made of layered brick. The children gathered themselves up at the top, reaching air and grasping the top bars, while she sunk deeper into the depths, exterior to the cage. Her hands pulled with all her remaining might in vain against the metal clasps behind her. Zora pushed her feet firmly upon the curved brick wall in a desperate renewed determination and she tried to gain traction, to crawl and inch upward, with her back against the long bars and her feet leveraged against the brick. But she could barely move. Her hands remained cuffed. She was stuck, and then her grip on the bars slipped. Casting her sight upward, she saw their legs treading water, but she went down. This pit, whatever it was, a conical brick-layered descent, went far down surely into a sucking, infinite pitch-black sea beneath.

Zora drifted deep down to a forever despair.

Then something yanked at the handcuffs around her wrists with inhuman ferocity from within the bars, pulled her back against the cage. They were hands, true hands with long fingers, though impossibly powerful. Zora couldn't see behind her at whatever being held her there with its hands in a vice around her wrists until, with a swift, short twist, the metal cracked and tore away. Zora twisted around, freed of the chair and clasps, to see what thing swam within that long vertical cage, what had a direct line to the children above.

She saw it, and its eyes saw hers. One long moment deep down in the swirling water they remained suspended together, regarding one another.

High cheek bones, long floating hair, pronounced chin and chiselled forehead, its eyes shone bright blue green above the neutral mouth of something almost human, with a serene human beauty yet vacant eyes that said nothing.

As fast as it started, water then spun in a swirling fury. Zora held her breath, desperate to hold on to life while the water exploded into a burst as the thing released her from its irresistible grip and heaved its mass around in a sudden pivoting summersault downward. Given one more chance, Zora writhed upward, kicked, frantic for air. She swam, reaching her hands and arms upward as the chair fell and twirled off below where the indiscernible mass rushed away, deeper down into utter blackness. From the shadowed last flap of a broad fin at the end of a hefty, muscular tail, she thought she saw the speed of a fish before it disappeared into the darkness.

Zora kicked to the surface, pulling herself upward at last where she gasped crisp night air.

The children hollered and shrieked while Zora swam, splashing her hands upon the surface until she arrived beside them where they huddled, hung on and treaded water on the other side, within the cage, which sat somehow suspended in the middle of this brick-layered pool, rising out of the surface of the water to provide just enough space for their heads and shoulders to float above the surface, thankfully able to breathe. They held one another and repeated, "Stay up, yes you can."

"God bless you and stay up, honeys."

Above, the late-night sky cleared of storm clouds. Spitting water, Zora looked up to a tall wall on one side of the pool, a market square on the other and an open sky with stars above. The last of the partiers packed their goods and departed through a far gate.

"Oh my God," she said slowly, knowing and disbelieving at once. It was the damaged, leaning pole across the pool with its long ragged ropes trailing the surface on the other side of the cage that convinced her.

This was the pool in the painting.

The children held the bars and asked themselves, "Where are we, I want Mommy." "We're outside," one said. Another cried in front of his friend who looked at him, silent in shock. Yet another: "We're away from there now."

"She made it," another kid exclaimed.

Another one, the solitary boy who'd stood farther from the others at one point, declared softly, "Guys. Know that painting they liked so much? We're in it now."

Some listened, some didn't, and those who paid attention to this — including Zora who knew kids could be smart, see things as they truly were, and accept the incredible — looked up and around the pool within the market square of the painting, mouths agape in shock.

An older girl reassured two younger ones who remained stunned, as they imagined what swam beneath the surface because a pale hand still grasped a bar beside them. The fingers that remained of Augustine gripped in rigor mortis, and the forearm stopped at a bloodied, ripped end floating its trails of skin upon the swirled surface whose disturbance was not of their doing.

That man was now gone.

Their little hands pulled at Zora's shirt, grabbed her long ponytail, so desperate were they to keep her alive. And they gathered to her, splashing on their side of the cage, reaching for her through the bars to keep her afloat, in the brick pool at the edge of the marketplace by the town's wall closest to the sea, asking what lurked deep in here and wondering, not yet speaking it aloud, when it would come back.

******

Midas followed Cisco through the door, feeling unsteady not just because he fell backward into a wall with the ship's sudden sway. He didn't know what could come next other than total failure.

He coughed through a red mist.

Cisco's face was set grim, and he sent a steady gaze into the foggy room, deciphering who was there, what it contained, and pointed his pistol into the red clouds.

"That's enough of this bullcrap," Cisco said into the room.

A blast of wind hit the ship again and cleared the mist somewhat to reveal a small taut ball of a man in a shining white suit.

"Caesar," said Midas. Water dripped from Caesar's soaked jacket and the rim of his fedora.

Midas gripped the mermaid statuette in his coat pocket. The stone felt hot, and the many minute scales of the mermaid's fins felt like silk.

Tubs from which red steam billowed sat upon a raised tile floor before him. Many of them had been shuttered at their top by a sheen of red energy, no doubt to preserve the abominable liquid within. The room lay in disarray. Beyond, glasses and bottles had splintered everywhere, chairs were jumbled around a bar at the far end, and white couches had slid to pile against it. And on the raised floor in the middle, the red viscous liquid drizzled from the baths that were open and still sizzling with hands hung limp from their edges, white and dead. They hadn't made it back, he thought, repulsed.

"You did this," said the thick, honeyed voice. Caesar emerged more clearly in his drenched white suit. He steadied himself between two tubs and panted beneath his bug-eyed brow.

"Where's my painting? You stole it," growled Midas. His eyes bulged, reddened with fury, redder than the foul fumes smoking from those awful basins amongst which Caesar stood, holding their edges with his shaking, tired hands.

"You have the mermaid, do you not?" Caesar said with a clenched effort. "Come, Midas, let me show you how to use it. Show you what must be done. And quickly. We haven't much time."

Cisco cocked his pistol at Caesar. "Stand back, Midas. I got this. Caesar," he said, "tell me where Zora is or I'll shoot you dead right now."

Midas stopped, stunned. "Zora? What, she's around here?"

From their right surged a tall thin man in a tattered red suit. His strong, bony hands clasped Cisco's throat and shoved him against the wall by the front door. Cisco manoeuvred his gun down as he choked under the power of this creature, who Midas saw as a man greatly changed. Close up once again to a Hallower, its stench and psychotic cruelty in its eyes, intent on murdering Cisco, Midas felt the same fear as when they glared at him that night from across the lawn and barked a gleeful, hungry, "Oh! Oh!" like they were half-animals.

Cisco gagged and the Hallower's long nails pierced his skin.

Midas pulled out the statuette and slammed its tail against the back of the Hallower's head just as Cisco's gun went off and its bullet tore through the Hallower's torso, narrowly missing Midas and flying into the room's far wall. The Hallower barked, went silent and slumped into the water accumulating on the floor. A pool of blood spread there and Cisco slumped too, still conscious and upright, holding his hand to a bleeding throat.

Midas stood back in shock. There was nothing he could do for the man. He turned to Caesar, not knowing what to do next other than to keep going.

"Bring me to the painting, and then I'll show you how to use it," Midas said to Caesar. "I've done it before. I have the key. See this?"

He would kick him in.

Caesar's face contorted. He held out his wrinkled palm. "And now we must finish this. The rest of the Hallowers shall come forth."

Midas resisted the temptation to argue with him. He walked to the edge of the raised floor, wary of the slider that might kill him with the ship's erratic swaying, for the shields of energy that had closed the tubs were failing, flickering on and off.

The wood of the ship moved, board by board, crunching in upon itself with a deafening series of cracks where planks snapped, and people on the decks screamed. A mast splintered and a collective pause silenced their terror during the long moment while it tumbled to the deck and crushed those unable to run.

"Give me the statuette," Caesar pressed. For the first time, Midas sensed emotion in the man, a grinding yearning and an abiding hatred. "Let me show you how to wield this awesome power."

The ship lurched sideways and Midas fell to his knees beside the raised floor.

"My Hallowers will return any moment, Midas. When they do, you will want to be my ally. And I see something changed in you since we last met. Don't I?" Caesar said, ever confident as he gripped the edge of a bath. "Your face. It's been a rough ride, has it? Did you bang it or get into a scuffle? Perhaps becoming one of them at last?"

Red liquid trickled from the baths and dripped along the raised floor where Midas held on to the edge. He stepped away and touched his face, wondering if he too was turning. But that couldn't possibly be. He looked back at the dead Hallower behind him, near Cisco's slumped figure.

"You've had a little taste of the Seeping yourself, haven't you?" Caesar said.

"Do you hear something?" He forced a laugh. "So close, as you approach, a distant roar that grows. So it is a thing, isn't it? It's something new that comes from outside and into you. Doesn't it, Midas? Influence? Midas." The slit of his mouth stretched wider. "It's the Seeping."

"Or a never-ending series of shitty choices." Midas retorted. "Show it to me and you can choose to let the Hallowers in or walk into the damn painting yourself and take a good look. Aren't you curious?"

Midas sought to recall Madame Blue's instructions, to make them coherent if ever they were. Or had he misunderstood all along? To trick Caesar, she said, and dump him into the maw of the beast on the other side. And somehow run back.

Midas stepped back from the raised tile floor and those baths, and then he heard a loud, sharp bang. Caesar's short rotund body flew back with the force of a bullet and fell against a tub, which splashed its red liquid all over him. He screamed in agony, a piercing that reduced quickly to a long, painful moan.

Just then, a massive force slammed the ship. Midas fell to the floor and to escape the spilling slider he dragged himself away toward the bar and the far door. He looked back at Cisco who leaned against the far wall, his outstretched arm with his pistol slowly lowering into the bloody pool in which he sat. His head slumped and he lay still. Caesar, surrounded by the baths whose slider drenched him as it spilled in gushing waves across the tiles, moaned again.

Water sprayed down from the ceiling, and through the distant and growing hollers, crashing waves and cracking wood that rose to an overwhelming screech, came the cries of children. "Stay up, honeys." Her voice, muffled, came from beyond the closed door beyond the bar.

"Zora," said Midas.

The ship lurched again and dipped sharply into a sea-sized trough. Caesar screamed as the shields upon the baths broke and they nearly emptied their slider all over him. Red mist engulfed his writhing body, and he disappeared for a moment until it cleared to reveal him lying on the floor, eyes open and frozen in death.

"Shit," said Midas, and he ran to the closed door, pulled at the stuck handle, pushed and shoulder-checked until it swung open.

There inside, Zora sat beside an open door of a cage full of children. The entire room flooded with swirling pools and water rained down. He wanted to run to her and embrace her and kiss her face, but the painting leaned upon the far wall and he'd already steeled himself against the crushing force from all around to do the deed — but Caesar was now dead. Throwing him in was only part of the task though, he reminded himself. Blue and Caesar were both right. The mermaid in his hand was a representation of a thing within that painting, a monstrous beast with powers akin to Blue, and she was Seeping this way. Worse, the Seeping might be invading his own mind. He sensed it along with the sudden bouts of incomprehensible, irrational fury that seized him, that came and went like the ship flipping back and forth from here to there. Unless they were all already there.

Water rained down, he heard the children screaming and as he glanced over at Zora and the children in the cage, for a flash he thought he saw them underwater. He was seeing them as an image separated from himself, as though that half of the room had become a painting's canvas itself, three-dimensional and real to the touch but in a separate reality, because for that brief flash they were within a cage treading water in the same brick pool as in the painting, clinging on.

That brief moment ended in a second and there they sat again, on the floor of this small square room sitting in a growing pool of water, rained upon by the lake, and the air shook under the cracking ship. Zora sat on the outside of the cage, huddled by the children congregated beside her on the inside.

We're really flipping over, he said to himself. *I have no more time.*

Midas gripped the statuette and held his hand back. It was hot, the scales soft now. It almost writhed but didn't, still remaining the beautiful stone that it was. He aimed and threw the statuette at the painting's canvas, only for it to emit a loud clap and flash of bright light as it bounced back to the floor.

He looked back at Zora who screamed something at him, but all he could hear was the unbearable roar of a massive waterfall spraying them as the two worlds collided, a Seeping becoming complete.

It might kill him, or more likely, as Blue said, trap him stuck in some hellish place with Ira, to be consumed by a ravenous beast. This moment, whether or not he'd become a Hallower himself, would be the moment when he'd reverse the Seeping. *If I'm selfless, if I think of the other, if I don't just take.*

So he ran to the base of the painting, picked up the fallen statuette, dug into the wet floor and propelled himself toward the canvas as he gripped the statuette and glared at the market square determined to take the risk.

Zora screamed through the rain to stop, barely hearing herself, "Don't do it, you can't!" even though it was incredible that he could lunge into a painting.

And then, the noise stopped.

Zora fell back into the churning water that had flooded the room, exhausted. *No, this can't be, let it stop, where did he go?*

"It's open," one of the children said. "Let's go."

The rain and flowing water slowed to a halt, the screams above deck ceased and the ship stilled. She pulled herself up, surrounded by children, and blinked at the dull, dissipating ache in her eye. Zora could barely see through the moonlit mist and heavy fog.

The ship bobbed upon a small wave. No one screamed. Nothing broke.

It settled.

"Hasn't he been a pain?" said the cheerful Hippias. Through the mist, a shadow of his pear-shaped trench coat hovered at the far door by the painting where Midas had disappeared. "Oh, lest I forget: thank you," he said with a fun bubble in his voice. "For buying the time, and so much else. Not to worry. Your eye will be fine. And you won't even shit it out." He chuckled. "So pleased." And he swished through the pool of water, stumbling as he went under the weight of the painting he'd picked up. As he turned with it, kicking the door further open with his foot, the painting's front canvas faced her as Hippias grunted and proceeded out the far door. Her heart sank in the second she saw her dear Midas standing by the pool, grasping the torn rope that had dangled from the bent pole as he pulled at it. Hippias kept walking and the painting receded deeper into the fog and out through the door.

The children chattered, "Whose mommy are you?"

That feeling beneath her skin returned as it curled up in a fit of freezing. "Midas?" she asked through the clearing mist. This was not real. Her tired eyes and the swirling mist must be playing tricks.

As her heart emptied with a new horror that Midas had disappeared somewhere, fallen into a dark nothingness, she said, swallowing the word, "No," and reached for their hands.

He had to be just outside that door. "Midas? Come back, Midas."

A child asked, "Who was that man?"

"A bad man, honeys," she said.

Another asked, "But the painting. What was it?"

"Once I imagined it like a mirror. Now I see it for what it is. A nightmare. One thing I promise you. The bad man is not going to keep it." Because Zora remembered their conversation a week ago when, if she remembered right, Midas said she had to have faith.

She stood with the children, and they walked from the room through the mess, down the hall. Out they marched in an organized line to freedom, and while the children kept asking questions, she felt herself deflecting them with empty claims that she didn't know the answer, haunted by the dawning thought that the painting was, in fact, a disguise. It wasn't what it or anyone said it was.

He must still be alive, she decided, for she along with the kids had apparently been there too, swallowed up then flipped back. There they had breathed. For the moment she felt a relief, and they walked out to the ruined promenades of the wrecked ship to see a hot rising sun that shone upon the settled waters by a very unsettled town.

THE END

Ingram Content Group UK Ltd.
Milton Keynes UK
UKHW011945080523
421401UK00004B/325

9 781771 805827